GAYLORD M

The Hidden Places

The Hidden Places

BERTRAND W. SINCLAIR

Sagebrush
Large Print Westerns

Library of Congress Cataloging-in-Publication Data
Sinclair, Bertrand W., 1881-1972.
    Hidden places / Bertrand W. Sinclair.
        p.   cm.
    ISBN 1-57490-496-5 (alk. paper)
 1. World War, 1914-1918—Veterans—Fiction. 2. Disfigured
persons—Fiction. 3. Vancouver (B.C.)—Fiction. 4. Blind
women—Fiction. 5. Large type books. I. Title.

PR9199.3.S5325H53 2003
813'.52—dc21   2003010606

Cataloging in Publication Data is available from
the British Library and the National Library of Australia.

Sagebrush Large Print Westerns are published in the United
States and Canada by Thomas T. Beeler, Publisher, PO Box 659,
Hampton Falls, New Hampshire 03844-0659. ISBN 1-57490-496-5

Published in the United Kingdom, Eire, and the Republic of
South Africa by Isis Publishing Ltd, 7 Centremead, Osney
Mead, Oxford OX2 0ES England. ISBN 0-7531-6919-3

Published in Australia and New Zealand by Bolinda Publishing
Pty Ltd, 17 Mohr Street, Tullamarine, Victoria, Australia, 3043
ISBN 1-74030-926-X

Manufactured by Sheridan Books in Chelsea, Michigan.

CHAPTER I

HOLLISTER STOOD IN THE MIDDLE OF HIS ROOM, staring at the door without seeing the door, without seeing the bulky shadow his body cast on the wall in the pale glow of a single droplight. He was seeing everything and seeing nothing; acutely, quiveringly conscious and yet oblivious to his surroundings by reason of the poignancy of his thought.

A feeling not far short of terror had folded itself about him like a shrouding fog.

It had not seized him unaware. For weeks he had seen it looming over him, and he had schooled himself to disregard a great deal which his perception was too acute to misunderstand. He had struggled desperately against the unescapable, recognizing certain significant facts and in the same breath denying their accumulated force in sheer self-defense.

A small dressing-table topped by an oval mirror stood against the wall beside his bed. Hollister took his unseeing gaze off the door with a start, like a man withdrawing his mind from wandering in far places. He sat down before the dressing-table and forced himself to look steadfastly, appraisingly, at the reflection of his face in the mirror—that which had once been a presentable man's countenance.

He shuddered and dropped his eyes. This was a trial he seldom ventured upon. He could not bear that vision long. No one could. That was the fearful implication which made him shrink. He, Robert Hollister, in the flush of manhood, with a body whose symmetry and vigor other men had envied, a mind that functioned

1

alertly, a spirit as nearly indomitable as the spirit of man may be, was like a leper among his own kind; he had become a something that filled other men with pitying dismay when they looked at him, that made women avert their gaze and withdraw from him in spite of pity.

Hollister snapped out the light and threw himself on his bed. He had known physical suffering, the slow, aching hours of tortured flesh, bodily pain that racked him until he had wished for death as a welcome relief. But that had been when the flame of vitality burned low, when the will to live had been sapped by bodily stress.

Now the mere animal instinct to live was a compelling force within him. He was young and strong, aching with his desire for life in its fullest sense. And he did not know how he was going to live and endure the manner of life he had to face, a life that held nothing but frustration and denial of all that was necessary to him, which was making him suffer as acutely as he had ever suffered in the field, under the knives of callous surgeons, in the shambles of the front line or the ether-scented dressing stations. There is morphine for a tortured body, but there is no opiate for agony of the spirit, the sharp-toothed pain that stabs at a lonely heart with its invisible lancet.

In the darkness of his room, with all the noisy traffic of a seaport city rumbling under his windows, Hollister lay on his bed and struggled against that terrifying depression which had seized him, that spiritual panic. It was real. It was based upon undeniable reality. He was no more captain of his soul than any man born of woman has ever been when he descends into the dark places. But he knew that he must shake off that feeling, or go mad, or kill himself. One of the three. He had known men to kill themselves for less. He had seen

2

wounded men beg for a weapon to end their pain. He had known men who, after months of convalescence, quitted by their own hand a life that no longer held anything for them.

And it was not because life held out any promise to Hollister that he lived, nor was it a physical fear of death, nor any moral scruple against self-destruction. He clung to life because instinct was stronger than reason, stronger than any of the appalling facts he encountered and knew he must go on encountering. He had to live, with a past that was no comfort, going on down the pathway of a future which he attempted not to see clearly, because when he did envisage it he was stricken with just such a panic as now overwhelmed him.

To live on and on, a pariah among his fellows because of his disfigurement. A man with a twisted face, a gargoyle of a countenance. To have people always shrink from him. To be denied companionship, friendship, love, to know that so many things which made life beautiful were always just beyond his reach. To be merely endured. To have women pity him—and shun him.

The sweat broke out on Hollister's face when he thought of all that. He knew that it was true. This knowledge had been growing on him for weeks. Tonight the full realization of what it meant engulfed him with terror. That was all. He did not cry out against injustice. He did not whine a protest. He blamed no one. He understood, when he looked at himself in the glass.

After a time he shook off the first paralyzing grip of this unnamable terror which had seized him with clammy hands, fought it down by sheer resolution. He was able to lie staring into the dusky spaces of his room and review the stirring panorama of his existence for the past four years. There was nothing that did not fill him with infinite regret—and there was nothing which by any conceivable effort he could have changed. He could not have escaped one of those calamities which had befallen him. He could not have left undone a single act that he had performed. There was an inexorable continuity in it all. There had been a great game. He had been one of the pawns.

Hollister shut his eyes. Immediately, like motion pictures projected upon a screen, his mind began to project visions. He saw himself kissing his wife goodbye. He saw the tears shining in her eyes. He felt again the clinging pressure of her arms, her cry that she would be so lonely. He saw himself in billets, poring over her letters. He saw himself swinging up the line with his company, crawling back with shattered ranks after a hammering, repeating this over and over again till it seemed like a nightmare in which all existence was comprised in blood and wounds and death and sorrow, enacted at stated intervals to the rumble of guns.

He saw himself on his first leave in London, when he found that Myra was growing less restive under his absence, when he felt proud to think that she was learning the lesson of sacrifice and how to bear up under it. He saw his second Channel crossing with a flesh wound in his thigh, when there seemed to his hyper-sensitive mind a faint perfunctoriness in her greeting. It was on this leave that he first realized how the grim business he was engaged upon was somehow rearing an impalpable wall between himself and this woman whom he still loved with a lover's passion after four years of marriage.

And he could see, in this mental cinema, whole searing sentences of the letter he received from her just before a big push on the Somme in the fall of '17—that letter in which she told him with child-like directness that he had grown dim and distant and that she loved another man. She was sure he would not care greatly. She was sorry if he did. But she could not help it. She had been so lonely. People were bound to change. It couldn't be helped. She was sorry—but—

And Hollister saw himself later lying just outside the lip of a shell crater, blind, helpless, his face a shredded smear when he felt it with groping fingers. He remembered that he lay there wondering, because of the darkness and the strange silence and the pain, if he were dead and burning in hell for his sins.

After that there were visions of himself in a German hospital, in a prison camp, and at last the armistice, and the Channel crossing once more. He was dead, they told him, when he tried in the chaos of demobilization to get in touch with his regiment, to establish his identity, to find his wife. He was officially dead. He had been so reported, so accepted eighteen months earlier. His wife had married again. She and her husband had vanished from England. And with his wife had vanished his assets, his estate, by virtue of a pre-war arrangement which he had never revoked.

He beheld himself upon the streets of London, one of innumerable stray dogs, ruined, deserted, disfigured, a bit of war's wreckage. He did not particularly consider himself a victim of injustice. He did not blame Myra. He was simply numbed and bewildered.

But that was before he grew conscious of what it meant to a sensitive man, a man in whom all warm human impulses flowed so strongly, to be penniless, to have all the dependable foundations of his life torn from under his feet, to be so disfigured that people shunned

5

him.

He had to gather up the broken pieces of his life, fit them together, go on as best he could. It did not occur to him at first to do otherwise, or that the doing would be hard. He had not foreseen all the strange shifts he would be put to, the humiliations he would suffer, the crushing weight of hopelessness which gathered upon him by the time he arrived on the Pacific Coast, where he had once lived, to which he now turned to do as men all over the war-racked earth were doing in the winter of 1919—cast about in an effort to adjust himself, to make a place for himself in civil life.

All the way across the continent of North America Hollister grew more and more restive under the accumulating knowledge that the horrible devastation of his features made a No Man's Land about him which few had the courage to cross. It was a fact. Here, upon the evening of the third day in Vancouver, a blind and indescribable fear seized upon him, a sickening conviction that although living, he was dead—dead in so far as the common, casual intimacies of daily intercourse with his fellows went. It was as if men and women were universally repulsed by that grotesquely distorted mask which served him for a face, as if at sight of it by common impulse they made off, withdrew to a safe distance, as they would withdraw from any loathsome thing.

Lying on his bed, Hollister flexed his arms. He arched his chest and fingered the muscular breadth of it in the darkness. Bodily, he was a perfect man. Strength flowed through him in continuous waves. He could feel within himself the surge of vast stores of energy. His brain functioned with a bright, bitter clearness. He could feel—ah, that was the hell of it. That quivering response

6

to the subtle nuances of thought! A profound change had come upon him, yet essentially he, the man, was unchanged. Except for those scars, the convoluted ridges of tissue, the livid patches and the ghastly hollows where once his cheeks and lips and forehead had been smooth and regular, he was as he had always been.

For a moment there came over him the wild impulse to rush out into the street, crying:

"You fools! Because my face is torn and twisted makes me no different from you. I still feel and think. I am as able to love and hate as you. Was all your talk about honorable scars just prattle to mislead the men who risked the scars? Is all your much advertised kindliness and sympathy for war-broken men a bluff?"

He smiled sadly. They would say he was mad. They would classify him as suffering from shell shock. A frock-coated committee would gravely recommend him for treatment in the mental hospital at Essondale. They would not understand. Hollister covered his face with a swift, tight clasping of his hands. Something rose chokingly in his throat. Into his eyes a slow, scalding wetness crept like a film. He set his teeth in one corner of his pillow.

CHAPTER II

WHEN HOLLISTER WAS EIGHTEEN YEARS OLD he had been briefly troubled by an affliction of his eyes brought on from overstudy. His father, at the time, was interested in certain timber operations on the coast of British Columbia. In these rude camps, therefore, young Hollister spent a year. During that twelve months books

7

were prohibited. He lived in the woods, restored the strength of his eyes amid that restful greenness, hardened a naturally vigorous body by healthy, outdoor labor with the logging crews. He returned home to go on with his University work in eastern Canada with unforgettable impressions of the Pacific coast, a boyish longing to go back to that region where the mountains receded from the sea in wave after wave of enormous height, where the sea lapped with green lips at the foot of the ranges and thrust winding arms back into the very heart of the land, and where the land itself, delta and slope and slide-engraved declivities, was clothed with great, silent forests, upon which man, with his axes and saws, his machinery, his destructiveness in the name of industry, had as yet made little more impression than the nibbling of a single mouse on the rim of a large cheese.

When he graduated he did return on a thirty days' vacation, which the lure of the semi-wild country prolonged for six months—a whole summer in which he resisted the importunities of his father to take his part in the business upon which rested the family fortune. Hollister never forgot that summer. He was young. He had no cares. He was free. All life spread before him in a vast illusion of unquestionable joyousness. There was a rose-pink tinge over these months in which he fished salmon and trout, climbed the frowning escarpments of the Coast Range, gave himself up to the spell of a region which is still potent with the charm of the wilderness untamed. There had always lingered in his receptive mind a memory of profound beauty, a stark beauty of color and outline, an unhampered freedom, opportunity as vast as the mountains that looked from their cool heights down on the changeful sea and the hushed forests, brooding in the sun and rain.

So he had come back again, after seven years, scarcely knowing why he came, except that the coast beckoned with a remote gesture, and that he desired to get as far as possible from the charnel house of Europe, and that he shrank from presenting himself among the acquaintances of his boyhood and the few distant relatives left him upon the Atlantic seaboard.

His father died shortly after Hollister married. He had left his son property aggregating several thousand dollars and a complicated timber business disorganized by his sudden death. Hollister was young, sanguine, clever in the accepted sense of cleverness. He had married for love—urged thereto by a headlong, unquestioning, uncritical passion. But there were no obstacles. His passion was returned. There was nothing to make him ponder upon what a devastating, tyrannical force this emotion which he knew as love might become, this blind fever of the blood under cover of which nature works her ends, blandly indifferent to the consequences.

Hollister was happy. He was ambitious. He threw himself with energy into a revival of his father's business when it came into his hands. His needs expanded with his matrimonial obligations. Considered casually—which was chiefly the manner of his consideration—his future was the future of a great many young men who begin life under reasonably auspicious circumstances. That is to say, he would be a success financially and socially to as great an extent as he cared to aspire. He would acquire wealth and an expanding influence in his community. He would lead a tolerably pleasant domestic existence. He would be proud of his wife's beauty, her charm; he would derive a soothing contentment from her affection. He would take pleasure in friendships. In the end, of course, at some far-off,

9

misty milepost, he would begin to grow old. Then he would die in a dignified manner, full of years and honors, and his children would carry on after him.

Hollister failed to reckon with the suavities of international diplomacy, with the forces of commercialism in relation to the markets of the world.

The war burst upon and shattered the placidity of his existence very much as the bombs from the first Zeppelins shattered the peace and security of London and Paris.

He reacted to the impetus of the German assault as young men of his class uniformly reacted. There was in Hollister's mind no doubt or equivocation about what he must do. But he did not embark upon this adventure joyously. He could not help weighing the chances. He understood that in this day and age he was a fortunate man. He had a great deal to lose. But he felt that he must go. He was not, however, filled with the witless idea that service with the Expeditionary Force was to be an adventure of some few months, a brief period involving some hardships and sharp fighting, but with an Allied Army hammering at the gates of Berlin as a grand finale. The slaughter of the first encounters filled him with the conviction that he should put his house in order before he entered that bloody arena out of which he might not emerge.

So that when he crossed the Channel the first time he had disentangled himself from his business at a great loss, in order to have all his funds available for his wife in case of the ultimate disaster.

Myra accompanied him to England, deferred their separation to the last hour. They could well afford that concession to their affection, they told each other. It was so hard to part.

It scarcely seemed possible that four years had gone winging by since then, yet in certain moods it seemed to Hollister as if an eternity had passed. Things had been thus and so; they had become different by agonizing processes.

He did not know where Myra was. He, himself, was here in Vancouver, alone, a stranger, a single speck of human wreckage cast on a far beach by the receding tides of war. He had no funds worth considering, but money was not as yet an item of consideration. He was not disabled. Physically he was more fit than he had ever been. The delicate mechanism of his brain was unimpaired. He had no bitterness—no illusions. His intellect was acute enough to suggest that in the complete shucking off of illusions lay his greatest peril. Life, as it faced him, the individual, appeared to be almost too grim a business to be endured without hopes and dreams. He had neither. He had nothing but moods.

He walked slowly down Granville Street in the blackest mood which had yet come upon him. It differed from that strange feeling of terror which had taken him unaware the night before. He had fallen easy prey then to the black shadows of forlornness. He was still as acutely aware of the barrier which his disfigurement raised between him and other men. But with that morbid awareness there rose also now, for the first time, resentment against the smug folk who glanced at him and hurriedly averted their eyes. Slowly, by imperceptible degrees, as the tide rises on a sloping shore, his anger rose.

The day was cold and sunny, a January morning with a touch of frost in the air. Men passed him, walking rapidly, clad in greatcoats. Women tripped by, wrapped in furs, eyes bright, cheeks glowing. And as they

11

passed, singly, in chattering pairs, in smiling groups, Hollister observed them with a growing fury. They were so thoroughly insulated against everything disagreeable. All of them. A great war had just come to a dramatic close, a war in which staggering numbers of men had been sacrificed, body and soul, to enable these people to walk the streets in comfortable security. They seemed so completely unaware of the significance of his disfigured face. It was simply a disagreeable spectacle from which they turned with brief annoyance.

Most of these men and women honored the flag. In a theater, at any public gathering, a display of the national colors caused the men to bare reverently their heads, the women to clap their hands with decorous enthusiasm. Without doubt they were all agreed that it was a sacred duty to fight for one's country. How peculiar and illogical then, he reflected, to be horrified at the visible results of fighting for one's country, of saving the world for democracy. The thing had had to be done. A great many men had been killed. A great number had lost their legs, their arms, their sight. They had suffered indescribable mutilations and disabilities in the national defense. These people were the nation. Those who passed him with a shocked glance at his face must be aware that fighting involves suffering and scars. It appeared as if they wished to ignore that. The inevitable consequences of war annoyed them, disturbed them, when they came face to face with those consequences.

Hollister imagined them privately thinking he should wear a mask.

After all, he was a stranger to these folk, although he was their countryman and a person of consequence until the war and Myra and circumstances conspired against him.

He stifled the resentment which arose from a realization that he must expect nothing else, that it was not injustice so much as stupidity. He reflected that this was natural. A cynical conclusion arose in his mind. There was no substance, after all, in this loose talk about sympathy and gratitude and the obligation of a proud country to those who had served overseas. Why should there be? He was an individual among other individuals who were unconsciously actuated by rampant individualism except in moments of peril, when stark necessity compelled them to social action. Otherwise it was every man for himself. Yes, it was natural enough. He was a stranger to these people. Except for the color of his skin, he was no more to them than a Hindoo or a Japanese. And doubtless the grotesque disarrangement of his features appalled them. How could they discern behind that caricature of a face the human desire for friendliness, the ache of a bruised spirit?

He deliberately clamped down the lid upon such reflections and bethought himself of the business which brought him along the street. Turning off the main thoroughfare, be passed half a block along a cross street and entered an office building. Ascending to the fourth floor, he entered an elaborate suite of offices which bore upon the ground glass of the entrance door this legend;

LEWIS AND COMPANY
SPECIALISTS IN B. C. TIMBER. INVESTMENTS

He inquired for Mr. Lewis, gave his card to a young woman who glanced at him once and thereafter looked anywhere but at him while he spoke. After a minute of waiting he was ushered into a private office. As he neared this door, Hollister happened to catch a

13

panoramic glimpse in a wall mirror. The eyes of half a dozen clerks and other persons in that room, both male and female, were fixed on him with the shocked and eager curiosity he had once observed upon the faces of a crowd gathered about the mangled victim of a street accident.

Mr. Lewis was a robust man, a few years older than Hollister. The cares of a rapidly developing business and certain domestic ties had prevented Mr. Lewis from offering himself upon the altar of his country. The responsibility of eight percent investments entrusted to his care was not easily shaken off. Business, of course, was a national necessity. However, since the armistice, Mr. Lewis had ceased to be either explanatory or inferentially apologetic—even in his own thought—for his inability to free himself from the demands of commerce during a critical period.

In any case he was there, sound in wind and limb, a tall, square-shouldered, ruddy man of thirty-five, seated behind an oak desk, turning Hollister's card over in his fingers with an anticipatory smile. Blankness replaced the smile. A sort of horrified wonder gleamed in his eyes. Hollister perceived that his face shocked the specialist in B. C. timber, filled Mr. Lewis with very mixed sensations indeed.

"You have my card. It is several years since we met. I dare say you find me unrecognizable," Hollister said bluntly. "Nevertheless I can identify myself to your satisfaction."

A peculiarity of Hollister's disfigurement was the immobility of his face. The shell which had mutilated him, the scalpels of the German field surgeons who had perfunctorily repaired the lacerations, had left the reddened, scar-distorted flesh in a rigid mold. He could

14

neither recognizably smile nor frown. His face, such as it was, was set in unchangeable lines. Out of this rigid, expressionless mask his eyes glowed, blue and bright, having escaped injury. They were the only key to the mutations of his mind. If Hollister's eyes were the windows of his soul, he did not keep the blinds drawn, knowing that few had the hardihood to peer into those windows now.

Mr. Lewis looked at him, looked away, and then his gaze came slowly back as if drawn by some fascination against which he struggled in vain. He did not wish to look at Hollister. Yet he was compelled to look. He seemed to find difficulty in speech, this suave man of affairs.

"I'm afraid I shouldn't have recognized you, as you say," he uttered, at last. "Have you—ah—"

"I've been overseas," Hollister answered the unspoken question. That strange curiosity, tinctured with repulsion! "The result is obvious."

"Most unfortunate," Mr. Lewis murmured. "But your scars are honorable. A brother of mine lost an arm at Loos."

"The brothers of a good many people lost more than their arms at Loos," Hollister returned dryly. "But that is not why I called. You recollect, I suppose, that when I was out here last I bought a timber limit in the Toba from your firm. When I went overseas I instructed you to sell. What was done in that matter?"

Mr. Lewis' countenance cleared at once. He was on his own ground again, dealing with matters in which he was competent, in consultation with a client whom he recalled as a person of consequence, the son of a man who had likewise been of considerable consequence. Personal undesirability was always discounted in the

15

investment field, the region of percentum returns. Money talked, in arrogant tones that commanded respect.

He pressed a button.

"Bring me," he ordered the clerk who appeared, "all correspondence relating to this matter," and he penciled a few sentences on a slip of paper.

He delved into the papers that were presently set before him.

"Ah, yes," he said. "Lot 2027 situated on the south slope of the Toba Valley. Purchased for your account July, 1912. Sale ordered October, 1914. We had some correspondence about that early in 1915, while you were in London. Do you recall it, Mr. Hollister?"

"Yes. You wrote that the timber market was dead, that any sale possible must be at a considerable sacrifice. Afterward, when I got to the front, I had no time to think about things like that. But I remember writing you to sell, even at a sacrifice."

"Yes, yes. Quite so," Mr. Lewis agreed. "I recall the whole matter very clearly. Conditions at that time were very bad, you know. It was impossible to find a purchaser on short notice. Early in 1917 there was a chance to sell, at a considerably reduced figure. But I couldn't get in touch with you. You didn't answer our cable. I couldn't take the responsibility of a sacrifice sale."

Hollister nodded. In 1917 he was a nameless convalescent in a German hospital; officially he was dead. Months before that such things as distant property rights had ceased to be of any moment. He had forgotten this holding of timber in British Columbia. He was too full of bitter personal misery to trouble about money.

16

"Failing to reach you we waited until we should hear from you—or from your estate." Mr. Lewis cleared his throat as if it embarrassed him to mention that contingency. "In war—there was that possibility, you understand. We did not feel justified; so much time had elapsed. There was risk to us in acting without verifying our instructions."

"So this property is still to be marketed. The carrying charges, as I remember, were small. I presume you carried them."

"Oh, assuredly," Mr. Lewis asserted. "We protected your interests to the very best of our ability."

"Well, find me a buyer for that limit as soon as you can," Hollister said abruptly. "I want to turn it into cash."

"We shall set about this at once," Mr. Lewis said. "It may take a little time—conditions, as a result of the armistice, are again somewhat unsettled in the logging industry. Airplane spruce production is dead—dead as a salt mackerel—and fir and cedar slumped with it. However we shall do our best. Have you a price in mind, Mr. Hollister, for a quick sale?"

"I paid ten thousand for it. On the strength of your advice as a specialist in timber investments," he added with a touch of malice. He had taken a dislike to Mr. Lewis. He had not been so critical of either men or motives in the old days. He had remembered Lewis as a good sort. Now he disliked the man, distrusted him. He was too smooth, too sleek. "I'll discount that twenty percent for a cash sale."

Mr. Lewis made a memorandum.

"Very good," said he, raising his head with an inquiring air, as if to say "If that is all—"

"If you will kindly identify me at a bank,"—Hollister

rose from his chair, "I shall cease to trouble you. I have a draft on the Bank of B. N. A. I do not know any one in Vancouver."

"No trouble, I assure you," Lewis hastened to assent, but his tone lacked heartiness, sincerity. It was only a little distance to the bank, but Lewis insisted on making the journey in a motorcar which stood at the curb. It was plain to Hollister that Mr. Lewis disliked the necessity of appearing in public with him, that he took this means of avoiding the crowded sidewalks, of meeting people. He introduced Hollister, excused himself on the plea of business pressure, and left Hollister standing before the teller's wicket.

This was not a new attitude to Hollister. People did that—as if he were a plague. There came into his mind—as he stood counting the sheaf of notes slid through a grill by a teller who looked at him once and thereafter kept his eyes averted—a paraphrase of a hoary quotation, "I am a monster of such frightful mien, as to be hated needs but to be seen." The rest of it, Hollister thought grimly, could never apply to him.

He put the money in his pocket and walked out on the street. It was a busy corner on a humming thoroughfare. Electric cars rumbled and creaked one behind another on the double tracks. Waves of vehicular traffic rolled by the curb. A current of humanity flowed past him on the sidewalk.

Standing there for a minute, Hollister felt again the slow rising of his resentment against these careless, fortunate ones. He could not say what caused that feeling. A look, a glance—the inevitable shrinking. He was morbidly sensitive. He knew that, knew it was a state of mind that was growing upon him. But from whatever cause, that feeling of intolerable isolation gave way to an inner fury.

As he stood there, he felt a wild desire to shout at these people, to curse them, to seize one of these dainty women by the arms, thrust his disfigured face close to hers and cry: "Look at me as if I were a man, not a monstrosity. I'm what I am so that you could be what you are. Look at me, damn you!"

He pulled himself together and walked on. Certainly he would soon run amuck if he did not get over feeling like that, if he did not master these impulses which bordered on insanity. He wondered if that inner ferment would drive him insane.

He went back to the second-rate hotel where he had taken refuge, depressed beyond words, afraid of himself, afraid of the life which lay in fragments behind him and spread away before him in terrifying drabness. Yet he must go on living. To live was the dominant instinct. A man did not put on or off the desire to live as he put on or off his coat. But life promised nothing. It was going to be a sorry affair. It struck Hollister with disheartening force that an individual is nothing—absolutely nothing—apart from some form of social grouping. And society, which had exacted so much from him, seemed peculiarly indifferent to the consequences of those imperative exactions, seemed wholly indifferent to his vital need.

And it was not reward or recognition of service performed that Hollister craved. He did not want to be pensioned or subsidized or to have medals pinned on him. What he wanted was chiefly to forget the war and what the war had visited upon him and others like him. Hollister suffered solely from that sense of being held outside the warm circle of human activities, fellowships, friendliness. If he could not overcome that barrier which people threw up around themselves at contact with him, if he could not occasionally know the sound of a friendly voice, he felt that he would very soon go mad. A man cannot go on forever enduring the pressure of the intolerable. Hollister felt that he must soon arrive at a crisis. What form it would take he did not know, and in certain moods he did not care.

On the landing at the end of the narrow corridor off which his room opened he met a man in uniform whom he recognized—a young man who had served under him in the Forty-fourth, who had won a commission on the field. He wore a captain's insignia now. Hollister greeted him by name.

"Hello, Tommy."

The captain looked at him. His face expressed nothing whatever. Hollister waited for that familiar shadow of distaste to appear. Then he remembered that, like himself, Rutherford must have seen thousands upon thousands of horribly mutilated men.

"Your voice," Rutherford remarked at length, "has a certain familiar sound. Still, I can't say I know you. What's the name?"

"Bob Hollister. Do you remember the bottle of Scotch we pinched from the Black Major behind the brick wall on the Albert Road? Naturally you wouldn't know me— with this face."

"Well," Rutherford said, as he held out his hand, "a fellow shouldn't be surprised at anything any more. I understood you'd gone west. Your face is mussed up a bit. Rotten luck, eh?"

Hollister felt a lump in his throat. It was the first time for months that any human being had met him on common ground. He experienced a warm feeling for Rutherford. And the curious thing about that was that

20

out of the realm of the subconscious rose instantly the remembrance that he had never particularly liked Tommy Rutherford. He was one of the wild men of the battalion. When they went up the line Rutherford was damnably cool and efficient, a fatalist who went about his grim business unmoved. Back in rest billets he was always pursuing some woman, unearthing surplus stores of whisky or wine, intent upon dubious pleasures—a handsome, self-centered debonair animal.

"My room's down here," Hollister said. "Come in and gas a bit—if you aren't bound somewhere."

"Oh, all right. I came up here to see a chap, but he's out. I have half an hour or so to spare." Rutherford stretched himself on Hollister's bed. They lit cigarettes and talked. And as they talked, Rutherford kept looking at Hollister's face, until Hollister at last said to him:

"Doesn't it give you the willies to look at me?"

Rutherford shook his head.

"Oh, no. I've got used to seeing fellows all twisted out of shape. You seem to be fit enough otherwise."

"I am," Hollister said moodily. "But it's a devil of a handicap to have a mug like this."

"Makes people shy off, eh? Women particularly. I can imagine," Rutherford drawled. "Tough luck, all right. People don't take very much stock in fellows that got smashed. Not much of a premium on disfigured heroes these days."

Hollister laughed harshly.

"No. We're at a discount. We're duds."

For half an hour they chatted more or less one-sidedly. Rutherford had a grievance which he took pains to air. He was on duty at Hastings Park, having been sent there a year earlier to instruct recruits, after recovering from a wound. He was the military man par

21

excellence. War was his game. He had been anxious to go to Siberia with the Canadian contingent which had just departed. And the High Command had retained him here to assist in the inglorious routine of demobilization. Rutherford was disgruntled. Siberia had promised new adventure, change, excitement.

The man, Hollister soon perceived, was actually sorry the war was over, sorry that his occupation was gone. He talked of resigning and going to Mexico, to offer his sword to whichever proved the stronger faction. It would be a picnic after the Western Front. A man could whip a brigade of those greasers into shape and become a power. There ought to be good chances for loot.

Yet Hollister enjoyed his company. Rutherford was genial. He was the first man for long to accept Hollister as a human being. He promised to look Hollister up again before he went away.

The world actually seemed cheerful to Hollister, after Rutherford had gone—until in moving about the room he caught sight of his face in the mirror."

CHAPTER III

ABOUT TEN DAYS LATER Tommy Rutherford walked into Hollister's room at eight in the evening. He laid his cap and gloves on the bed, seated himself, swung his feet to and fro for a second, and reached for one of Hollister's cigarettes.

"It's a hard world, old thing," he complained. "Here was I all set for an enjoyable winter. Nice people in Vancouver. All sorts of fetching affairs on the tapis. And I'm to be demobilized myself next week. Chucked out into the blooming street with a gratuity and a couple of medals. Damn the luck."

He remained absorbed in his own reflections for a minute, blowing smoke rings with meticulous care.

"I wonder if a fellow could make it go in Mexico?" he drawled.

Hollister made no comment.

"Oh, well, hang it, sufficient unto the day is the evil thereof," he remarked, with an abrupt change of tone. "I'm going to a hop at the Granada presently. Banish dull care and all that, for the time being, anyway."

His gaze came to an inquiring rest on Hollister.

"What's up, old thing?" he asked lightly. "Why so mum?"

"Oh, nothing much," Hollister answered.

"Bad thing to get in the dumps," Rutherford observed sagely. "You ought to keep a bottle of Scotch handy for that."

"Drink myself into a state of mind where the world glitters and becomes joyful, eh? No, I don't fancy your prescription. I'd be more apt to run amuck."

"Oh, come now," Rutherford remonstrated. "It isn't so bad as that. Cheer up, old man. Things might be worse, you know."

"Oh, hell!" Hollister exploded.

After which he relapsed into sullen silence, to which Rutherford, frankly mystified and somewhat inclined to resent this self-contained mood, presently left him.

Hollister was glad when the man went away. He had a feeling of relief when the door closed and retreating footsteps echoed down the hall. He had grasped at a renewal of Rutherford's acquaintance as a man drowning in a sea of loneliness would grasp at any friendly straw. And Rutherford, Hollister quickly realized, was the most fragile sort of straw. The man was a profound, non-thinking egotist, the adventurer pure and simple, whose mentality never rose above grossness of one sort and another, in spite of a certain outward polish. He could tolerate Hollister's mutilated countenance because he had grown accustomed to horrible sights—not because he had any particular sympathy for a crippled, mutilated man's misfortune, or any understanding of such a man's state of feeling. To Rutherford that was the fortune of war. So many were killed. So many crippled. So many disfigured. It was luck. He believed in his own luck. The evil that befell other men left him rather indifferent. That was all. When Hollister once grasped Rutherford's attitude, he almost hated the man.

He sat now staring out the window. A storm had broken over Vancouver that day. Tonight it was still gathering force. The sky was a lowering, slate-colored mass of clouds, spitting squally bursts of rain that drove in wet lines against his window and made the street below a glistening area shot with tiny streams and shallow puddles that were splashed over the curb by rolling motor wheels. The wind droned its ancient, melancholy chant among the telephone wires, shook with its unseen, powerful hands a row of bare maples across the way, rattled the windows in their frames. Now and then, in a momentary lull of the wind, a brief cessation of the city noises, Hollister could hear far off the beat of the Gulf seas bursting on the beach at English Bay, snoring in the mouth of False Creek. A dreary, threatening night that fitted his mood.

He sat pondering over the many-horned dilemma upon which he hung impaled. He had done all that a man could do. He had given the best that was in him, played the game faithfully, according to the rules. And

24

the net result had been for him the most complete disaster. So far as Myra went, he recognized that domestic tragedy as a natural consequence. He did not know, he was unable to say if his wife had simply been a weak and shallow woman, left too long alone, thrown too largely on her own resources in an environment so strongly tinctured by the highpitched and reckless spirit generated by the war. He had always known that his wife—women generally were the same, he supposed—was dominated by emotional urges, rather than cold reason. But that had never struck him as of great significance. Women were like that. A peculiar obtuseness concealed from him, until now, that men also were much the same. He was, himself. When his feelings and his reason came into conflict, it was touch and go which should triumph. The fact remained that for a long time the war had separated them as effectually as a divorce court. Hollister had always had a hazy impression that Myra was the sort of woman to whom love was necessary, but he had presumed that it was the love of a particular man, and that man himself. This, it seemed, was a mistake, and he had paid a penalty for making that mistake.

So he accepted this phase of his unhappiness without too much rancor. Myra had played fair, he perceived. She had told him what to expect. And the accident of a misleading report had permitted her to follow her bent with a moral sanction. That she had bestowed herself and some forty thousand dollars of his money on another man was not the thing Hollister resented. He resented only the fact that her glow of love for him had not endured, that it had gone out like an untended fire. But for some inscrutable reason that had happened. He had built a dreamhouse on an unstable foundation. It had tumbled down. Very well. He accepted that.

But he did not accept this unuttered social dictum that he should be kept at arm's length because he had suffered a ghastly disarrangement of his features while acting as a shield behind which the rest of society rested secure. No, he would never accept that as a natural fact. He could not.

No one said that he was a terrible object which should remain in the background along with family skeletons and unmentionable diseases. He was like poverty and injustice—present but ignored. And this being shunned and avoided, as if he were something which should go about in furtive obscurity, was rapidly driving Hollister to a state approaching desperation.

For he could not rid himself of the social impulse any more than a healthy man can rid himself of the necessity for food and drink at certain intervals. If Hollister had been so crushed in body and mind that his spirit was utterly quenched, if his vitality had been so drained that he could sit passive and let the world go by unheeded, then he would have been at peace.

He had seen men like that—many of them—content to sit in the sun, to be fed and let alone. Their hearts were broken as well as their bodies.

But except for the distortion of his face, he returned as he had gone away, a man in full possession of his faculties, his passions, his strength. He could not be passive either physically or mentally. His mind was too alert, his spirit too sensitive, his body too crammed with vitality to see life go swinging by and have no hand in its manifestations and adventures.

Yet he was growing discouraged. People shunned him, shrank from contact. His scarred face seemed to dry up in others the fountain of friendly intercourse. If

26

he were a leper or a man convicted of some hideous crime, his isolation could not be more complete. It was as if the sight of him affected men and women with a sense of something unnatural, monstrous. He sweated under this. But he was alive, and life was a reality to him, the will to live a dominant force. Unless he succumbed in a moment of madness, he knew that he would continue to struggle for life and happiness because that was instinctive, and fundamental instincts are stronger than logic, reason, circumstance.

How he was going to make his life even tolerably worth living was a question that harassed him with disheartening insistence as he watched through his window the slanting lines of rain and listened to the mournful cadences of the wind.

"I must get to work at something," he said to himself. "If I sit still and think much more—"

He did not carry that last sentence to its logical conclusion. Deliberately he strove to turn his thought out of the depressing channels in which it flowed and tried to picture what he should set about doing.

Not office work; he could not hope for any inside position such as his experience easily enabled him to fill. He knew timber, the making and marketing of it, from top to bottom. But he could not see himself behind a desk, directing or selling. His face would frighten clients. He smiled; that rare grimace he permitted himself when alone. Very likely he would have to accept the commonest sort of labor, in a mill yard, or on a booming ground, among workers not too sensitive to a man's appearance.

Staring through the streaming window, Hollister looked down on the traffic flow in the street, the hurrying figures that braved the storm in pursuit of

27

pleasure or of necessity, and while that desperate loneliness gnawed at him, he felt once more a sense of utter defeat, of hopeless isolation—and for the first time he wished to hide, to get away out of sight and hearing of men.

It was a fugitive impulse, but it set his mind harking back to the summer he had spent holidaying along the British Columbia coast long ago. The tall office buildings, with yellow window squares dotting the black walls, became the sun-bathed hills looking loftily down on rivers and bays and inlets that he knew. The wet floor of the street itself became a rippled arm of the sea, stretching far and silent between wooded slopes where deer and bear and all the furtive wild things of the forest went their accustomed way.

Hollister had wandered alone in those hushed places, sleeping with his face to the stars, and he had not been lonely. He wondered if he could do that again.

He sat nursing those visions, his imagination pleasantly quickened by them, as a man sometimes finds ease from care in dreaming of old days that were full of gladness. He was still deep in the past when he went to bed. And when he arose in the morning, the far places of the B. C. coast beckoned with a more imperious gesture, as if in those solitudes lay a sure refuge for such as he.

And why not, he asked himself? Here in this pushing seaport town, among the hundred and fifty thousand souls eagerly intent upon their business of gaining a livelihood, of making money, there was not one who cared whether he came or went, whether he was glad or sad, whether he had a song on his lips or the blackest gloom in his heart. He had done his bit as a man should. In the doing he had been broken in a cruel variety of ways. The war machine had chewed him up and spat him out on the scrap heap. None of these hale, unmaimed citizens cared to be annoyed by the sight of him, of what had happened to him.

And he could not much longer endure this unapproachableness, this palpable shrinking. He could not much longer bear to be in the midst of light and laughter, of friendly talk and smiling faces, and be utterly shut off from any part in it all. He was in as evil a case as a man chained to a rock and dying of thirst, while a clear, cold stream flowed at his feet. Whether he walked the streets or sat brooding in his room, he could not escape the embittered consciousness that all about him there was a great plenty of kindly fellowship which he craved and which he could not share because war had stamped its iron heel upon his face.

Yes, the more he thought about it, the more he craved the refuge of silence and solitude. If he could not escape from himself, at least he could withdraw from this feast at which he was a death's-head. And so he began to cast about him for a place to go, for an objective, for something that should save him from being purely aimless. In the end it came into his mind that he might go back and look over this timber in the valley of the Toba River, this last vestige of his fortune which remained to him by pure chance. He had bought it as an investment for surplus funds. He had never even seen it. He would have smiled, if his face had been capable of smiling, at the irony of his owning ten million feet of Douglas fir and red cedar—material to build a thousand cottages—he who no longer owned a roof to shelter his head, whose cash resources were only a few hundred dollars.

Whether Lewis sold the timber or not, he would go

29

and see it. For a few weeks he would be alone in the woods, where men would not eye him askance, nor dainty, fresh-faced women shrink from him as they passed.

CHAPTER IV

THE STEAMER BACKED AWAY FROM A FLOAT of which Hollister was the sole occupant. She swung in a wide semicircle, pointed her bluff bow down the Inlet, and presently all that he could see of her was the tip of her masts over a jutting point and the top of her red funnel trailing a pennant of smoke, black against a gray sky.

Hollister stood looking about him. He was clad like a logger, in thick mackinaws and heavy boots, and the texture of his garments was appropriate to the temperature, the weather. He seemed to have stepped into another latitude—which in truth he had, for the head of Toba Inlet lies a hundred and fifty miles northwest of Vancouver, and the thrust of that narrow arm of the sea carries it thirty miles into the glacial fastnesses of the Coast Range. The rain that drenched Vancouver became snow here. The lower slopes were green with timber which concealed the drifts that covered the rocky soil. A little higher certain clear spaces bared the whiteness, and all the tree tops, the drooping boughs, carried a burden of clinging snow. Higher still lifted grim peaks capped with massive snow banks that even midsummer heat could never quite dispel. But these upper heights were now hidden in clouds and wraiths of frost fog, their faces shrouded in this winter veil which—except for rare bursts of sunshine or sweeping northwest wind—would not be lifted till the vernal equinox.

It was very cold and very still, as if winter had laid a compelling silence on everything in the land. Except the faint slapping of little waves against the ice-encrusted, rocky shore, and the distant, harsh voices of some wheeling gulls, there was no sound or echo of a sound, as he stood listening.

Yet Hollister was not oppressed by this chill solitude. In that setting, silence was appropriate. It was merely unexpected. For so long Hollister had lived amid blaring noises, the mechanical thunder and lightning of the war, the rumble of industry, the shuffle and clatter of crowds, he had forgotten what it was like to be alone—and in the most crowded places he had suffered the most grievous loneliness. For the time being he was unconscious of his mutilation, since there was no one by to remind him by look or act. He was only aware of a curious interest in what he saw, a subdued wonder at the majestic beauty and the profound hush, as if he had been suddenly transferred from a place where life was maddeningly, distractingly clamorous to a spot where life was mute.

The head of Toba is neither a harbor nor a bay. One turns out of the island-studded Gulf of Georgia into an arm of the sea a mile in breadth. The cliffs and mountains grow higher, more precipitous mile by mile, until the Inlet becomes a chasm with the salt water for its floor. On past frowning points, around slow curves, boring farther and farther into the mainland through a passage like a huge tunnel, the roof of which has been blown away. Then suddenly there is an end to the sea. Abruptly, a bend is turned, and great mountains bar the way, peaks that lift from tidewater to treeless heights, formidable ranges bearing upon their rocky shoulders

31

the lingering remains of a glacial age. The Inlet ends there, the seaway barred by these frowning declivities.

Hollister remembered the head of Toba after a fashion. He had the lay of the land in his mind. He had never seen it in midwinter, but the snow, the misty vapors drifting along the mountain sides, did not confuse him.

From the float he now perceived two openings in the mountain chain. The lesser, coming in from the northwest, was little more than a deep and narrow gash in the white-clad hills. On his right opened the broader valley of the Toba River, up which he must go.

For a space of perhaps five minutes Hollister stood gazing about him. Then he was reminded of his immediate necessities by the chill that crept over his feet—for several inches of snow overlaid the planked surface of the landing float.

Knowing what he was about when he left Vancouver, Hollister had brought with him a twenty foot Hudson Bay freight canoe, a capacious shoal-water craft with high topsides. He slid this off the float, loaded into it sundry boxes and packages, and taking his seat astern, paddled inshore to where the rising tide was ruffled by the outsetting current of a river.

Here, under the steep shoulder of a mountain, rows of piles stood gaunt above the tide flats. When Hollister had last seen the mouth of the Toba, those same piles had been the support of long boom-sticks, within which floated hundreds of logs. On the flat beside the river there had stood the rough shacks of a logging camp. Donkey engines were puffing and grunting in the woods. Now the booming ground was empty, save for those decaying, teredo-eaten sticks, and the camp was a tumbledown ruin when he passed. He wondered if the

32

valley of the Toba were wholly deserted, if the forests of virgin timber covering the delta of that watercourse had been left to their ancient solitude. But he did not stop to puzzle over this. In ten minutes he was over the sandy bar at the river's mouth. The sea was hidden behind him. He passed up a sluggish waterway lined by alder and maple, covered with dense thickets, a jungle in which flourished the stalwart salmonberry and the thorny sticks of the devil's club. Out of this maze of undergrowth rose the tall brown columns of Douglas fir, of red cedar, of spruce and hemlock with their drooping boughs. Sloughs branched off in narrow laterals, sheeted with thin ice, except where the current kept it open, and out of these open patches flocks of wild duck scattered with a whir of wings. A mile upstream he turned a bend and passed a Siwash rancheria. The bright eyes of little brown-faced children peered shyly out at him from behind stumps. He could see rows of split salmon hung by the tail to the beams of an open-fronted smokehouse. Around another bend he came on a buck deer standing knee-deep in the water, and at the sight of him the animal snorted, leaped up the bank and vanished as silently as a shadow.

Hollister marked all these things without ceasing to ply his paddle. His objective lay some six miles upstream. But when he came at last to the upper limit of the tidal reach he found in this deep, slack water new-driven piling and freshly strung boom-sticks and acres of logs confined therein; also a squat motor tugboat and certain lesser craft moored to these timbers. A little back from the bank he could see the roofs of buildings.

He stayed his paddle a second to look with a mild curiosity. Then he went on. That human craving for companionship which had gained no response in the cities of two continents had left him for the time being. For that hour he was himself, sufficient unto himself. Here probably a score of men lived and worked. But they were not men he knew. They were not men who would care to know him—not after a clear sight of his face.

Hollister did not say that to himself in so many words. He was only subconsciously aware of this conclusion. Nevertheless it guided his actions. Through long, bitter months he had rebelled against spiritual isolation. The silent woods, the gray river, the cloud-wrapped hills seemed friendly by comparison with mankind—mankind which had marred him and now shrank from its handiwork.

So he passed by this community in the wilderness, not because he wished to but because he must.

Within half a mile he struck fast water, long straight reaches up which he gained ground against the current by steady strokes of the paddle, shallows where he must wade and lead his craft by hand. So he came at last to the Big Bend of the Toba River, a great S curve where the stream doubled upon itself in a mile-wide flat that had been stripped of its timber and lay now an unlovely vista of stumps, each with a white cap of snow.

On the edge of this, where the river swung to the southern limit of the valley and ran under a cliff that lifted a thousand foot sheer, he passed a small house. Smoke drifted blue from the stovepipe. A pile of freshly chopped firewood lay by the door. The dressed carcass of a deer hung under one projecting eave. Between two stumps a string of laundered clothes waved in the down-river breeze. By the garments Hollister knew a woman must be there. But none appeared to watch him pass. He did not halt, although the short afternoon was merging

34

into dusk and he knew the hospitality of those who go into lonely places to wrest a living from an untamed land. But he could not bear the thought of being endured rather than welcomed. He had suffered enough of that. He was in full retreat from just that attitude. He was growing afraid of contact with people, and he knew why he was afraid.

When the long twilight was nearly spent, he gained the upper part of the Big Bend and hauled his canoe out on the bank. A small flat ran back to the mouth of a canyon, and through the flat trickled a stream of clear water.

Hollister built a fire on a patch of dry ground at the base of a six-foot fir. He set up his tent, made his bed, cooked his supper, sat with his feet to the fire, smoking a pipe.

After four years of clamor and crowds, he marveled at the astonishing contentment which could settle on him here in this hushed valley, where silence rested like a fog. His fire was a red spot with a yellow nimbus. Beyond that ruddy circle, valley and cliff and clouded sky merged into an impenetrable blackness. Hollister had been cold and wet and hungry. Now he was warm and dry and fed. He lay with his feet stretched to the fire. For the time he almost ceased to think, relaxed as he was into a pleasant, animal well-being. And so presently he fell asleep.

In winter, north of the forty-ninth parallel, and especially in those deep clefts like the Toba, dusk falls at four in the afternoon, and day has not grown to its full strength at nine in the morning. Hollister had finished his breakfast before the first gleam of light touched the east. When day let him see the Alpine crevasses that notched the northern wall of the valley, he buckled on a belt that carried a sheath-ax, took up his rifle and began first of all a cursory exploration of the flat on which he camped.

It seemed to him that in some mysterious way he was beginning his life all over again—that life which his reason, with cold, inexorable logic, had classified as a hopeless ruin. He could not see wherein the ruin was lessened by embarking upon this lone adventure into the outlying places. Nevertheless, something about it had given a fillip to his spirits. He felt that he would better not inquire too closely into this; that too keen self-analysis was the evil from which he had suffered and which he should avoid. But he said to himself that if he could get pleasure out of so simple a thing as a canoe trip in a lonely region, there was hope for him yet. And in the same breath he wondered how long he could be sustained by that illusion.

He had a blueprint of the area covering the Big Bend. That timber limit which he had lightly purchased long ago, and which unaccountably went begging a purchaser, lay south and a bit west from where he set up his camp. He satisfied himself of that by the blueprint and the staking description. The northeast corner stake should stand not a great way back from the river bank.

He had to find a certain particularly described cedar tree, thence make his way south to a low cliff, at one extreme of which he should find a rock cairn with a squared post in its center. From that he could run his boundary lines with a pocket compass, until he located the three remaining corners.

Hollister found cedars enough, but none that pointed the way to a low cliff and a rock cairn. He ranged here and there, and at last went up the hillside which rose here so steeply as to be stiff climbing. It bore here and there a massive tree, rough-barked pillars rising to a branchy head two hundred feet in the air. But for the most part the slope was clothed with scrubby hemlock and thickets of young fir and patches of hazel, out of which he stirred a great many grouse and once a deer.

But if he found no stakes to show him the boundaries of his property, he gained the upper rim of the high cliff which walled the southern side of the Big Bend, and all the valley opened before him. Smoke lifted in a pale spiral from the house below his camp. Abreast of the log boom he had passed in the river, he marked the roofs of several buildings, and back of the clearings in the logged-over land opened white squares against the dusky green of the surrounding timber. He perceived that a considerable settlement had arisen in the lower valley, that the forest was being logged off, that land was being cleaned and cultivated. There was nothing strange in that. All over the earth the growing pressure of population forced men continually to invade the strongholds of the wilderness. Here lay fertile acres, water, forests to supply timber, the highway of the sea to markets. Only labor—patient, unremitting labor—was needed to shape all that great valley for cultivation. Cleared and put to the plow, it would produce abundantly. A vast, fecund area out of which man, withdrawing from the hectic pressure of industrial civilization, could derive sustenance—if he possessed sufficient hardihood to survive such hardships and struggle as his forefathers had for their common lot.

Hollister ranged the lower part of the hillside until hunger drove him back to camp. And, as it sometimes happens that what a man fails to come upon when he seeks with method and intent he stumbles upon by accident, so now Hollister, coming heedlessly downhill,

37

found the corner stake he was seeking. With his belt-axe he blazed a trail from this point to the flat below, so that he could find it again.

He made no further explorations that afternoon. He spent a little time in making his camp comfortable in ways known to any outdoor man. But when day broke clear the following morning he was on the hill, compass in hand, bearing due west from the original stake. He found the second without much trouble. He ran a line south and east and north again and so returned to his starting point by noon with two salient facts outstanding in his mind.

The first was that he suspected himself of having bought a poke which contained a pig of doubtful value. This, if true, made plain the difficulty of resale, and made him think decidedly unpleasant things of "Lewis and Company, Specialists in B. C. Timber." The second was that some one, within recent years, had cut timber on his limit. And it was his timber. The possessive sense was fairly strong in Hollister, as it usually is in men who have ever possessed any considerable property. He did not like the idea of being cheated or robbed. In this case there was superficial evidence that both these things had happened to him.

So when he had cooked himself a meal and smoked a pipe, he took to the high ground again to verify or disprove these unwelcome conclusions. In that huge and largely inaccessible region which is embraced within the boundaries of British Columbia, in a land where the industrial lifeblood flows chiefly along two railways and three navigable streams, there are many great areas where the facilities of transportation are much as they were when British Columbia was a field exploited only by trappers and traders. Settlement is still but a fringe upon the borders of the wilderness. Individuals and corporations own land and timber which they have never seen, sources of material wealth acquired cheaply, with an eye to the future. Beyond the railway belts, the navigable streams, the coastwise passages where steamers come and go, there lies a vast hinterland where canoe and pack-sack are still the mainstay of the traveler.

In this almost primeval region the large-handed fashion of primitive transactions is still in vogue. Men traffic in timber and mineral stakings on the word of other men. The coastal slopes and valleys are dotted with timber claims which have been purchased by men and corporations in Vancouver and New York and London and Paris and Berlin, bought and traded "sight unseen" as small boys swap jackknives. There flourishes in connection with this, on the Pacific coast, the business of cruising timber, a vocation followed by hardy men prepared to go anywhere, any time, in fair weather or foul. Commission such a man to fare into such a place, cruise such and such areas of timber land, described by metes and bounds. This resourceful surveyor-explorer will disappear. In the fullness of weeks he will return, bearded and travel-worn. He will place in your hands a report containing an estimate of so many million feet of standing fir, cedar, spruce, hemlock, with a description of the topography, an opinion on the difficulty or ease of the logging chance.

On the British Columbia coast a timber cruiser's report comes in the same category as a bank statement or a chartered accountant's audit of books; that is to say, it is unquestionable, an authentic statement of fact.

Within the boundaries defined by the four stakes of the limit Hollister owned there stood, according to the original cruising estimate, eight million feet of merchantable timber, half fir, half red cedar. The Douglas fir covered the rocky slopes and the cedar lined the gut of a deep hollow which split the limit midway. It was classed as a fair logging chance, since from that corner which dipped into the flats of the Toba a donkey engine with its mile-long arm of steel cable could snatch the logs down to the river, whence they would be floated to the sea and towed to the Vancouver sawmills.

Hollister had been guided by the custom of the country. He had put a surplus fund of cash into this property in the persuasion that it would resell at a profit, or that it could ultimately be logged at a still greater profit. And this persuasion rested upon the cruising estimate and the uprightness of "Lewis and Company, Specialists in B. C. Timber, Investments, Etc."

But Hollister had a practical knowledge of timber himself, acquired at first hand. He had skirted his boundaries and traversed the fringes of his property, and he saw scrubby, undersized trees where the four-foot trunks of Douglas fir should have lifted in brown ranks. He had looked into the bisecting hollow from different angles and marked magnificent cedars—but too few of them. Taken with the fact that Lewis had failed to resell even at a reduced price, when standing timber had doubled in value since the beginning of the war, Hollister had grave doubts, which, however, he could not establish until he went over the ground and made a rough estimate for himself.

This other matter of timber cutting was one he could settle in short order. It roused his curiosity. It gave him a touch of the resentment which stirs a man when he suspects himself of being the victim of pillaging vandals. No matter that despair had recently colored his mental vision; the sense of property right still functioned unimpaired. To be marred and impoverished and shunned as if he were a monstrosity were accomplished facts which had weighed upon him, an intolerable burden. He forgot that now. There was nothing much here to remind him. He was free to react to this new sense of outrage, this new evidence of mankind's essential unfairness.

In the toll taken of his timber by these unwarranted operations there was little to grieve over, he discovered before long. He had that morning found and crossed, after a long, curious inspection, a chute which debouched from the middle of his limit and dipped towards the river bottom apparently somewhere above his camp. He knew that this shallow trough built of slender poles was a means of conveying shingle-bolts from the site of cutting to the water that should float them to market. Earlier he had seen signs of felling among the cedars, but only from a distance. He was not sure he had seen right until he discovered the chute.

So now he went back to the chute and followed its winding length until it led into the very heart of the cedars in the hollow. Two or three years had elapsed since the last tree was felled. Nor had there ever been much inroad on the standing timber. Some one had begun operations there and abandoned the work before enough timber had been cut to half repay the labor of building that long chute.

Nor was that all. In the edge of the workings the branches and litter of harvesting those hoary old cedars had been neatly cleared from a small level space. And on this space, bold against the white carpet of snow, stood a small log house.

Hollister pushed open the latched door and stepped into the musty desolation of long abandoned rooms. It

41

was neatly made, floored with split cedar, covered by a tight roof of cedar shakes. Its tiny-paned windows were still intact. Within, it was divided into two rooms. There was no stove and there had never been a stove. A rough fireplace of stone served for cooking. An iron bar crossed the fireplace and on this bar still hung the fire-blackened pothooks. On nails and shelves against the wall pans still hung and dishes stood thick with dust. On a homemade bunk in one corner lay a mattress which the rats had converted to their own uses, just as they had played havoc with papers scattered about the floor and the oilcloth on the table.

Hollister passed into the other room. This had been a bedroom, a woman's bedroom. He guessed that by the remnants of fabric hanging over the windows, as well as by a skirt and sunbonnet which still hung from a nail. Here, too, was a bedstead with a rat-ruined mattress. And upon a shelf over the bed was ranged a row of books, perhaps two dozen volumes, which the rats had somehow respected—except for sundry gnawing at the bindings.

Hollister took one down. He smiled; that is to say, his eyes smiled and his features moved a little out of their rigid cast. Fancy finding the *contes* of August Strindberg, the dramatist, that genius of subtle perception and abysmal gloom, here in this forsaken place. Hollister fluttered the pages. Writing on the fly-leaf caught his eye. There was a date and below that:

Doris Cleveland—Her Book

He took down the others, one by one—an Iliad, a Hardy novel, "The Way of All Flesh" between "Kim" and "The Pilgrim Fathers", a volume of Swinburne rubbing shoulders with a California poet who sang of gibbous moons, "The Ancient Lowly" cheek by jowl with "Two

Years Before the Mast." A catholic collection, with strong meat sandwiched between some of the rat-gnawed covers. And each bore on the flyleaf the inscription of the first, written in a clear firm hand: Doris Cleveland— Her Book.

Hollister put the last volume back in place and stood staring at the row. Who was Doris Cleveland and why had she left her books to the rats?

He gave over his wonder at the patently unanswerable, went out into the living room, glanced casually over that once more, and so to the outside where the snow crisped under his feet now that the sun had withdrawn behind the hills. About the slashed area where the cedars had fallen, over stumps and broken branches and the low roof of the cabin, the virgin snow laid its softening whiteness, and the tall trees enclosed the spot with living green. A hidden squirrel broke out with brisk scolding, a small chirruping voice in a great silence. Here men had lived and worked and gone their way again. The forest remained as it was before. The thickets would soon arise to conceal man's handiwork.

Hollister shook off this fleeting impression of man's impermanence, and turned downhill lest dark catch him in the heavy timber and make him lose his way.

CHAPTER V

A WIND BEGAN TO SIGH AMONG THE TREES as Hollister made his way downhill. Over his evening fire he heard it grow to a lusty gale that filled the valley all night with moaning noises. Fierce gusts scattered the ashes of his fire and fluttered the walls of his tent as though some strong-lunged giant were huffing and puffing to blow his house down. At daylight the wind died. A sky banked solid with clouds began to empty upon the land a steady downpour of rain. All through the woods the sodden foliage dripped heavily. The snow melted, pouring muddy cataracts out of each gully, making tiny cascades over the edge of every cliff. Snowbanks slipped their hold on steep hillsides high on the north valley wall. They gathered way and came roaring down out of places hidden in the mist. Hollister could hear these slides thundering like distant artillery. Watching that grim façade across the river he saw, once or twice during the day, those masses plunge and leap, ten thousand tons of ice and snow and rock and crushed timber shooting over ledge and precipice to end with fearful crashing and rumbling in the depth of a steep-walled gorge.

He was tied to his camp. He could not stir abroad without more discomfort than he cared to undergo. Every bush, every bough, would precipitate upon him showers of drops at the slightest touch. He sat by his fire in the mouth of the tent and smoked and thought of the comfortable cabin up in the cedar hollow, and of Doris Cleveland's books. He began by reflecting that he might have brought one down to read. He ended before nightfall of a dull, rain-sodden day with a resolution to move up there when the weather cleared. A tent was well enough, but a house with a fireplace was better.

The rain held forty-eight hours without intermission. Then, as if the clouds had discharged their aqueous cargo and rode light as unballasted ships, they lifted in aerial fleets and sailed away, white in a blue sky. The sun, swinging in a low arc, cocked a lazy eye over the southern peaks, and Hollister carried his first pack-load up to the log cabin while the moss underfoot, the tree trunks, the green blades of the salal, and the myriad stalks of the low thickets were still gleaming with the white frost that came with a clearing sky.

He began with the idea of carrying up his blankets and three or four days' food. He ended by transporting up that steep slope everything but his canoe and the small tent. It might be, he said to himself as he lugged load after load, just a whim, a fancy, but he was free to act on a whim or a fancy, as free as if he were in the first blush of careless, adventurous youth—freer, because he had none of the impatient hopes and urges and dreams of youth. He was finished, he told himself in a transient mood of bitterness. Why should he be governed by practical considerations? He was here, alone in the unsentient, uncritical forest. It did not matter to any one whether he came or stayed. To himself it mattered least of all, he thought. There was neither plan nor purpose nor joy in his existence, save as he conceived the first casually, or snatched momentarily at the other in such simple ways as were available to him here—here where at least there was no one and nothing to harass him, where he was surrounded by a wild beauty that comforted him in some fashion beyond his understanding.

When he had brought the last of his food supply up to the cabin, he hauled the canoe back into a thicket and covered it with the glossy green leaves of the salal. He folded his tent in a tight bundle and strung it to a bough with a wire, out of reach of the wood rats.

These tasks completed, he began his survey of the standing timber on his limit.

At best he could make only a rough estimate, less accurate than a professional crusier's would be, but sufficient to satisfy him. In a week he was reasonably

45

certain that the most liberal estimate left less than half the quantity of merchantable timber for which he had paid good money. The fir, as a British Columbia logging chance, was all but negligible. What value resided there lay in the cedar alone.

By the time he had established this, the clear, cold, sunny days came to an end. Rain began to drizzle half-heartedly out of a murky sky. Overnight the rain changed to snow, great flat flakes eddying soundlessly earthward in an atmosphere uncannily still. For two days and a night this ballet of the snowflakes continued, until valley and slope and the high ridges were two feet deep in the downy white.

Then the storm which had been holding its breath broke with singular fury. The frost bared its teeth. The clouds still volleyed, but their discharge now filled the air with harsh, minute particles that stung bare skin like hot sand blown from a funnel. The wind shrieked its whole tonal gamut among the trees. It ripped the clinging masses of snow from drooping bough and exposed cliff and flung it here and there in swirling clouds. And above the treble voices of the storm Hollister, from the warm security of the cabin, could hear the intermittent rumbling of terrific slides. He could feel faint tremors in the earth from the shock of the arrested avalanche.

This elemental fury wore itself out at last. The wind shrank to chill whisperings. But the sky remained gray and lowering, and the great mountain ranges—white again from foot to crest, save where the slides had left gashes of brown earth and bare granite—were wrapped in winter mists, obscuring vapors that drifted and opened and closed again. Hollister could stir abroad once more. His business there was at an end. But he considered with reluctance a return to Vancouver. He was not happy. He was merely passive. It did not matter to anyone where he went. It did not matter much to himself. He was as well here as elsewhere until some substantial reason or some inner spur rowelled him into action.

Here there was no one to look askance at his disfigurement. He was less alone than he would be in town, for he found a subtle sense of companionship in this solitude, as if the dusky woods and those grim, aloof peaks accepted him for what he was, discounting all that misfortune which had visited him in the train of war. He knew that was sheer fantasy, but a fantasy that lent him comfort.

So he stayed. He had plenty of material resources, a tight warm house, food. He had reckoned on staying perhaps a month. He found now that his estimate of a month's staples was away over the mark. He could subsist two months. With care he could stretch it to three, for there was game on that southern slope—deer and the white mountain goat and birds. He hunted the grouse at first, but that gave small return for ammunition expended, although the flesh of the blue and willow grouse is pleasant fare. When the big storm abated he looked out one clear dawn and saw a buck deer standing in the open. At a distance of sixty yards he shot the animal, not because he hankered to kill, but because he needed meat. So under the cabin eaves he had quarters of venison, and he knew that he could go abroad on that snowy slope and stalk a deer with ease. There was a soothing pleasantness about a great blaze crackling in the stone fireplace. And he had Doris Cleveland's books.

Yes, Hollister reiterated to himself, it was better than

a bedroom off the blank corridor of a second-rate hotel and the crowded streets that were more merciless to a stricken man than these silent places. Eventually he would have to go back. But for the present—well, he occupied himself wholly with the present, and he did not permit himself to look far beyond.

From the deerskin he cut a quantity of fine strips and bent into oval shape two tough sticks of vine maple. Across these he strung a web of rawhide, thus furnishing himself with a pair of snowshoes which were a necessity now that the snow lay everywhere knee-deep and in many places engulfed him to the waist when he went into the woods.

It pleased him to go on long snowshoe hikes. He reached far up the ridges that lifted one after another behind his timber. Once he gained a pinnacle, a solitary outstanding hummock of snow-bound granite rising above all the rest, rising above all the surrounding forest. From this summit he gained an eagle's view. The long curve of Toba Inlet wound like a strip of jade away down to where the islands of the lower gulf spread with channels of the sea between. He could see the twin Redondas, Cortez, Raza, the round blob that was Hernando—a picturesque nomenclature that was the inheritance of Spanish exploration before the time of Drake. Beyond the flat reaches of Valdez, Vancouver Island, an empire in itself, lifted its rocky backbone, a misty purple against the western sky. He watched a steamer, trailing a black banner of smoke, slide through Baker Pass.

Out there men toiled at fishing; the woods echoed with the ring of their axes and the thin twanging of their saws; there would be the clank of machinery and the hiss of steam. But it was all hidden and muffled in those

48

vast distances. He swung on his heel. Far below, the houses of the settlement in the lower Toba sent up blue wisps of smoke. To his right ran with many a twist and turn the valley itself, winding away into remote fastnesses of the Coast Range, a strip of level, fertile, timbered land, abutted upon by mountains that shamed the Alps for ruggedness—mountains gashed by slides, split by gloomy crevasses, burdened with glaciers which in the heat of summer spewed foaming cataracts over cliffs a thousand foot sheer.

"Where the hill-heads split the tide
Of green and living air,
I would press Adventure hard
To her deepest lair.

"I would let the world's rebuke
Like a wind go by,
With my naked soul laid bare
To the naked sky."

Out of some recess in his memory, where they had fixed themselves long before, those lines rose to Hollister's lips. And he looked a long time before he turned downhill.

A week passed. Once more the blustery god of storms asserted his dominion, leaving the land, when he passed, a foot deeper in snow. If he had elected to stay there from choice, Hollister now kept close to his cabin from necessity, for passage with his goods to the steamer landing would have been a journey of more hardships than he cared to undertake. The river was a sheet of ice except over the shallow rapids. Cold winds whistled up and down the Toba. Once or twice on clear days he

49

climbed laboriously to a great height and felt the cold pressure of the northwest wind as he stood in the open; and through his field glasses he could see the Inlet and the highroads of the sea past the Inlet's mouth all torn by surging waves that reared and broke in flashing crests of foam. So he sat in the cabin and read Doris Cleveland's books one after another—verse, philosophy, fiction—and when physical inaction troubled him he cut and split and piled firewood far beyond his immediate need. He could not sit passive too long. Enforced leisure made too wide a breach in his defenses, and through that breach the demons of brooding and despondency were quick to enter. When neither books nor self-imposed tasks about the cabin served, he would take his rifle in hand, hook on the snowshoes, and trudge far afield in the surrounding forest.

On one of these journeys he came out upon the rim of the great cliff which rose like a wall of masonry along the southern edge of the flats in the Big Bend. It was a clear day. Hollister had a pair of very powerful binoculars. He gazed from this height down on the settlement, on the reeking chimneys of those distant houses, on the tiny black objects that were men moving against a field of white. He could hear a faint whirring which he took to be the machinery of a sawmill. He could see on the river bank and at another point in the near-by woods the feathery puff of steam. He often wondered about these people, buried, like himself, in this snowblanketed and mountain-ringed remoteness. Who were they? What manner of folk were they? He trifled with this curiosity. But it did not seriously occur to him that by two or three hours' tramping he could answer these idle speculations at first hand. Or if it did occur to him he shrank from the undertaking as one shrinks from a dubious experiment which has proved a failure in former trials.

But this day, under a frosty sky in which a February sun hung listless, Hollister turned his glasses on the cabin of the settler near his camp. He was on the edge of the cliff, so close that when he dislodged a fragment of rock it rolled over the brink, bounded once from the cliff's face, and after a lapse that grew to seconds struck with a distant thud among the timber at the foot of the precipice. Looking down through the binoculars it was as if he sat on the topmost bough of a tall tree in the immediate neighborhood of the cabin, although he was fully half a mile distant. He could see each garment of a row on a line. He could distinguish colors—a blue skirt, the deep green of salal and second-growth cedar, the weathered hue of the walls.

And while he stared a woman stepped out of the doorway and stood looking, turning her head slowly until at last she gazed steadily up over the cliff-brow as if she might be looking at Hollister himself. He sat on his haunches in the snow, his elbows braced on his knees, and trained the powerful lenses upon her. In a matter of half a minute her gaze shifted, turned back to the river. She shrugged her shoulders, or perhaps it was a shiver born of the cold, and then went back inside.

Hollister rested the binoculars upon his knee. His face did not alter. Facile expression was impossible to that marred visage. Pain or anger or sorrow could no longer write its message there for the casual beholder to read. The thin, twisted remnants of his lips could tighten a little, and that was all.

But his eyes, which had miraculously escaped injury, could still glow with the old fire, or grow dull and lifeless, giving some index to the mutations of his mind. And those darkly blue eyes, undimmed beacons amid the wreckage of his features, burned and gleamed now with a strange fire.

The woman who had been standing there staring up the hillside, with the sun playing hide and seek in her yellow hair, was Myra Hollister, his wife.

CHAPTER VI

HOLLISTER SAT IN THE SNOW, his gaze fixed upon this house on the river bank, wrestling with all the implications of this incredible discovery. He could neither believe what he had seen nor deny the evidence of his vision. He kept watch, with the glasses ready to fix upon the woman if she emerged again. But she did not reappear. The cold began to chill his body, to stiffen his limbs. He rose at last and made his way along the cliff, keeping always a close watch on the house below until he came abreast of his own quarters and turned reluctantly into the hollow where the cedars masked the log cabin.

He cooked a meal and ate his food in a mechanical sort of abstraction, troubled beyond measure, rousing himself out of periods of concentration in which there seemed, curiously, to be two of him present—one questioning and wondering, the other putting forward critical and sneering answers, pointing out the folly of his wonder.

In the end he began to entertain a real doubt not only of the correctness of his sight, but also of his sanity. For it was clearly impossible, his reason insisted, that Myra would be pioneering in those snowy solitudes, that she should live in a rude shack among stumps on the fringe of a wilderness. She had been a creature of luxury. Hollister could not conceive a necessity for her doing this. He had so arranged his affairs when he went to France that she had access to and complete control of his fortune. When she disclosed to him by letter the curious transformation of her affections, he had not revoked that arrangement. In the bewildering shock of that disclosure his first thought had not been a concern for his property. And the official report of him as killed in action which followed so soon after had allowed her to reap the full benefit of this situation. When she left London, if indeed she had left London, with her new associate in the field of emotion she had at least forty-five thousand dollars in negotiable securities.

And if so—then why?

Hollister's reason projected him swiftly and surely out of pained and useless speculation into forthright doing. From surety of what he had seen he passed to doubt, to uneasiness about himself: for if he could not look at a fair-haired woman without seeing Myra's face, then he must be going mad. He must know beyond any equivocation.

There was a simple way to know, and that way Hollister took while the embers of his noonday fire still glowed red on the hearth. He took his glasses and went down to the valley floor.

It would have been a simple matter and the essence of directness to walk boldly up and rap at the door. Certainly he would not be recognized. He could account for himself as a traveler in need of matches, some trifling thing to be borrowed. The wilderness is a destroyer of conventions. The passer-by needs to observe no ceremony. He comes from nowhere and

53

passes into the unknown, unquestioned as to his name, his purpose, or his destination. That is the way of all frontiers.

But Hollister wished to see without being seen. He did not know why. He did not attempt to fathom his reluctance for open approach. In the social isolation which his disfigurement had inflicted upon him, Hollister had become as much guided by instinct in his actions and impulses as by any coldly reasoned process. He was moved to his stealthy approach now by an instinct which he obeyed as blindly as the crawling worm.

He drew up within fifty yards of the house, moving furtively through thickets that screened him, and took up his post beside a stump. He peered through the drooping boughs of a clump of young cedar. There, in perfect concealment, hidden as the deer hides to let a roving hunter pass, Hollister watched with a patience which was proof against cold, against the discomfort of snow that rose to his thighs.

For an hour he waited. Except for the wavering smoke from the stovepipe, the place might have been deserted. The house was one with the pervading hush of the valley. Hollister grew numb. But he held his post. And at last the door opened and the woman stood framed in the opening.

She poised for an instant on the threshold, looking across the river. Her gaze pivoted slowly until it encompassed the arc of a half-circle, so that she faced Hollister squarely. He had the binoculars focused on her face. It seemed near enough to touch. Then she took a step or two gingerly in the snow, and stooping, picked up a few sticks from a pile of split wood. The door closed upon her once more.

Hollister turned upon the instant, retraced his steps across the flat, gained the foot of the steep hill and climbed step by step with prodigious effort in the deep snow until he reached the cabin.

He had reaffirmed the evidence of his eyes, and was no longer troubled by the vague fear that a disordered imagination had played him a disturbing trick. He had looked on his wife's face beyond a question. He accepted this astounding fact as a man must accept the indubitable. She was here in the flesh—this fair-haired, delicate-skinned woman whose arms and lips had once been his sure refuge. Here, in a rude cabin on the brink of a frozen river, chance had set her neighbor to him. To what end Hollister neither knew nor wished to inquire. He said to himself that it did not matter. He repeated this aloud.

He believed it to be true. How *could* it matter now?

But he found that it did matter in a way that he had not reckoned upon. For he found that he could not ignore her presence there. He could not thrust her into the outer darkness beyond the luminous circle of his thoughts. She haunted him with a troublesome insistence. He had loved her. She had loved him. If that love had gone glimmering, there still remained memory from which he could not escape, memories of caresses and embraces, of mutual passion, of all they had been to each other through a time when they desired only to be all things to each other. These things arose like ghosts out of forgotten chambers in his mind. He could not kill memory, and since he was a man, a physically perfect man, virile and unspent, memory tortured him.

He could not escape the consequences of being, the dominant impulses of life. No normal man can. He may think he can. He may rest secure for a time in that belief—but it will fail him. And of this Hollister now became aware.

He made every effort to shake off this new besetment, this fresh assault upon the tranquility he had attained. But he could not abolish recollection. He could not prevent his mind from dwelling upon this woman who had once meant so much to him, nor his flesh from responding to the stimulus of her nearness. When a man is thirsty he must drink. When he is hungry food alone can satisfy that hunger. And there arose in Hollister that ancient sex-hunger from which no man may escape.

It had been dormant in him for a time; dormant but not dead. In all his life Hollister had never gone about consciously looking upon women with a lustful eye. But he understood life, its curious manifestations, its sensory demands, its needs. For a long time pain, grief, suffering of body and anguish of mind had suppressed in him every fluttering of desire. He had accepted that apparent snuffing out of passion thankfully. Where, he had said to himself when he thought of this, where would he find such a woman as he could love who would find pleasure in the embrace of a marred thing like himself? Ah, no. He had seen them shrink too often from mere sight of his twisted face. The fruits of love were not for the plucking of such as he. Therefore he was glad that the urge of sex no longer troubled him. Yet here in a brief span, amid these silent hills and dusky forests where he had begun to perceive that life might still have compensations for him, this passivity had been overthrown, swept away, destroyed. He could not look out over the brow of that cliff without thinking of the woman in the valley below. He could not think of her without the floodgates of his recollection loosing their torrents. He had slept with her head pillowed in the crook of his arm. He had been wakened by the warm pressure of her lips on his. All the tender intimacies of their life together had lurked in his subconsciousness, to rise and torture him now.

And it was torture. He would tramp far along those slopes and when he looked too long at some distant peak he would think of Myra. He would sit beside his fireplace with one of Doris Cleveland's books in his hand and the print would grow blurred and meaningless. In the glow of the coals Myra's face would take form and mock him with a seductive smile. Out of the gallery of his mind pictures would come trooping, and in each the chief figure was that fair-haired woman who had been his wife. At night while he slept, he was hounded by dreams in which the conscious repression of his waking hours went by the board and he was delivered over to the fantastic deviltries of the subconscious.

Hollister had never been a sentimental fool, nor a sensualist whose unrestrained passions muddied the streams of his thought. But he was a man, aware of both mind and body. Neither functioned mechanically. Both were complex. By no effort of his will could he command the blood in his veins to course less hotly. By no exercise of any power he possessed could he force his mind always to do his bidding. He did not love this woman whose nearness so profoundly disturbed him. Sometimes he hated her consciously, with a volcanic intensity that made his fingers itch for a strangling grip upon her white throat. She had ripped up by the roots his faith in life and love at a time when he sorely needed that faith, when the sustaining power of some such faith was his only shield against the daily impact of bloodshed and suffering and death, of all the nerve-shattering accompaniments of war.

Yet he suffered from the spur of her nearness, those haunting pictures of her which he could not bar out of his mind, those revived memories of alluring tenderness, of her clinging to him with soft arms and laughter on her lips.

He would stand on the rim of the cliff, looking down at the house by the river, thinking the unthinkable, attracted and repulsed, a victim to his imagination and the fever of his flesh, until it seemed to him sometimes that in the loaded chamber of his rifle lay the only sure avenue of escape from these vain longings, from unattainable desire.

Slowly a desperate resolution formed within his seething brain, shadowy at first, recurring again and again with insistent persuasion, until it no longer frightened him as it did at first, no longer made him shrink and feel a loathing of himself.

She was his wife. She had ceased to care for him. She had given herself to another man. No matter, she was still his. Legally, beyond any shadow of a doubt. The law and the Church had joined them together. Neither man nor God had put them asunder, and the law had not released them from their bonds. Then, if he wanted her, why should he not take her?

Watching the house day after day, hours at a stretch, Hollister brooded over this new madness. But it no longer seemed to him madness. It came to seem fit and proper, a matter well within his rights. He postulated a hypothetical situation; if he, officially dead, resurrected himself and claimed her, who was there to say him nay if he demanded and exacted a literal fulfilment of her solemn covenant to "love, honor, and obey?" She herself? Hollister snapped his fingers. The man she lived with? Hollister dismissed him with an impatient gesture.

The purely animal man, which is never wholly extinguished, which merely lurks unsuspected under centuries of cultural veneer to rise lustily when slowly acquired moralities shrivel in the crucible of passion, now began to actuate Hollister with a strange cunning, a ferocity of anticipation. He would repossess himself of this fair-haired woman. And she should have no voice in the matter. Very well. But how?

That was simplicity itself. No one knew such a man as he was in the Toba country. All these folk in the valley below went about unconscious of his existence in that cabin well hidden among the great cedars. All he required was the conjunction of a certain kind of weather and the absence of the man. Falling snow to cover the single track that should lead to this cabin, to bury the dual footprints that should lead away. The absence of the man was to avoid a clash: not because Hollister feared that; simply because in his mind the man was not a factor to be considered, except as the possibility of his interference should be most easily avoided. Because if he did interfere he might have to kill him, and that was a complication he did not wish to invoke. Somehow he felt no grudge against this man, no jealousy.

The man's absence was a common occurrence. Hollister had observed that nearly every day he was abroad in the woods with a gun. For the obscuring storm, the obliterating snowfall, he would have to wait.

All this, every possible contingency, took form as potential action in his obsessed mind—with neither perception nor consideration of consequences. The consummation alone urged him. The most primitive instinct swayed him. The ultimate consequences were as nothing.

This plan was scarcely formed in Hollister's brain before he modified it. He could not wait for that happy conjunction of circumstances which favored action. He must create his own circumstances. This he readily perceived as the better plan. When he sought a way it was revealed to him.

A few hundred yards above the eastern limit of the flat where his canoe was cached, there jutted into the river a low, rocky point. From the river back to the woods the wind had swept the bald surface of this little ridge clear of snow. He could go down over those sloping rocks to the glare ice of the river. He could go and come and leave no footprints, no trace. There would be no mark to betray, unless a searcher ranged well up the hillside and so came upon his track. And if a man, searching for this woman, bore up the mountain side and came at last to the log cabin—what would he find? Only another man who had arisen after being dead and had returned to take possession of his own!

Hollister threw back his head and burst into sardonic laughter. It pleased him, this devastating jest which he was about to perpetrate upon his wife and her lover.

From the seclusion of the timber behind this point of rocks he set himself to watch through his glasses the house down the river. The second day of keeping this vigil he saw the man leave the place, gun in hand, cross on the river ice and vanish in the heavy timber of that wide bottom land. Hollister did not know what business took him on these recurrent absences; hunting, he guessed, but he had noted that the man seldom returned before late in the afternoon, and sometimes not till dusk.

He waited impatiently for an hour. Then he went down to the frozen river. Twenty minutes' rapid striding brought him to the door of the house.

The place was roughly built of split cedar. A door and a window faced the river. The window was uncurtained, a bald square of glass. The sun had grown to some little strength. The air that morning had softened to a balminess like spring. Hollister had approached unseen over snow softened by this warmth until it lost its frosty crispness underfoot. Now, through the uncurtained window, his gaze marked a section of the interior, and what he saw stayed the hand he lifted to rap on the door.

A man young, smooth-faced, dark almost to swarthiness, sat on a bench beside a table on which stood the uncleared litter of breakfast. And Myra sat also at the table with one corner of it between them. She leaned an elbow on the board and nursed her round chin in the palm of that hand, while the other was imprisoned between the two clasped hands of the man. He was bending over this caught hand, leaning eagerly toward her, speaking rapidly.

Myra sat listening. Her lips were slightly parted. Her eyelids drooped. Her breast rose and fell in a slow, rhythmic heave. Otherwise she was motionless and faintly smiling, as if she were given up to some blissful languor. And the man spoke on, caressing her imprisoned hand, stroking it, looking at her with the glow of conquest in his hot eyes.

Hollister leaned on the muzzle of his grounded rifle, staring through the window. He could see their lips move. He could hear faintly the tense murmur of the man's voice. He saw the man bend his head and press a kiss on the imprisoned hand.

He turned softly and went down the bank to the river and walked away over the ice. When he had put five hundred yards between himself and that house, he turned to look back. He put his hand to his face and wiped away drops of sweat, a clammy exudation that broke out all over his body very much as if he had just become aware of escaping by a hair's breadth some imminent and terrible disaster. In truth that was precisely his feeling—as if he had been capering madly on the brink of some fearful abyss which he could not see until it was revealed to him in a terrifying flash.

He shivered. His ego grovelled in the dirt. He had often smiled at theories of dual personality. But standing there on the frozen stream with the white hills looming high above the green-forested lowlands he was no longer sure of anything, least of all whether in him might lurk a duality of forces which could sway him as they would. Either that, or he had gone mad for a while, a brief madness born of sex-hunger, of isolation, of brooding over unassuaged bitterness.

Perhaps he might have done what he set out to do if the man had not been there. But he did not think so now. The brake of his real manbood had begun to set upon those wild impulses before he drew up to the door and looked in the window. What he saw there only cleared with a brusque hand the cobwebs from his brain.

Fundamentally, Hollister hated trickery, deceit, unfairness, double-dealing. In his normal state he would neither lie, cheat, nor steal. He had grown up with a natural tendency to regard his own ethics as the common attribute of others. There had somehow been born in him, or had developed as an intrinsic part of his character early in life, a child-like, trustful quality of faith in human goodness. And that faith had begun to reel under grievous blows dealt it in the last four years.

Myra was not worth the taking, even if he had a legal and moral right to take her (not that he attempted to justify himself now by any such sophistry). She could not be faithful, it seemed, even to a chosen lover. The man into whose eyes she gazed with such obvious complaisance was not the man she lived with in that house on the river bank. Hollister had watched him through the glasses often enough to know. He was a tall, ruddy-faced man, a big man and handsome. Hollister had looked at him often enough, reckoning him to be an Englishman, the man Myra married in London, the man for whom she had conceived such a passion that she had torn Hollister's heart by the brutal directness of her written avowal. Hollister had watched him swinging his ax on the woodpile, going off on those long tramps in the bottom land. He might be within gunshot of the house at this moment.

Hollister found himself pitying this man. He found himself wondering if it had always been that way with Myra, if she were the helpless victim of her own senses. There were women like that. Plenty of them. Men too. Sufferers from an overstimulated sexuality. He could not doubt that. He suspected that he was touched with it himself.

What a muddle life was, Hollister reflected sadly, looking down from the last opening before he plunged into the cedar grove that hid the log cabin. Here, amid this wild beauty, this grandeur of mountain and forest, this silent land virginal in its winter garment, human passion, ancient as the hills themselves, functioned in the old, old way.

But he did not expend much thought on mere generalizations. The problem of Myra and her lovers was no longer his problem; their passions and pains were not his. Hollister understood very clearly that he had escaped an action that might have had far-reaching

63

consequences. He was concerned with his escape and also with the possible recurrence of that strange obsession, or mood, or madness, or whatever it was that had so warped his normal outlook that he could harbor such thoughts and plan such deeds. He did not want to pass through that furnace again.

He had had enough of the Toba Valley. No, he modified that. The valley and the sentinel peaks that stood guard over it, the lowlands duskily green and full of balsamy odors from the forest, was still a goodly place to be. But old sins and sorrows and new, disturbing phases of human passion were here at his elbow to dispel the restful peace he had won for a little while. He must escape from that.

To go was not so simple as his coming. The river was frozen, that watery highway closed. But he solved the problem by knowledge gained in those casual wanderings along the ridge above the valley. He knew a direct way of gaining the Inlet head on foot.

So he spent a last night before the fireplace, staring silently into the dancing blaze, seeing strange visions in the glowing coals, lying down to heavy, dreamless sleep at last in his bunk.

At daybreak he struck out westward along the great cliff that frowned on the Big Bend, his blankets and a small emergency supply of food in a bulky pack upon his shoulders. When the sheer face of the cliff ran out to a steep, scrubbily timbered hillside, he dropped down to the valley floor and bore toward the river through a wide flat. Here he moved through a forest of cedar and spruce so high and dense that no ray of sun ever penetrated through those interlocked branches to warm the earth in which those enormous trunks were rooted. Moss hung in streamers from the lower boughs. It was dusky there in full day. The wild things of the region made this their sanctuary. Squirrels scolded as he passed. The willow grouse tamely allowed him to approach within twenty feet before they fluttered to the nearest thicket. The deep snow was crisscrossed by the tracks of innumerable deer driven down from the highlands by the deeper snow above.

For a time, in this shadowy temple of the pagan gods, Hollister was forced to depend on a pocket compass to hold a course in the direction he wished to go. But at last he came out in a slashing, a place where loggers had been recently at work. Here a donkey engine stood black and cold on its skids, half-buried in snow. Beyond this working a clear field opened, and past the field he saw the outline of the houses on the river bank and he bore straight for these to learn upon what days the steamer touched the head of Toba and how he might best gain that float upon which he had disembarked two months before.

CHAPTER VII

HOLLISTER STOWED HIS PACK IN THE SMOKING ROOM and stood outside by the rail, watching the Toba Valley fall astern, a green fissure in the white rampart of the Coast Range. Chance, the inscrutable arbiter of human destinies, had directed him that morning to a man cutting wood on the bank of the river close by that cluster of houses where other men stirred about various tasks, where there must have been wives and mothers, for he saw a dozen children at play by a snow fort.

"Steamer?" the man answered Hollister's inquiry. "Say, if you want to catch her, you just about got time.

65

Two fellows from here left awhile ago. If you hurry, maybe you can catch 'em. If you catch 'em before they get out over the bar, they'll give you a lift to the float. If you don't, you're stuck for a week. There's only one rowboat down there."

Hollister had caught them.

He took a last, thoughtful look. Over the vessel's bubbling wake he could see the whole head of the Inlet deep in winter snows—a white world, coldly aloof in its grandeur. It was beautiful, full of the majesty of serene distances, of great heights. It stood forth clothed with the dignity of massiveness, of permanence. It was as it had been for centuries, calm and untroubled, unmoved by floods and slides, by fires and slow glacial changes. Yes, it was beautiful and Hollister looked a long time, for he was not sure he would see it again. He had a canoe and a tent cached in that silent valley, but for these alone he would not return. Neither the ownership of that timber which he now esteemed of doubtful value nor the event of its sale would require his presence there.

He continued to stare with an absent look in his eyes until a crook in the Inlet hid those white escarpments and outstanding peaks, and the Inlet walls—themselves lifting to dizzy heights that were shrouded in rolling mist—marked the limit of his visual range. The ship's bell tinkled the noon hour. A white-jacketed steward walked the decks, proclaiming to all and sundry that luncheon was being served. Hollister made his way to the dining saloon.

The steamer was past Salmon Bay when he returned above decks to lean on the rail, watching the shores flit by, marking with a little wonder the rapid change in temperature, the growing mildness in the air as the

66

steamer drew farther away from the gorge-like head of Toba with its aerial ice fields and snowy slopes. Twenty miles below Salmon Bay the island-dotted area of the Gulf of Georgia began. There a snowfall seldom endured long, and the teeth of the frost were blunted by eternal rains. There the logging camps worked full blast the year around, in sunshine and drizzle and fog. All that region bordering on the open sea bore a more genial aspect and supported more people and industries in scattered groups than could be found in any of those lonely inlets.

Hollister was not thinking particularly of these things. He had eaten his meal at a table with half a dozen other men. In the saloon probably two score others applied themselves, with more diligence than refinement, to their food. There was a leavening of women in this male mass of loggers, fishermen, and what-not. A buzz of conversation filled the place. But Hollister was not a participant. He observed casual, covert glances at his disfigured face, that disarrangement of his features and marring of his flesh which made men ill at ease in his presence. He felt a recurrence of the old protest against this. He experienced a return of that depression which had driven him out of Vancouver. It was a disheartenment from which nothing in the future, no hope, no dream, could deliver him. He was as he was. He would always be like that. The finality of it appalled him.

After a time he became aware of a young woman leaning, like himself, against the rail a few feet distant. He experienced a curious degree of self-consciousness as he observed her. The thought crossed his mind that presently she would look at him and move away. When she did not, his eyes kept coming back to her with the involuntary curiosity of the casual male concerning the strange female. She was of medium height, well-formed, dressed in a well-tailored gray suit. Under the edges of a black velvet turban her hair showed glossy brown in a smooth roll. She had one elbow propped on the rail and her chin nestled in the palm. Hollister could see a clean-cut profile, the symmetrical outline of her nose, one delicately colored cheek above the gloved hand and a neckpiece of dark fur.

He wondered what she was so intent upon for so long, leaning immobile against that wooden guard. He continued to watch her. Would she presently bestow a cursory glance upon him and withdraw to some other part of the ship? Hollister waited for that with moody expectation. He found himself wishing to hear her voice, to speak to her, to have her talk to him. But he did not expect any such concession to a whimsical desire.

Nevertheless the unexpected presently occurred. The girl moved slightly. A hand-bag slipped from under her arm to the deck. She half-turned, seemed to hesitate. Instinctively, as a matter of common courtesy to a woman, Hollister took a step forward, picked it up. Quite as instinctively he braced himself, so to speak, for the shocked look that would gather like a shadow on her piquant face.

But it did not come. The girl's gaze bore imperturbably upon him as he restored the handbag to her hand. The faintest sort of smile lurked about the corners of a pretty mouth. Her eyes were a cloudy gray. They seemed to look out at the world with a curious impassivity. That much Hollister saw in a fleeting glance.

"Thanks, very much," she said pleasantly. Hollister

68

resumed his post against the rail. His movement had brought him nearer, so that he stood now within arm's length, and his interest in her had awakened, become suddenly intense. He felt a queer thankfulness, a warm inward gratefulness, that she had been able to regard his disfigurement unmoved. He wondered how she could. For months he had encountered women's averted faces, the reluctant glances of mingled pity and distaste which he had schooled himself to expect and endure but which he never ceased to resent. This girl's uncommon selfpossession at close contact with him was a puzzle as well as a pleasure. A little thing, to be sure, but it warmed Hollister. It was like an unexpected gleam of sunshine out of a sky banked deep with clouds.

Presently, to his surprise, the girl spoke to him. "Are we getting near the Channel Islands?" She was looking directly at him, and Hollister was struck afresh with the curious quality of her gaze, the strangely unperturbed directness of her eyes upon him. He made haste to answer her question.

"We'll pass between them in another mile. You can see the western island a little off our starboard bow."

"I should be very glad if I could, but I shall have to take your word for its being there."

"I'm afraid I don't quite understand."

A smile spread over her face at the puzzled tone.

"I'm blind," she explained, with what struck Hollister as infinite patience. "If my eyes were not sightless, I shouldn't have to ask a stranger about the Channel Islands. I used to be able to see them well enough."

Hollister stared at her. He could not associate those wide gray eyes with total darkness. He could scarcely make himself comprehend a world devoid of light and color, an existence in which one felt and breathed and

69

had being amid eternal darkness. Yet for the moment he was selfish enough to feel glad. And he said so, with uncharacteristic impulsiveness.

"I'm glad you can't see," he found himself saying. "If you could—"

"What a queer thing to say," the girl interrupted. "I thought every one always regarded a blind person as an object of pity."

There was an unmistakably sardonic inflection in the last sentence.

"But you don't find it so, eh?" Hollister questioned eagerly. He was sure he had interpreted that inflection. "And you sometimes resent that attitude, eh?"

"I daresay I do," the girl replied, after a moment's consideration. "To be unable to see is a handicap. At the same time to have pity drooled all over one is sometimes irritating. But why did you just say you were glad I was blind?"

"I didn't mean that. I meant that I was glad you couldn't see *me*," he explained. "One of Fritz's shells tore my face to pieces. People don't like to look at the result. Women particularly. You can't see my wrecked face, so you don't shudder and pass on. I suppose that is why I said that the way I did."

"I see. You feel a little bit glad to come across some one who doesn't know whether your face is straight or crooked? Some one who accepts you sight unseen, as she would any man who spoke and acted courteously? Is that it?"

"Yes," Hollister admitted. "That's about it."

"But your friends and relatives?" she suggested softly.

"I have no relatives in this country," he said. "And I have no friends anywhere, now."

70

She considered this a moment, rubbing her cheek with a gloved forefinger. What was she thinking about, Hollister wondered?

"That must be rather terrible at times. I'm not much given to slopping over, but I find myself feeling sorry for you—and you are only a disembodied voice. Your fix is something like my own," she said at last. "And I have always contended that misery loves company."

"You were right in that, too," Hollister replied. "Misery wants pleasant company. At least, that sort of misery which comes from isolation and unfriendliness makes me appreciate even chance companionship."

"Is it so bad as that?" she asked quickly. The tone of her voice made Hollister quiver, it was so unexpected, so wistful.

"Just about. I've become a stray dog in this old world. And it used to be a pretty good sort of a world for me in the old days. I'm not whining. But I do feel like kicking. There's a difference, you know."

He felt ashamed of this mild outburst as soon as it was uttered. But it was true enough, and he could not help saying it. There was something about this girl that broke down his reticence, made him want to talk, made him feel sure he would not be misunderstood.

She nodded.

"There is a great difference. Any one with any spirit will kick if there is anything to kick about. And it's always shameful to whine. You don't seem like a man who *could* whine."

"How can you tell what sort of man I am?" Hollister inquired. "You just said that I was only a disembodied voice."

She laughed, a musical low-toned chuckle that pleased him.

71

"One gets impressions," she answered. "Being sightless sharpens other faculties. You often have very definite impressions in your mind about people you have never seen, don't you?"

"Oh, yes," he agreed. "I daresay every one gets such impressions."

"Sometimes one finds those impressions are merely verified by actual sight. So there you are. I get a certain impression of you by the language you use, your tone, your inflections—and by a something else which in those who can see is called intuition, for lack of something more definite in the way of a term."

"Aren't you ever mistaken in those impressionistic estimates of people?"

She hesitated a little.

"Sometimes—not often. That sounds egotistic, but really it is true."

The steamer drew out of the mouth of Toba Inlet. In the widening stretch between the mainland and the Redondas a cold wind came whistling out of Homfray Channel. Hollister felt the chill of it through his mackinaw coat and was moved to thought of his companion's comfort.

"May I find you a warm place to sit?" he asked. "That's an uncomfortable breeze. And do you mind if I talk to you? I haven't talked to any one like you for a long time."

She smiled assent.

"Ditto to that last," she said.

"You aren't a western man, are you?" she continued, as Hollister took her by the arm and led her toward a cabin abaft the wheelhouse on the boat deck, a roomy lounging place unoccupied save by a fat woman taking a midday nap in one corner, her double chin sunk on her ample bosom.

"No," he said. "I'm from the East. But I spent some time out here once or twice, and I remembered the coast as a place I liked. So I came back here when the war was over and everything gone to pot—at least where I was concerned. My name is Hollister."

"Mine," she replied, "is Cleveland." Hollister looked at her intently.

"Doris Cleveland—her book," he said aloud. It was to all intents and purposes a question.

"Why do you say that?" the girl asked quickly. "And how do you happen to know my given name?"

"That was a guess," he answered. "Is it right?"

"Yes—but—"

"Let me tell you," he interrupted. "It's queer, and still it's simple enough. Two months ago I went into Toba Inlet to look at some timber about five miles up the river from the mouth. When I got there I decided to stay awhile. It was less lonesome there than in the racket and hustle of a town where I knew no one and nobody wanted to know me. I made a camp, and in looking over a stretch of timber on a slope that runs south from the river I found a log cabin—"

"In a hollow full of big cedars back of the cliff along the south side of the Big Bend?" the girl cut in eagerly. "A log house with two rooms, where some shingle-bolts had been cut—with a bolt-chute leading downhill?"

"The very same," Hollister continued. "I see you know the place. And in this cabin there was a shelf with a row of books, and each one had written on the flyleaf, 'Doris Cleveland—Her Book.' "

"My poor books," she murmured. "I thought the rats had torn them to bits long ago."

"No. Except for a few nibbles at the binding.

73

Perhaps," Hollister said whimsically, "the rats knew that some day a man would need those books to keep him from going crazy, alone there in those quiet hills. They were good books, and they would give his mind something to do besides brooding over past ills and an empty future."

"They did that for you?" she asked.

"Yes. They were all the company I had for two months. I often wondered who Doris Cleveland was and why she left her books to the rats—and was thankful that she did. So you lived up there?"

"Yes. It was there I had my last look at the sun shining on the hills. I daresay the most vivid pictures I have in my mind are made up of things there. Why, I can see every peak and gorge yet, and the valley below with the river winding through and the beaver meadows in the flats—all those slides and glaciers and waterfalls—cascades like ribbons of silver against green velvet. I loved it all—it was so beautiful."

She spoke a little absently, with the faintest shadow of regret, her voice lingering on the words. And after a momentary silence she went on:

"We lived there nearly a year, my two brothers and I. I know every rock and gully within two miles of that cabin. I helped to build that little house. I used to tramp around in the woods alone. I used to sit and read, and sometimes just dream, under those big cedars on hot summer afternoons. The boys thought they would make a little fortune in that timber. Then one day, when they were felling a tree, a flying limb struck me on the head—and I was blind; in less than two hours of being unconscious I woke up, and I couldn't see anything— like that almost," she snapped her finger. "On top of that my brothers discovered that they had no right to cut

74

timber there. Things were going badly in France, too. So they went overseas. They were both killed in the same action, on the same day. My books were left there because no one had the heart to carry them out. It was all such a muddle. Everything seemed to go wrong at once. And you found them and enjoyed having them to read. Isn't it curious how things that seem so incoherent, so unnecessary, so disconnected, sometimes work out into an orderly sequence, out of which evil comes to some and good to others? If we could only forestall Chance! Blind, blundering, witless Chance!"

Hollister nodded, forgetting that the girl could not see. For a minute they sat silent. He was thinking how strange it was that he should meet this girl whose books he had been poring over all these weeks. She had a mind, he perceived. She could think and express her thoughts in sentences as clean-cut as her face. She made him think, thrust him face to face with an abstraction. Blind, blundering, witless Chance! Was there nothing more than that? What else was there?

"You make me feel ashamed of myself," he said at last. "Your luck has been worse than mine. Your handicap is greater than mine—at least you must feel it so. But you don't complain. You even seem quite philosophic about it. I wish I could cultivate that spirit. What's your secret?"

"Oh, I'm not such a marvel," she said, and the slight smile came back to lurk around the corners of her mouth. "There are times when I rebel—oh, desperately. But I get along very nicely as a general thing. One accepts the inevitable. I comfort myself with the selfish reflection that if I can't see a lot that I would dearly love to see, I am also saved the sight of things that are mean and sordid and disturbing. If I seem cheerful I daresay

75

it's because I'm strong and healthy and have grown used to being blind. I'm not nearly so helpless as I may seem. In familiar places and within certain bounds, I can get about nearly as well as if I could see."

The steamer cleared the Redondas, stood down through Desolation Sound and turned her blunt nose into the lower gulf just as dark came on. Hollister and Doris Cleveland sat in the cabin talking. They went to dinner together, and if there were curious looks bestowed upon them Hollister was too engrossed to care and the girl, of course, could not see those sidelong, unspoken inquiries. After dinner they found chairs in the same deck saloon and continued their conversation until ten o'clock, when drowsiness born of a slow, rolling motion of the vessel drove them to their berths.

The drowsiness abandoned Hollister as soon as he turned in. He lay wakeful, thinking about Doris Cleveland. He envied her courage and fortitude, the calm assurance with which she seemed to face the world which was all about her and yet hidden from her sight. She was really an extraordinary young woman, he decided.

She was traveling alone. For several months she had been living with old friends of the family on Stuart Island, close by the roaring tiderace of the Euclataw Rapids. She was returning there, she told Hollister, after three weeks or so in Vancouver. The steamer would dock about daylight the following morning. When Hollister offered to see her ashore and to her destination, she accepted without any reservations. It comforted Hollister's sadly bruised ego to observe that she even seemed a trifle pleased.

"I have once or twice got a steward to get me ashore and put me in a taxi," she said. "But if you don't mind,

76

Mr. Hollister."

And Hollister most decidedly did not mind. Doris Cleveland had shot like a pleasant burst of colorful light across the grayest period of his existence, and he was loath to let her go.

He dropped off to sleep at last, to dream, strangely enough and with astonishing vividness, of the cabin among the great cedars with the snow banked white outside the door. He saw himself sitting beside the fireplace poring over one of Doris Cleveland's books. And he was no longer lonely, because he was not alone.

He smiled at himself, remembering this fantasy of the subconscious mind, when the steward's rap at the door wakened him half an hour before the steamer docked.

CHAPTER VIII

QUARTERED ONCE MORE IN THE CITY he had abandoned two months earlier, Hollister found himself in the grip of new desires, stirred by new plans, his mind yielding slowly to the conviction that life was less barren than it seemed. Or was that, he asked himself doubtfully, just another illusion which would uphold him for awhile and then perish? Not so many weeks since, a matter of days almost, life, so far as he was concerned, held nothing, promised nothing. All the future years through which he must live because of the virility of his body seemed nothing but a dismal fog in which he must wander without knowing where he went or what lay before him.

Now it seemed that he had mysteriously acquired a starting point and a goal. He was aware of a new impetus. And since life had swept away a great many illusions which he had once cherished as proven reality, he did not shrink from or misunderstand the cause underlying this potent change in his outlook. He pondered on this. He wished to be sure. And he did not have to strain himself intellectually to understand that Doris Cleveland was the outstanding factor in this change.

Each time he met her, he breathed a prayer of thanks for her blindness, which permitted her to accept him as a man instead of shrinking from him as a monster. Just as the man secure in the knowledge that he possesses the comfort and security of a home can endure with fortitude the perils and hardships of a bitter trial, so Hollister could walk the streets of Vancouver now, indifferent to the averted eyes, the quick glance of reluctant pity. He could get through the days without brooding. Loneliness no longer made him shudder with its clammy touch.

For that he could thank Doris Cleveland, and her alone. He saw her nearly every day. She was the straw to which he, drowning, clung with all his might. The most depressing hours that overtook him were those in which he visualized her floating away beyond his reach.

To Hollister, as he saw more of her, she seemed the most remarkable woman he had ever known. Her loss of sight had been more than compensated by an extraordinary acuteness of mental vision. The world about her might now be one of darkness, but she had a precise comprehension of its nature, its manifestations, its complexities. He had always taken blindness as a synonym for helplessness, a matter of uncertain groping, of timidities, of despair. He revised that conclusion sharply in her case. He could not associate the most remote degree of helplessness with Doris Cleveland when they walked, for instance, through

Stanley Park from English Bay to Second Beach. That broad path, with the Gulf swell muttering along the bouldery shore on one side and the wind whispering in the lofty branches of tall trees on the other, was a favorite haunt of theirs on crisp March days. The buds of the pussy willow were beginning to burst. Birds twittered in dusky thickets. Even the gulls, wheeling and darting along the shore, had a new note in their raucous crying. None of these first undertones of the spring symphony went unmarked by Doris Cleveland. She could hear and feel. She could respond to subtle, external stimuli. She could interpret her thoughts and feelings with apt phrases, with a whimsical humor—sometimes with an appealing touch of wistfulness.

At the Beach Avenue entrance to the park she would release herself from the hand by which Hollister guided her through the throngs on the sidewalks or the traffic of the crossings, and along the open way she would keep step with him easily and surely, her cheeks glowing with the brisk movement; and she could tell him with uncanny exactness when they came abreast of the old elk paddock and the bowling greens, or the rock groynes and bathhouse at Second Beach. She knew always when they turned the wide curve farther out, where through a fringe of maple and black alder there opened a clear view of all the Gulf, with steamers trailing their banners of smoke and the white pillar of Point Atkinson lighthouse standing guard at the troubled entrance to Howe Sound.

No, he could not easily fall into the masculine attitude of a protector, of guiding and bending a watchful care upon a helpless bit of desirable femininity that clung to him with confiding trust. Doris Cleveland was too buoyantly healthy to be a clinging vine. She had too hardy an intellectual outlook. Her mind was like her body, vigorous, resilient, unafraid. It was hard sometimes for Hollister to realize fully that to those gray eyes so often turned on him it was always night— or at best a blurred, unrelieved dusk.

In the old, comfortable days before the war, Hollister, like many other young men, accepted things pretty much as they came without troubling to scrutinize their import too closely. It was easy for him, then, to overlook the faint shadows than ran before coming events. It had been the most natural thing in the world to drift placidly until in more or less surprise he found himself caught fairly in a sweeping current. Some of the most important turns in his life had caught him unprepared for their denouement, left him a trifle dizzy as he found himself committed irrevocably to this or that.

But he had not survived four years of bodily and spiritual disaster without an irreparable destruction of the sanguine, if more or less nebulous assurance that God was in his heaven and all was well with the world. He had been stricken with a wariness concerning life, a reluctant distrust of much that in his old easy-going philosophy seemed solid as the hills. He was disposed to a critical and sometimes pessimistic examination of his own feelings and of other people's actions.

So love for Doris Cleveland did not steal upon him like a thief in the night. From the hour when he put her in the taxi at the dock and went away with her address in his pocket, he was keenly alive to the definite quality of attraction peculiar to her. When he was not thinking of her, he was thinking of himself in relation to her. He found himself involved in the most intimate sort of speculation concerning her. From the beginning he did not close his eyes to a possibility which might become a fact. Six months earlier he would honestly have denied that any woman could linger so tenaciously in his mind, a lovely vision to gladden and disturb him in love's paradoxical way. Yet step by step he watched himself approaching that dubious state, dreading a little the drift toward a definite emotion, yet reluctant to draw back.

When Doris went about with him, frankly finding a pleasure in his company, he said to himself that it was a wholly unwise proceeding to set too great store by her. Chance, he would reflect sadly, had swung them together, and that same blind chance would presently swing them far apart. This daily intimacy of two beings, a little out of it among the medley of other beings so highly engrossed in their own affairs, would presently come to an end. Sitting beside her on a shelving rock in the sun, Hollister would think of that and feel a pang. He would say to himself also, a trifle cynically, that if she could see him as he was, perhaps she would be like the rest: he would never have had the chance to know her, to sit beside her hearing the musical ripple of her voice when she laughed, seeing the sweetness of her face as she turned to him, smiling. He wondered sometimes what she really thought of him, how she pictured him in her mind. She had very clear mental pictures of everything she touched or felt, everything that came within the scope of her understanding—which covered no narrow field. But Hollister never quite had the courage to ask her to describe what image of him she carried in her mind.

For a month he did very little but go about with Doris, or sit quietly reading a book in his room. March drew to a close. The southern border of Stanley Park which faced the Gulf over English Bay continued to be their haunt on every sunny afternoon, save once or twice when they walked along Marine Drive to where the sands of the Spanish Bank lay bared for a mile offshore at ebb tide.

If it rained, or a damp fog blew in from the sea, Hollister would pick out a motion-picture house that afforded a good orchestra, or get tickets to some available concert, or they would go and have tea at the Granada where there was always music at the tea hour in the afternoon. Doris loved music. Moreover she knew music, which is a thing apart from merely loving melodious sounds. Once, at the place where she was living, the home of a married cousin, Hollister heard her play the piano for the first time. He listened in astonishment, forgetting that a pianist does not need to see the keyboard and that the most intricate movements may be memorized. But he did not visit that house often. The people there looked at him a little askance. They were courteous, but painfully self-conscious in his presence—and Hollister was still acutely sensitive about his face.

By the time that April Fool's Day was a week old on the calendar, Hollister began to be haunted by a gloomy void which would engulf him soon, for Doris told him one evening that in another week she was going back to the Euclataws. She had already stretched her visit to greater length than she intended. She must go back.

They were sitting on a bench under a great fir that overlooked a deserted playground, emerald green with new grass. They faced a sinking sun, a ball of molten fire on the far crest of Vancouver Island. Behind them the roar of traffic on downtown streets was like the faint murmur of distant surf.

"In a week," Hollister said. If there was an echo of regret in his voice he did not try to hide it. "It has been

82

the best month I have spent for a long, long time."

"It has been a pleasant month," Doris agreed.

They fell silent. Hollister looked away to the west where the deep flame-red of low, straggling clouds shaded off into orange and pale gold that merged by imperceptible tints into the translucent clearness of the upper sky. The red ball of the sun showed only a small segment above the mountains. In ten minutes it would be gone. From the east dusk walked silently down to the sea.

"I shall be sorry when you are gone," he said at last.

"And I shall be sorry to go," she murmured, "but—"

She threw out her hands in a gesture of impotence, of resignation.

"One can't always be on a holiday."

"I wish we could," Hollister muttered. "You and I."

The girl made no answer. And Hollister himself grew dumb in spite of a pressure of words within him, things that tugged at his tongue for utterance. He could scarcely bear to think of Doris Cleveland beyond sound of his voice or reach of his hand. He realized with an overwhelming certainty how badly he needed her, how much he wanted her—not only in ways that were sweet to think of, but as a friendly beacon in the murky, purposeless vista of years that stretched before him. Yes, and before her also. They had not spent all those hours together without talking of themselves. No matter that she was cheerful, that youth gave her courage and a ready smile, there was still a finality about blindness that sometimes frightened her. She, too, was aware— and sometimes afraid—of drab years running out into nothingness.

Hollister sat beside her visualizing interminable tomorrows in which there would be no Doris Cleveland;

in which he would go his way vainly seeking the smile on a friendly face, the sound of a voice that thrilled him with its friendly tone.

He took her hand and held it, looking down at the soft white fingers. She made no effort to withdraw it. He looked at her, peering into her face, and there was nothing to guide him. He saw only a curious expectancy and a faint deepening of the color in her cheeks.

"Don't go back to the Euclataws, Doris," he said at last. "I love you. I want you. I need you. Do you feel as if you liked me—enough to take a chance?

"For it is a chance," he finished abruptly. "Life together is always a chance for the man and woman who undertake it. Perhaps I surprise you by breaking out like this. But when I think of us each going separate ways—"

He held her hand tightly imprisoned between his, bending forward to peer closely at her face. He could see nothing of astonishment or surprise. Her lips were parted a little. Her expression, as he looked, grew different, inscrutable, a little absent even, as if she were lost in thought. But there was arising a quiver in the fingers he held which belied the emotionless fixity of her face.

"I wonder if it is such a desperate chance?" she said slowly. "If it is, why do you want to take it?"

"Because the alternative is worse than the most desperate chance I could imagine," he answered. "And because I have a longing to face life with you, and a dread of it alone. You can't see my ugly face which frightens off other people, so it doesn't mean anything to you. But you can hear my voice. You can feel me near you. Does it mean anything to you? Do you wish I could always be near you?"

He drew her up close to him. She permitted it, unresisting, that strange, thoughtful look still on her face.

"Tell me, do you want me to love you—or don't you care?" he demanded.

For a moment Doris made no answer.

"You're a man," she said then, very softly, a little breathlessly. "And I'm a woman. I'm blind—but I'm a woman. I've been wondering how long it would take you to find that out."

CHAPTER IX

NOT UNTIL HOLLISTER HAD LEFT DORIS at her cousin's home and was walking back downtown did a complete realization of what he had done and pledged himself to do burst upon him. When it did, he pulled up short in his stride, as if he had come physically against some forthright obstruction. For an instant he felt dazed. Then a consuming anger flared in him—anger against the past by which he was still shackled.

But he refused to be bound by those old chains whose ghostly clanking arose to harass him in this hour when life seemed to be holding out a new promise, when he saw happiness beckoning, when he was dreaming of pleasant things. He leaned over the rail on the Granville Street drawbridge, watching a tug pass through, seeing the dusky shape of the small vessel, hearing the ripple of the flood tide against the stone piers, and scarcely conscious of the bridge or the ship or the gray dimness of the sea, so profound was the concentration of his mind on this problem. It did not perplex him; it maddened him. He whispered a defiant protest to himself and walked on. He was able to think more calmly when he reached his room. There were the facts, the simple, undeniable facts, to be faced withou7t shrinking—and a decision to be made.

For months Hollister, when he thought of the past, thought of it as a slate which had been wiped clean. He was dead, officially dead. His few distant relatives had accepted the official report without question. Myra had accepted it, acted upon it. Outside the British War Office no one knew, no one dreamed, that he was alive. He had served in the Imperials. He recalled the difficulties and delays of getting his identity reestablished in the coldly impersonal, maddeningly deliberate, official departments which dealt with his case. He had succeeded. His back pay had been granted. A gratuity was still forthcoming. But Hollister knew that the record of his case was entangled with miles of red tape. He was dead—killed in action. It would never occur to the British War Office to seek publicity for the fact that he was not dead. There was no machinery for that purpose. Even if there were such machinery, there was no one to pull the levers. Nothing was ever set in motion in the War Office without pulling a diversity of levers. So much for that. Hollister, recalling his experience in London, smiled sardonically at thought of the British War Office voluntarily troubling itself about dead men who came to life. The War Office would not know him. The War Office did not know men. It only knew identification numbers, regiments, ranks, things properly documented, officially assigned. It was disdainful of any casual inquiry; it would shunt such from official to official, from department to department, until the inquirer was worn out, his patience, his fund of postage and his time alike exhausted.

No, the British War Office would neither know nor

care nor tell.

Surely the slate was sponged clean. Should he condemn himself and Doris Cleveland to heartache and loneliness because of a technicality? To Hollister it seemed no more than that. Myra had married again. Would she—reckoning the chance that she learned he was alive—rise up to denounce him? Hardly. His own people? They were few and far away. His friends? The war had ripped everything loose, broken the old combinations, scattered the groups. There was, for Hollister, nothing left of the old days. And he himself was dead—officially dead.

After all, it narrowed to himself and Doris Cleveland and an ethical question.

He did not shut his eyes to the fact that for him this marriage would be bigamy; that their children would be illegitimate in the eyes of the law if legal scrutiny ever laid bare their father's history; nor that by all the accepted dictums of current morality he would be leading an innocent woman into sin. But current morality had ceased to have its old significance for Hollister. He had seen too much of it vaporized so readily in the furnace of the war. Convention had lost any power to dismay him. His world had used him in its hour of need, had flung him into the Pit, and when he crawled out maimed, discouraged, stripped of everything that had made life precious, this world of his fellows shunned him because of what he had suffered in their behalf. So he held himself under no obligation to be guided by their moral dictums. He was critical of accepted standards because he had observed that an act might be within the law and still outrage humanity; it might be legally sanctioned and socially approved and spread intolerable misery in its wake. Contrariwise, he could conceive a thing beyond the law being meritorious in itself. With the Persian tent-maker, Hollister had begun to see that "A hair, perhaps, divides the false and true."

There was no falsity in his love, in his aching desire to lay hold of happiness out of the muddle of his life, to bestow happiness if he could upon a woman who like himself had suffered misfortune. Within him there was the instinct to clutch firmly this chance which lay at hand. For Hollister the question was not, "Is this thing right or wrong in the eyes of the world?" but "Is it right for her and for me?" And always he got the one answer, the answer with which lovers have justified themselves ever since love became something more than the mere breeding instinct of animals.

Hollister could not see himself as a man guilty of moral obliquity if he let the graveyard of the past retain its unseemly corpse without legal exhumation and examination, and the delivering of a formal verdict upon what was already an accomplished fact.

Nevertheless, he forced himself to consider just what it would mean to take that step. Briefly it would be necessary for him to go to London, to secure documentary evidence. Then he must return to Canada, enter suit against Myra, secure service upon her here in British Columbia. There would be a trial and a temporary decree; after the lapse of twelve months a divorce absolute.

He was up against a stone wall. Even if he nerved himself to public rattling of the skeleton in his private life, he did not have the means. That was final. He did not have money for such an undertaking, even if he beggared himself. That was a material factor as inexorable as death. Actual freedom he had in full measure. Legal freedom could only be purchased at a price—and he did not have the price.

Perhaps that decided Hollister. Perhaps he would have made that decision in any case. He had no friends to be shocked. He had no reputation to be smirched. He was, he had said with a bitter wistfulness, a stray dog. And Doris Cleveland was in very much the same position. Two unfortunates cleaving to each other, moved by a genuine human passion. If they could be happy together, they had a right to be together. Hollister challenged his reason to refute that cry of his heart.

He disposed finally of the last uncertainty—whether he should tell Doris. And a negative to that rose instantly to his lips. The past was a dead past. Let it remain dead—buried. Its ghost would never rise to trouble them. Of that he was very sure.

Hollister went to bed, but not to sleep. He heard a great clock somewhere in the town strike twelve and then one, while he still lay staring up at the dusky ceiling. But his thoughts had taken a pleasanter road. He had turned over the pages of his life history, scanned them with a gloomy and critical eye, and cast them with decisive finality into the waste basket. He was about to begin a new book, the book of the future. It was pleasant to contemplate what he and Doris Cleveland together would write on those blank pages. To hope much, to be no longer downcast, to be able to look forward with eagerness. There was a glow in that like good wine.

And upon that he slept.

Morning brought him no qualms or indecisions. But it did bring him to a consideration of very practical matters, which yesterday's emotional crisis had overshadowed. That is to say, Hollister began to take stock of the means whereby they two should live. It was not an immediately pressing matter, since he had a few hundred dollars in hand, but he was not short-sighted and he knew it would ultimately become so. Hence, naturally, his mind turned once more to that asset which had been one factor in bringing him back to British Columbia, the timber limit he owned in the Toba Valley.

He began to consider that seriously. Its value had shrunk appreciably under his examination. He had certainly been tricked in its purchase and he did not know if he had any recourse. He rather thought there should be some way of getting money back from people who obtained it under false pretenses. The limit, he was quite sure, contained less than half the timber Lewis and Company had solemnly represented it to carry. He grew uneasy thinking of that. All his eggs were in that wooden basket.

He found himself anxious to know what he could expect, what he could do. There was a considerable amount of good cedar there. It should bring five or six thousand dollars, even if he had to accept the fraud and make the best of it. When he reflected upon what a difference the possession or lack of money might mean to himself and Doris, before long, all his acquired and cultivated knowledge of business affairs began to spur him to some action. As soon as he finished his breakfast he set off for the office of the "Timber Specialist." He already had a plan mapped out. It might work and it might not, but it was worth trying.

As he walked down the street, Hollister felt keenly, for the first time in his thirty-one years of existence, how vastly important mere bread and butter may become. He had always been accustomed to money.

Consequently he had very few illusions either about money as such or the various methods of acquiring money. He had undergone too rigorous a business training for that. He knew how easy it was to make money with money—and how difficult, how very nearly impossible it was for the penniless man to secure more than a living by his utmost exertion. If this timber holding *should* turn out to be worthless, if it should prove unsalable at any price, it would be a question of a job for him, before so very long. With the handicap of his face! With that universal inclination of people to avoid him because they disliked to look on the direct result of settling international difficulties with bayonets and high explosives and poison gas, he would not fare very well in the search for a decent job. Poverty had never seemed to present quite such a sinister face as it did to Hollister when he reached this point in his self-communings.

Mr. Lewis received him with a total lack of the bland dignity Hollister remembered. The man seemed uneasy, distracted. His eyes had a furtive look in them. Hollister, however, had not come there to make a study of Mr. Lewis' physiognomy or manner.

"I went up to Toba Inlet awhile ago and had a look over that timber limit of mine," he began abruptly. "I'd like to see the documents bearing on that, if you don't mind."

Mr. Lewis looked at him uncertainly, but he called a clerk and issued an order. While the clerk was on his mission to the files Lewis put a few questions which Hollister answered without disclosing what he had in mind. It struck him, though, that the tone of Mr. Lewis' inquiry bordered upon the anxious.

Presently the clerk returned with the papers. Hollister

took them up. He selected the agreement of sale, a letter or two, the original cruiser's estimate, a series of tax receipts, held them in his hand and looked at Lewis.

"You haven't succeeded in finding a buyer, I suppose?"

"In the winter," Lewis replied, "there is very little stir in timber."

"There is going to be some sort of stir in this timber before long," Hollister said.

The worried expression deepened on Mr. Lewis' face.

"The fact is," Hollister continued evenly, "I made a rough survey of that timber, and found it away off color. You represented it to contain so many million feet. It doesn't. Nowhere near. I appear to have been rather badly stung, and I really don't wonder it hasn't been resold. What do you propose to do about this?"

Mr. Lewis made a gesture of deprecation.

"There must be some mistake, Mr. Hollister."

"No doubt of that," Hollister agreed dryly. "The point is, who shall pay for the mistake?"

Mr. Lewis looked out of the window. He seemed suddenly to be stricken with an attitude of remoteness. It occurred to Hollister that the man was not thinking about the matter at all.

"Well?" he questioned sharply.

The eyes of the specialist in timber turned back to him uneasily.

"Well?" he echoed.

Hollister put the documents in his pocket. He gathered up those on the desk and put them also in his pocket. He was angry because he was baffled. This was a matter of vital importance to him, and this man seemed able to insulate himself against either threat or suggestion.

92

"My dear sir," Lewis expostulated. Even his protest was half-hearted, lacked honest indignation.

Hollister rose.

"I'm going to keep these," he said irritably. "You don't seem to take much interest in the fact that you have laid yourself open to a charge of fraud, and that I am going to do something about it if you don't."

"Oh, go ahead," Lewis broke out pettishly. "I don't care what you do."

Hollister stared at him in amazement. The man's eyes met his for a moment, then shifted to the opposite wall, became fixed there. He sat half turned in his chair. He seemed to grow intent on something, to become wrapped in some fog of cogitation, through which Hollister and his affairs speared only as inconsequential phantoms.

In the doorway Hollister looked back over his shoulder. The man sat mute, immobile, staring fixedly at the wall.

Down the street Hollister turned once more to look up at the gilt-lettered windows. Something had happened to Mr. Lewis. Something had jolted the specialist in British Columbia timber and paralyzed his business nerve centers. Some catastrophe had overtaken him, or impended, beside which the ugly matter Hollister laid before him was of no consequence.

But it was of consequence to Hollister, as vital as the breaker of water and handful of ship's biscuits is to castaways in an open boat in midocean. It angered him to feel a matter of such deep concern brushed aside. He walked on down the street, thinking what he should do. Midway of the next block, a firm name, another concern which dealt in timber, rose before his eyes. He entered the office.

"Mr. MacFarlan or Mr. Lee," he said to the desk man.

A short, stout individual came forward, glanced at Hollister's scarred face with that involuntary disapproval which Hollister was accustomed to catch in people's expression before they suppressed it out of pity or courtesy, or a mixture of both.

"I am Mr. MacFarlan."

"I want legal advice on a matter of considerable importance," Hollister came straight to the point. "Can you recommend an able lawyer—one with considerable experience in timber litigation preferred?"

"I can. Malcolm MacFarlan, second floor Sibley Block. If it's legal business relating to timber, he's your man. Not because he happens to be my brother," MacFarlan smiled broadly, "but because he knows his business. Ask any timber concern. They'll tell you."

Hollister thanked him, and retraced his steps to the office building he had just quitted. In an office directly under the Lewis quarters he introduced himself to Malcolm MacFarlan, a bulkier, less elderly duplicate of his brother the timber broker. Hollister stated his case briefly and clearly. He put it in the form of a hypothetical case, naming no names.

MacFarlan listened, asked questions, nodded understanding.

"You could recover on the ground of misre-presentation," he said at last. "The case, as you state it, is clear. It could be interpreted as fraud and hence criminal if collusion between the maker of the false estimate and the vendor could be proven. In any case the vendor could be held accountable for his misrepresentation of value. Your remedy lies in a civil suit—provided an authentic cruise established your estimate of such a small quantity of merchantable

94

timber. I should say you could recover the principal with interest and costs. Always provided the vendor is financially responsible."

"I presume they are. Lewis and Company sold me this timber. Here are the papers. Will you undertake this matter for me?"

MacFarlan jerked his thumb towards the ceiling.

"This Lewis above me?"

"Yes."

Hollister laid the documents before MacFarlan. He ran through them, laid them down and looked reflectively at Hollister.

"I'm afraid," he said slowly, "you are making your move too late."

"Why?" Hollister demanded uneasily.

"Evidently you aren't aware what has happened to Lewis? I take it you haven't been reading the papers?"

"I haven't," Hollister admitted. "What has happened?"

"His concern has gone smash," MacFarlan stated. "I happen to be sure of that, because I'm acting for two creditors. A receiver has been appointed. Lewis himself is in deep. He is at present at large on bail, charged with unlawful conversion of moneys entrusted to his care. You have a case, clear enough, but—" he threw out his hands with a suggestive motion—"they're bankrupt."

"I see," Hollister muttered. "I appear to be out of luck, then."

"Unfortunately, yes," MacFarlan continued. "You could get a judgment against them. But it would be worthless. Simply throwing good money after bad. There will be half a dozen other judgments recorded against them, a dozen other claims put in, before you could get action. Of course, I could proceed on your

95

behalf and let you in for a lot of costs, but I would rather not earn my fees in that manner. I'm satisfied there won't be more than a few cents on the dollar for anybody."

"That seems final enough," Hollister said. "I am obliged to you, Mr. MacFarlan."

He went out again into a street filled with people hurrying about their affairs in the spring sunshine. So much for that, he reflected, not without a touch of contemptuous anger against Lewis. He understood now the man's troubled absorption: With the penitentiary staring him in the face—

At any rate the property was not involved. Whatever its worth, it was his, and the only asset at his command. He would have to make the best of it, dispose of it for what he could get. Meantime, Doris Cleveland began to loom bigger in his mind than this timber limit. He suffered a vast impatience until he should see her again. He had touches, this morning, of incredulous astonishment before the fact that he could love and be loved. He felt once or twice that this promise of happiness would prove an illusion, something he had dreamed, if he did not soon verify it by sight and speech.

He was to call for her at two o'clock. They had planned to take a Fourth Avenue car to the end of the line and walk thence past the Jericho Club grounds and out a driveway that left the houses of the town far behind, a road that went winding along the gentle curve of a shore line where the Gulf swell whispered or thundered, according to the weather.

Doris was a good walker. On the level road she kept step without faltering or effort, holding Hollister's hand, not because she needed it for guidance, but because it

96

was her pleasure.

They came under a high wooded slope.

"Listen to the birds," she said, with a gentle pressure on his fingers. "I can smell the woods and feel the air soft as a caress. I can't see the buds bursting, or the new, pale-green leaves, but I know what it is like. Sometimes I think that beauty is a feeling, instead of a fact. Perhaps if I could see it as well as feel it—still, the birds wouldn't sing more sweetly if I could see them there swaying on the little branches, would they, Bob?"

There was a wistfulness, but only a shadow of regret in her tone. And there were no shadows on the fresh, young face she turned to Hollister. He bent to kiss that sweet mouth, and he was again thankful that she had no sight to be offended by his devastated features. His lips, unsightly as they were, had power to stir her. She blushed and hid her face against his coat.

They found a dry log to sit upon, a great tree trunk cast by a storm above high-water mark. Now and then a motor whirred by, but for the most part the drive lay silent, a winding ribbon of asphalt between the sea and the wooded heights of Point Grey. English Bay sparkled between them and the city. Beyond the purple smoke-haze driven inland by the west wind rose the white crests of the Capilanos, an Alpine background to the seaboard town. Hollister could hear the whine of sawmills, the rumble of trolley cars, the clang of steel in a great shipyard—and the tide whispering on wet sands at his feet, the birds twittering among the budding alders. And far as his eyes could reach along the coast there lifted enormous, saw-toothed mountains. They stood out against a sapphire sky with extraordinary vividness, with remarkable brilliancy of color, with an austere dignity.

Hollister put his arm around the girl. She nestled

97

close to him. A little sigh escaped her lips.

"What is it, Doris?"

"I was just remembering how I lay awake last night," she said, "thinking, thinking until my brain seemed like some sort of machine that would run on and on grinding out thoughts till I was worn out."

"What about?" he asked.

"About you and myself," she said simply. "About what is ahead of us. I think I was a little bit afraid."

"Of me?"

"Oh, no," she tightened her grip on his hand. "I can't imagine myself being afraid of *you*. I like you too much. But—but—well, I was thinking of myself, really; of myself in relation to you. I couldn't help seeing myself as a handicap. I could see you beginning to chafe finally under the burden of a blind wife, growing impatient at my helplessness—which you do not yet realize—and in the end—oh, well, one can think all sorts of things in spite of a resolution not to think."

It stung Hollister.

"Good God," he cried, "you don't realize it's only the fact you *can't* see me that makes it possible. Why, I've clutched at you the way a drowning man clutches at anything. That I should get tired of you, feel you as a burden—it's unthinkable. I'm thankful you're blind. I shall always be glad you can't see. If you could—what sort of picture of me have you in your mind?"

"Perhaps not a very clear one," the girl answered slowly. "But I hear your voice, and it is a pleasant one. I feel your touch, and there is something there that moves me in the oddest way. I know that you are a big man and strong. Of course I don't know whether your eyes are blue or brown, whether your hair is fair or dark—and I don't care. As for your face I can't possibly imagine it

98

as terrible, unless you were angry. What are scars? Nothing, nothing. I can't see them. It wouldn't make any difference if I could."

"It would," he muttered. "I'm afraid it would."

Doris shook her head. She looked up at him, with that peculiarly direct, intent gaze which always gave him the impression that she did see. Her eyes, the soft gray of a summer rain cloud—no one would have guessed them sightless. They seemed to see, to be expressive, to glow and soften.

She lifted a hand to Hollister's face. He did not shrink while those soft fingers went exploring the devastation wrought by the exploding shell. They touched caressingly the scarred and vivid flesh. And they finished with a gentle pat on his cheek and a momentary, kittenish rumpling of his hair.

"I cannot find so very much amiss," she said. "Your nose is a bit awry, and there is a hollow in one cheek. I can feel scars. What does it matter? A man is what he thinks and feels and does. I am the maimed one, really. There is so much I can't do, Bob. You don't realize it yet. And we won't always be living this way, sitting idle on the beach, going to a show, having tea in the Granada. I used to run and swim and climb hills. I could have gone anywhere with you—done anything—been as good a mate as any primitive woman. But my wings are clipped. I can only get about in familiar surroundings. And sometimes it grows intolerable. I rebel. I rave—and wish I were dead. And if I thought I was hampering you, and you were beginning to regret you had married me—why, I couldn't bear it. That's what my brain was buzzing with last night."

"Do any of those things strike you as serious obstacles now—when I have my arms around you?"

99

Hollister demanded.

She shook her head.

"No. Really and truly right now I'm perfectly willing to take any sort of chance on the future—if you're in it," she said thoughtfully. "That's the sort of effect you have on me. I suppose that's natural enough."

"Then we feel precisely the same," Hollister declared. "And you are not to have any more doubts about me. I tell you, Doris, that besides wanting you, I *need* you. I can be your eyes. And for me, you will be like a compass to a sailor in a fog—something to steer a course by. So let's stop talking about whether we're going to take the plunge. Let's talk about how we're going to live, and where."

A whimsical expression rippled across the girl's face, a mixture of tenderness and mischief.

"I've warned you," she said with mock solemnity. "Your blood be upon your own head."

They both laughed.

CHAPTER X

"WHY NOT GO IN THERE and take that cedar out yourself?" Doris suggested.

They had been talking about that timber limit in the Toba, the possibility of getting a few thousand dollars out of it, and how they could make the money serve them best.

"We could live there. I'd love to live there. I loved that valley. I can see it now, every turn of the river, every canyon, and all the peaks above. It would be like getting back home."

"It is a beautiful place," Hollister agreed. He had a

100

momentary vision of the Toba as he saw it last: a white-floored lane between two great mountain ranges; green, timbered slopes that ran up to immense declivities; glaciers; cold, majestic peaks scarred by winter avalanches. He had come a little under the spell of those rugged solitudes then. He could imagine it transformed by the magic of summer. He could imagine himself living there with this beloved woman, exacting a livelihood from those hushed forests and finding it good.

"I've been wondering about that myself," he said. "There is a lot of good cedar there. That bolt chute your brothers built could be repaired. If they expected to get that stuff out profitably, why shouldn't I? I'll have to look into that."

They were living in a furnished flat. If they had married in what people accustomed to a certain formality of living might call haste they had no thought of repenting at leisure, or otherwise. They were, in fact, quite happy and contented. Marriage had shattered no illusions. If, indeed, they cherished any illusory conceptions of each other, the intimacy of mating had merely served to confirm those illusions, to shape them into realities. They were young enough to be ardent lovers, old enough to know that love was not the culmination, but only an ecstatic phase in the working out of an inexorable natural law.

If Doris was happy, full of high spirits, joyfully abandoned to the fulfillment of her destiny as a woman, Hollister too was happier than he had considered it possible for him ever to be again. But, in addition, he was supremely grateful. Life for him as an individual had seemed to be pretty much a blank wall, a drab, colorless routine of existence; something he could not voluntarily give up, but which gave nothing, promised nothing, save monotony and isolation and, in the end, complete despair. So that his love for this girl, who had given herself to him with the strangely combined passion of a mature woman and the trusting confidence of a child, was touched with gratitude. She had put out her hand and lifted him from the pit. She would always be near him, a prop and a stay. Sometimes it seemed to Hollister a miracle. He would look at his face in the mirror and thank God that she was blind. Doris said that made no differ ence, but he knew better. It made a difference to eyes that could see, however tolerantly.

In Hollister, also, there revived the natural ambition to get on, to grasp a measure of material security, to make money. There were so many ways in which money was essential, so many desirable things they could secure and enjoy together with money. Making a living came first, but beyond a mere living he began to desire comfort, even luxuries, for himself and his wife. He had made tentative plans. They had discussed ways and means; and the most practical suggestion of all came now from his wife's lips.

Hollister went about town the next few days, diligently seeking information about prices, wages, costs and methods. He had a practical knowledge of finance, and a fair acquaintance with timber operations generally, so that he did not waste his own or other men's time. He met a rebuff or two, but he learned a great deal which he needed to know, and he said to Doris finally:

"I'm going to play your hunch and get that timber out myself. It will pay. In fact, it is the only way I'll ever get back the money I put into that, so I really haven't much choice in the matter."

"Good!" Doris said. "Then we go to the Toba to live. When?"

"Very soon—if we go at all. There doesn't seem to be much chance to sell it, but there is some sort of returned soldiers' cooperative concern working in the Big Bend, and MacFarlan and Lee have had some correspondence with their head man about this limit of mine. He is going to be in town in a day or two. They may buy."

"And if they do?"

"Well, then, we'll see about a place on Valdez Island at the Euclataws, where I can clear up some land and grow things, and fish salmon when they run, as we talked about."

"That would be nice, and I dare say we would get on very well," Doris said. "But I'd rather go to the Toba."

Hollister did not want to go to the Toba. He would go if it were necessary, but when he remembered that fair-haired woman living in the cabin on the river bank, he felt that there was something to be shunned. Myra was like a bad dream too vividly remembered. There was stealing over Hollister a curious sense of something unreal in his first marriage, in the war, even in the strange madness which had briefly afflicted him when he discovered that Myra was there. He could smile at the impossibility of that recurring, but he could not smile at the necessity of living within gunshot of her again. He was not afraid. There was no reason to be afraid. He was officially dead. No sense of sin troubled him. He had put all that behind him. It was simply a distaste for living near a woman he had once loved, with another whom he loved with all the passion he had once lavished on Myra, and something that was truer and tenderer. He wanted to shut the doors on the past forever. That was why he did not wish to go back to the Toba. He

103

only succeeded in clearly defining that feeling when it seemed that he must go—unless this prospective sale went through—because he had to use whatever lever stood nearest his hand. He had a direct responsibility, now, for material success. As the laborer goes to his work, distasteful though it may be, that he may live, that his family may be fed and clothed, so Hollister knew that he would go to Toba Valley and wrest a compensation from that timber with his own hands unless a sale were made.

But it failed to go through. Hollister met his man in MacFarlan's office—a lean, weather-beaten man of sixty, named Carr. He was frank and friendly, wholly unlike the timber brokers and millmen Hollister had lately encountered.

"The fact is," Carr said after some discussion, "we aren't in the market for timber in the ordinary, speculative sense. I happen to know that particular stand of cedar, or I wouldn't be interested. We're a body of returned men engaged in making homes and laying the foundation for a competence by our joint efforts. You would really lose by selling out to us. We would only buy on stumpage. If you were a broker I would offer you so much, and you could take it or leave it. It would be all one to us. We have a lot of standing timber ourselves. But we're putting in a shingle mill now. The market looks good, and what we need is labor and shingle bolts, not standing timber. I would suggest you go in there with two or three men and get the stuff out yourself. We'll take all the cedar on your limit, in bolts on the river bank at market prices, less cost of towage to Vancouver. You can make money on that, especially if shingles go up."

There seemed a force at work compelling Hollister to

this move. He reflected upon it as he walked home. Doris wanted to go; this man Carr encouraged him to go. He would be a fool not to go when opportunity beckoned, yet he hesitated; there was a reluctance in his mind. He was not afraid, and yet he was. Some vague peril seemed to lurk like a misty shadow at his elbow. Nothing that he had done, nothing that he foresaw himself doing, accounted for that, and he ended by calling himself a fool. Of course, he would go. If Myra lived there—well, no matter. It was nothing to him, nothing to Doris. The past was past; the future theirs for the making. So he went once more up to Toba Inlet, when late April brought spring showers and blossoming shrubs and soft sunny days to all the coast region. He carried with him certain tools for a purpose, axes, crosscut saws, iron wedges, a froe to flake off uniform slabs of cedar. He sat on the steamer's deck and thought to himself that he was in vastly different case to the last time he had watched those same shores slide by in the same direction. Then he had been in full retreat, withdrawing from a world which for him held nothing of any value. Now it held for him a variety of desirable things, which to have and to hold he need only make effort; and that effort he was eager to put forth, was now indeed putting forth if he did no more than sit on the steamer's deck, watching green shore and landlocked bays fall astern, feeling the steady throb of her engines, hearing the swish and purl of a cleft sea parting at the bow in white foam, rippling away in a churned wake at her stern.

He felt a mild regret that he went alone, and the edge of that was dulled by the sure knowledge that he would not long be alone, only until such time as he could build a cabin and transport supplies up to the flat above the

Big Bend, to that level spot where his tent and canoe were still hidden, where he had made his first camp, and near where the bolt chute was designed to spit its freight into the river.

It was curious to Hollister—the manner in which Doris could see so clearly this valley and river and the slope where his timber stood. She could not only envision the scene of their home and his future operations, but she could discuss these things with practical wisdom. They had talked of living in the old cabin where he had found her shelf of books, but there was a difficulty in that—of getting up the steep hill, of carrying laboriously up that slope each item of their supplies, their personal belongings, such articles of furniture as they needed; and Doris had suggested that they build their house in the flat and let his men, the bolt cutters, occupy the cabin on the hill.

He had two hired woodsmen with him, tools, food, bedding. When the steamer set them on the float at the head of Toba Inlet, Hollister left the men to bring the goods ashore in a borrowed dugout and himself struck off along a line blazed through the woods which, one of Carr's men informed him, led out near the upper curve of the Big Bend.

A man sometimes learns a great deal in the brief span of a few minutes. When Hollister disembarked he knew the name of one man only in Toba Valley, the directing spirit of the settlement, Sam Carr, whom he had met in MacFarlan's office. But there were half a dozen loggers meeting the weekly steamer. They were loquacious men, without formality in the way of acquaintance. Hollister had more than trail knowledge imparted to him. The name of the man who lived with his wife at the top of the Big Bend was Mr. J. Harrington Bland;

the logger said that with a twinkle in his eye, a chuckle as of inner amusement. Hollister understood. The man was a round peg in this region of square holes; otherwise he would have been Jack Bland, or whatever the misplaced initial stood for. They spoke of him further as "the Englishman." There was a lot of other local knowledge bestowed upon Hollister, but "the Englishman" and his wife—who was a "pippin" for looks—were still in the forefront of his mind when the trail led him out on the river bank a few hundred yards from their house. He passed within forty feet of the door. Bland was chopping wood; Myra sat on a log, her tawny hair gleaming in the sun. Bland bestowed upon Hollister only a casual glance, as he strode past, and went on swinging his axe; and Hollister looking impersonally at the woman, observed that she stared with frank curiosity. He remembered that trait of hers. He had often teased her about it in those days when it had been an impossible conception that she could ever regard seriously any man but himself. Men had always been sure of a very complete survey when they came within Myra's range, and men had always fluttered about her like moths drawn to a candle flame. She had that mysterious quality of attracting men, pleasing them—and of making other girls hate her in the same degree. She used to laugh about that.

"I can't help it if I'm popular," she used to say, with a mischievous smile, and Hollister had fondly agreed with that. He remembered that it flattered his vanity to have other men admire his wife. He had been so sure of her affections, her loyalty; but that had passed like melting snow, like dew under the morning sun. A little loneliness, a few months of separation, had done the trick.

Hollister shrugged his shoulders. He had no feeling in

the matter. She could not possibly know him; she would not wish to know him if she could. His problems were nowise related to her. But he knew too much to be completely indifferent. His mind kept turning upon what her life had been, and what it must be now. He was curious. What had become of the money? Why did she and her English husband bury themselves in a rude shack by a river that whispered down a lonely valley?

Hollister's mind thrust these people aside, put them out of consideration, when he reached the flat and found his canoe where he left it, his tiny silk tent suspended intact from the limb. He ranged about the flat for an hour or so. He had an impression of it in his mind from his winter camp there; also he had a description of it from Doris, and her picture was clearer and more exact in detail than his. He found the little falls that trickled down to a small creek that split the flat. He chose tentatively a site for their house, close by a huge maple which had three sets of initials cut deeply in the bark where Doris told him to look.

Then he dragged the canoe down to the river, and slid it afloat and let the current bear him down. The air was full of pleasant odors from the enfolding forest. He let his eyes rest thankfully upon those calm, majestic peaks that walled in the valley. It was even more beautiful now than he had imagined it could be when the snow blanketed hill and valley, and the teeth of the frost gnawed everywhere. It was less aloof; it was as if the wilderness wore a smile and beckoned with friendly hands.

The current and his paddle swept him down past the settlement, past a busy, grunting sawmill, past the booming ground where brown logs floated like droves of sheep in a yard, and he came at last to where his woodsmen waited with the piled goods on a bank above tidewater.

All the rest of that day, and for many days thereafter, Hollister was a busy man. There was a pile of goods to be transported upstream, a house to be fashioned out of raw material from the forest, the shingle-bolt chute to be inspected and repaired, the work of cutting cedar to be got under way, all in due order. He became a voluntary slave to work, clanking his chains of toil with that peculiar pleasure which comes to men who strain and sweat toward a desired end. As literally as his hired woodsmen, he earned his bread in the sweat of his brow, spurred on by a vision of what he sought to create—a home and so much comfort as he could grasp for himself and a woman.

The house arose as if by magic—the simple magic of stout arms and skilled hands working with axe and saw and iron wedges. One of Hollister's men was a lean, saturnine logger, past fifty, whose life had been spent in the woods of the Pacific Coast. There was no trick of the axe Hayes had not mastered, and he could perform miracles of shaping raw wood with neat joints and smooth surfaces.

Two weeks from the day Hayes struck his axe blade into the brown trunk of a five-foot cedar and said laconically, "She'll do", that ancient tree had been transformed into timbers, into boards that flaked off smooth and straight under iron wedges, into neat shakes for a rain-tight roof, and was assembled into a two-roomed cabin. This was furnished with chairs and tables and shelves, hewn out of the raw stuff of the forest. It stood in the middle of a patch of earth cleared of fallen logs and thicket. Its front windows gave on the Toba River, slipping down to the sea. A maple spread friendly

109

arms at one corner, a lordly tree that would blaze crimson and russet-brown when October came again. All up and down the river the still woods spread a deep-green carpet on a floor between the sheer declivity of the north wall and the gentler, more heavily timbered slope of the south. Hollister looked at his house when it was done and saw that it was good. He looked at the rich brown of the new-cleared soil about it, and saw in his mind flowers growing there, and a garden.

And when he had quartered his men in the cabin up the hill and put them to work on the cedar, he went back to Vancouver for his wife.

CHAPTER XI

A WEEK OF HOT SUNSHINE had filled the Toba River bank full of roily water when Hollister breasted its current again. In midstream it ran full and strong. Watery whisperings arose where swirls boiled over sunken snags. But in the slow eddies and shoal water under each bank the gray canoe moved upstream under the steady drive of Hollister's paddle.

Doris sat in the bow. Her eyes roved from the sunglittering stream to the hills that rose above the tree-fringed valley floor, as if sight had been restored to her so that her eyes could dwell upon the green-leaved alder and maple, the drooping spruce bows, the vastness of those forests of somber fir where the deer lurked in the shadows and where the birds sang vespers and matins when dusk fell and dawn came again. There were meadow larks warbling now on stumps that dotted the floor of the Big Bend, and above the voices of those yellow-breasted singers and the watery murmuring of the river there arose now and then the shrill, imperative blast of a donkey engine.

"Where are we now, Bob?"

"About half a mile below the upper curve of the Big Bend," Hollister replied.

Doris sat silent for awhile. Hollister, looking at her, was stricken anew with wonder at her loveliness, with wonder at the contrast between them. Beauty and the beast, he said to himself. He knew without seeing. He did not wish to see. He strove to shut away thought of the devastation of what had once been a man's goodly face. Doris' skin was like a child's, smooth and soft and tinted like a rose petal. Love, he said to himself, had made her bloom. It made him quake to think that she might suddenly see out of those dear, blind eyes. Would she look and shudder and turn away? He shook off that ghastly thought. She would never see him. She could only touch him, feel him, hear the tenderness of his voice, know his guarding care. And to those things which were realities she would always respond with an intensity that thrilled him and gladdened him and made him feel that life was good.

"Are you glad you're here?" he asked suddenly.

"I would pinch you for such a silly question if it weren't that I would probably upset the canoe," Doris laughed. "Glad?"

"There must be quite a streak of pure barbarian in me," she said after a while. "I love the smell of the earth and the sea and the woods. Even when I could see, I never cared a lot for town. It would be all right for awhile, then I would revolt against the noise, the dirt and smoke, the miles and miles of houses rubbing shoulders against each other, and all the thousands of people scuttling back and forth, like—well, it seems

111

sometimes almost as aimless as the scurrying of ants when you step on their hill. Of course it isn't. But I used to feel that way. When I was in my second year at Berkeley I had a brain storm like that. I took the train north and turned up at home—we had a camp running on Thurlow Island then. Daddy read the riot act and sent me back on the next steamer. It was funny—just an irresistible impulse to get back to my own country, among my own people. I often wonder if it isn't some such instinct that keeps sailors at sea, no matter what the sea does to them. I have sat on that ridge"—she pointed unerringly to the first summit above Hollister's timber, straight back and high above the rim of the great cliff south of the Big Bend—"and felt as if I had drunk a lot of wine; just to be away up in that clear still air, with not a living soul near and the mountains standing all around like the pyramids."

"Do you know that you have a wonderful sense of direction, Doris?" Hollister said. "You pointed to the highest part of that ridge as straight as if you could see it."

"I do see it," she smiled, "I mean I know where I am, and I have in my mind a very clear picture of my surroundings always, so long as I am on familiar ground."

Hollister knew this to be so, in a certain measure, on a small scale. In a room she knew Doris moved as surely and rapidly as he did himself. He had dreaded a little lest she should find herself feeling lost and helpless in this immensity of forest and hills which sometimes made even him feel a peculiar sense of insignificance. It was a relief to know that she turned to this wilderness which must be their home with the eagerness of a child throwing itself into its mother's arms. He perceived that she had indeed a clear image of the Toba in her mind.

She was to give further proof of this before long.

They turned the top of the Big Bend. Here the river doubled on itself for nearly a mile and crossed from the north wall of the valley to the south. Where the channel straightened away from this loop Hollister had built his house on a little flat running back from the right-band bank. A little less than half a mile below, Bland's cabin faced the river just where the curve of the S began. They came abreast of that now. What air currents moved along the valley floor shifted in from the sea. It wafted the smoke from Bland's stovepipe gently down on the river's shining face.

Doris sniffed.

"I smell wood smoke," she said. "Is there a fire on the flat?"

"Yes, in a cook's stove," Hollister replied. "There is a shack here."

She questioned him and he told her of the Blands—all that he had been told, which was little enough. Doris displayed a deep interest in the fact that a woman, a young woman, was a near neighbor, as nearness goes on the British Columbia coast.

From somewhere about the house Myra Bland appeared now. To avoid the heavy current, Hollister hugged the right-hand shore so that he passed within a few feet of the bank, within speaking distance of this woman with honey-colored hair standing bareheaded in the sunshine. She took a step or two forward. For an instant Hollister thought she was about to exercise the immemorial privilege of the wild places and hail a passing stranger. But she did not call or make any sign. She stood gazing at them, and presently her husband joined her and together they watched. They were still looking when Hollister gave his last backward glance, then turned his attention to the reddish-yellow gleam of new-riven timber which marked his own dwelling. Twenty minutes later he slid the gray canoe's forefoot up on a patch of sand before his house.

"We're here," he said. "Home—such as it is—it's home."

He helped her out, guided her steps up to the level of the bottomland. He was eager to show her the nest he had devised for them. But Doris checked him with her hand.

"I hear the falls," she said. "Listen!"

Streaming down through a gorge from melting snowfields the creek a little way beyond plunged with a roar over granite ledges. The few warm days had swollen it from a whispering sheet of spray to a deep-voiced cataract. A mist from it rose among the deep green of the fir.

"Isn't it beautiful—beautiful?" Doris said. "There"— she pointed—"is the canyon of the Little Toba coming in from the south. There is the deep notch where the big river comes down from the Chilcotin, and a ridge like the roof of the world rising between. Over north there are mountains and mountains, one behind the other, till the last peaks are white cones against the blue sky. There is a bluff straight across us that goes up and up in five-hundred-foot ledges like masonry, with hundred-foot firs on each bench that look like toy trees from here.

"I used to call that gorge there"—her pointing finger found the mark again—"The Black Hole. It is always full of shadows in summer, and in winter the slides rumble and crash into it with a noise like the end of the world. Did you ever listen to the slides muttering and grumbling last winter when you were here, Bob?"

114

"Yes, I used to hear them day and night."

They stood silent a second or two. The little falls roared above them. The river whispered at their feet. A blue-jay perched on the roof of their house and began his harsh complaint to an unheeding world, into which a squirrel presently broke with vociferous reply. An up-river breeze rustled the maple leaves, laid cooling fingers from salt water on Hollister's face, all sweaty from his labor with the paddle.

He could see beauty where Doris saw it. It surrounded him, leaped to his eye whenever his eye turned—a beauty of woods and waters, of rugged hills and sapphire skies. And he was suddenly filled with a great gladness that he could respond to this. He was quickened to a strange emotion by the thought that life could still hold for him so much that seemed good. He put one arm caressingly, protectingly, across his wife's shoulder, over the smooth, firm flesh that gleamed through thin silk.

She turned swiftly, buried her face against his breast and burst into tears, into a strange fit of sobbing. She clung to him like a frightened child. Her body quivered as if some unseen force grasped and shook her with uncontrollable power. Hollister held her fast, dismayed, startled, wondering, at a loss to comfort her.

"But I *can't* see it," she cried. "I'll never see it again. Oh, Bob, Bob! Sometimes I can't stand this blackness. Never to see you—never to see the sun or the stars—never to see the hills, the trees, the grass. Always to grope. Always night—night—night without beginning or end."

And Hollister still had no words to comfort her. He could only hold her close, kiss her glossy brown hair, feeling all the while a passionate sympathy—and yet conscious of a guilty gladness that she could not see

115

him—that she could not look at him and be revolted and draw away. He knew that she clung to him now as the one clear light in the darkness. He was not sure that she (or any other woman) would do that if she could see him as he really was.

Her sobs died in her throat. She leaned against him passively for a minute. Then she lifted her face and smiled.

"It's silly to let go like that," she said. "Once in awhile it comes over me like a panic. I wonder if you will always be patient with me when I get like that. Sometimes I fairly rave. But I won't do it often. I don't know why I should feel that way now. I have never been so happy. Yet that feeling came over me like a suffocating wave. I am afraid your wife is rather a temperamental creature, Bob."

She ended with a laugh and a pout, to which Hollister made appropriate response. Then he led her into the house and smiled—or would have smiled had his face been capable of that expression—at the pleasure with which her hands, which she had trained to be her organs of vision, sought and found doors and cupboards, chairs, the varied equipment of the kitchen. He watched her find her way about with the uncanny certainty of the sightless, at which he never ceased to marvel. When she came back at last to where he sat on a table, swinging one foot while he smoked a cigarette, she put her arms around him and said:

"It's a cute little house, Bob. The air here is like old wine. The smell of the woods is like heaven, after soot and smoke and coal gas. I'm the happiest woman in the whole country."

Hollister looked at her. He knew by the glow on her face that she spoke as she felt, that she *was* happy, that

116

he had made her so. And he was proud of himself for a minute, as a man becomes when he is conscious of having achieved greatness, however briefly.

Only he was aware of a shadow. Doris leaned against him talking of things they would do, of days to come. He looked over her shoulder through the west window and his eye rested on Bland's cabin, where another woman lived who had once nestled in his arms and talked of happiness. Yes, he was conscious of the shadow, of regrets, of something else that was nameless and indefinable—a shadow. Something that was not and yet still might be troubled him vaguely.

He could not tell why. Presently he dismissed it from his mind.

CHAPTER XII

HOLLISTER LIKENED HIMSELF AND DORIS, more than once in the next few days, to two children in a nursery full of new toys. He watched the pride and delight which Doris bestowed upon her house and all that it contained, the satisfaction with which she would dwell upon the comforts and luxuries that should be added to it when the cedars on the hill began to produce revenue for them.

For his own part he found himself eager for work, taking a pleasure far beyond his expectation in what he had set himself to do, here in the valley of the Toba. He could shut his eyes and see the whole plan work out in ordered sequence—the bolt chute repaired, the ancient cedars felled, sawed into four-foot lengths, split to a size, piled by the chute and all its lateral branches. Then, when a certain quantity was ready, they would be

117

cast one after another into that trough of smooth poles which pitched sharply down from the heart of his timber to the river. One after another they would gather way, slipping down, faster and faster, to dive at last with a great splash into the stream, to accumulate behind the confining boom-sticks until they were rafted to the mill, where they would be sawn into thin sheets to make tight roofs on houses in distant towns. And for the sweat that labor with axe and saw wrung from his body, and for the directing power of his brain, he would be rewarded with money which would enable him to satisfy his needs. For the first time in his life Hollister perceived both the complexity and the simplicity of that vast machine into which modern industry has grown. In distant towns other men made machinery, textiles, boots, furniture. On inland plains where no trees grew, men sowed and reaped the wheat which passed through the hands of the miller and the baker and became a nation's daily bread. The axe in his hand was fashioned from metallic ore dug by other men out of the bowels of the earth. He was fed and clothed by unseen hands. And in return he, as they did, levied upon nature's store of raw material and paid for what he got with timber, rough shaped to its ultimate uses by the labor of his hands.

All his life Hollister had been able to command money without effort. Until he came back from the war he did not know what it meant to be poor. He had known business as a process in which a man used money to make more money. He had been accustomed to buy and sell, to deal with tokens rather than with things themselves. Now he found himself at the primitive source of things and he learned, a little to his astonishment, the pride of definitely planned creative work. He began to understand that lesson which many men never learn, the pleasure of pure achievement even in simple things.

For two or three days he occupied himself at various tasks on the flat. He did this to keep watch over Doris, to see that she did not come to grief in this unfamiliar territory. But he soon put aside those first misgivings, as he was learning to put aside any fear of the present or of the future, which arose from her blindness. His love for her had not been borne of pity. He had never thought of her as helpless. She was too vivid, too passionately alive in body and mind to inspire him with that curiously mixed feeling which the strong bestow upon the maimed and the weak. But there were certain risks of which he was conscious, no matter that Doris laughingly disclaimed them. With a stick and her ears and fingers she could go anywhere, she said; and she was not far wrong, as Hollister knew.

Within forty-eight hours she had the run of the house and the cleared portion of land surrounding. She could put her hand on every item of her kitchen equipment. She could get kindling out of the wood box; light a fire in the stove as well as he. All the stock of food staples lay in an orderly arrangement of her own choice on the kitchen shelves. She knew every object in the two rooms, each chair and box and stool, the step at the front door, the short path to the river bank, the trunk of the branchy maple, the rugged bark of a great spruce behind the house, as if within her brain there existed an exact diagram of the whole and with which as a guide she could move within those limits as swiftly and surely as Hollister himself.

He never ceased to wonder at the mysterious delicacies of touch and hearing which served her so well in place of sight. But he accepted the fact, and once she had mastered her surroundings Hollister was free to take up his own work, no matter where it led him. Doris insisted that he should. She had a sturdy soul that seldom leaned and never thought of clinging. She could laugh, a deep-throated chuckling laugh, and sometimes, quite unexpectedly, she could go about the house singing. And if now and then she rebelled with a sudden, furious resentment against the long night that shut her in, that, as she said herself, was just like a small black cloud passing swiftly across the face of the sun.

Hollister began at the bottom of the chute, as he was beginning at the bottom of his fortune, to build up again. Where it was broken he repaired it. Where it had collapsed under the weight of snow or of fallen trees he put in a new section. His hands grew calloused and the muscles of his back and shoulders grew tough with swinging an axe, lugging and lifting heavy poles. The sun burned the scar-tissue of his face to a brown like that on the faces of his two men, who were piling the cut cedar in long ricks among the green timber while he got the chute ready to slide the red, pungent-smelling blocks downhill. Sometimes, on a clear still day when he was at the house, he would hear old Bill Hayes' voice far off in the woods, very faint in the distance, shrilling the fallers' warning, *"Timb-r-r-r."* Close on that he would hear a thud that sent tremors running through the earth, and there would follow the echo of crashing boughs all along the slope. Once he said lightly to Doris:

"Every time one of those big trees goes down like that it means a hundred dollars' worth of timber on the ground."

And she laughed back:

"We make money when cedar goes up, and we make money when cedar comes down. Very nice."

May passed and June came to an end; with it Hollister also came to the end of his ready money. It had all gone into tools, food, wages, all his available capital sunk in the venture. But the chute was ready to run bolts. They poured down in a stream till the river surface within the boom-sticks was a brick-colored jam that gave off a pleasant aromatic smell.

Then Hollister and his two men cast off the boom, let the current sweep it down to Carr's new shingle mill below the Big Bend. When the bolts were tallied in, Hollister got a check. He sat with pad and pencil figuring for half an hour after he came home, after his men had each shouldered a fifty-pound pack of supplies and gone back up the hill. He gave over figuring at last.

The thing was profitable. More so than he had reckoned. He got up and went into the kitchen where Doris was rolling pie crust on a board.

"We're off," he said, putting an arm around her. "If we can keep this up all summer, I'll build a new wing on the house and bring you in a piano to play with this winter."

Hollister himself now took a hand at cutting cedar. Each morning he climbed that steep slope to the works, and each night he came trudging down; and morning and night he would pause at a point where the trail led along the rim of a sheer cliff, to look down on the valley below, to look down on the roof of his own house and upon Bland's house farther on. Sometimes smoke streamed blue from Bland's stovepipe. Sometimes it stood dead, a black cylinder above the shake roof. Sometimes one figure and sometimes two moved about the place; more often no one stirred. But that was as near as the Blands had come in eight weeks. Hollister had an unspoken hope that they would remain distant, no matter that Doris occasionally wondered about this woman who lived around the river's curve, what she was like and when she would meet her. Hollister knew nothing of Bland, nothing of Myra. He did not wish to know. It did not matter in the least, he assured himself. He was dead and Myra was married. All that old past was as a book long out of print. It could not possibly matter if by chance they came in contact. Yet he had a vague feeling that it did matter—a feeling for which he could not account. He was not afraid; he had no reason to be afraid. Nevertheless he gazed sometimes from the cliff top down on the cabin where Bland and Myra lived, and something stirred him so that he wished them gone.

He came off the hill one evening in the middle of June to find a canoe drawn up on the beach, two Siwashes puttering over a camp fire, and a tall, wirily slender, fair-haired man who might have been anywhere between twenty-seven and thirty-five sitting in the front doorway, talking to Doris.

Hollister noted the expression on the man's face when their eyes met. But he did not mind. He was used to that. He was becoming indifferent to what people thought of his face, because what they thought no longer had power to hurt him, to make him feel that sickening depression, to make him feel himself kin to those sinners who were thrust into the outer darkness. Moreover, he knew that some people grew used to the wreckage of his features. That had been his experience with his two woodsmen. At first they looked at him askance. Now they seemed as indifferent to his disfigurement as they were to the ragged knots and old fire-scars on the trees they felled. Anyway, it did not matter to Hollister.

But this fair-haired man went on talking, looking all the

while at Hollister, and his look seemed to say, "I know your face is a hell of a sight, but I am not disturbed by it, and I don't want you to think I am disturbed." Behind the ragged mask of his scars Hollister smiled at this fancy. Nevertheless he accepted his interpretation of that look as a reality and found himself moved by a curious feeling of friendliness for this stranger whom he had never seen before, whom he might never see again—for that was the way of casual travelers up and down the Toba. They came out of nowhere, going up river or down, stopped perhaps to smoke a pipe, to exchange a few words, before they moved on into the hushed places that swallowed them up.

The man's name was Lawanne. He was bound up-stream, after grizzly bear.

"I was told of an Englishman named Bland who is quite a hunter. I stopped in here, thinking this was his place and that I might get him to go on with me," he said to Hollister.

"That's Bland's place down there," Hollister explained.

"So Mrs. Hollister was just telling me. There didn't seem to be anybody about when I passed. It doesn't matter much, anyway," he laughed. "The farther I get into this country, the less keen I am to hunt. It's good enough just to loaf around and look at."

Lawanne had supper with them. Hollister asked him, not only as a matter of courtesy but with a genuine feeling that he wanted this man to break bread with them. He could not quite understand that sudden warmth of feeling for a stranger. He had never in his life been given to impulsive friendliness. The last five years had not strengthened his belief in friendships. He had seen too many fail under stress. But he liked this man. They sat outside after supper and Doris joined them there. Lawanne was not talkative. He was given to long silences in which he sat with eyes fixed on river or valley or the hills above, in mute appreciation.

"Do you people realize what a panoramic beauty is here before your eyes all the time?" he asked once. "It's like a fairyland to me. I must see a lot of this country before I go away. And I came here quite by chance."

"Which is, after all, the way nearly everything happens," Doris said.

"Oh," Lawanne turned to her, "You think so? You don't perceive the Great Design, the Perfect Plan, in all that we do?"

"Do you?" she asked.

He laughed.

"No. If I did I should sit down with folded hands, knowing myself helpless in the inexorable grip of destiny. I should always be perfectly passive."

"If you tried to do that you could not remain passive long. The unreckonable element of chance would still operate to make you do this or that. You couldn't escape it; nobody can."

"Then you don't believe there is a Destiny that shapes our ends, rough-hew them how we will?" Lawanne said lightly.

Doris shook her head.

"Destiny is only a word. It means one thing to one person, something else to another. It's too abstract to account for anything. Life's a puzzle no one ever solves, because the factors are never constant. When we try to account for this and that we find no fixed law, nothing but what is subject to the element of chance—which can't be reckoned. Most of us at different times hold our own fate, temporarily at least, in our own hands without knowing it, and some insignificant happening does this

124

or that to us. If we had done something else it would all be different."

"Your wife," Lawanne observed to Hollister, "is quite a philosopher."

Hollister nodded. He was thinking of this factor of chance. He himself had been a victim of it. He had profited by it. And he wondered what vagaries of chance were still to bestow happiness or inflict suffering upon him in spite of his most earnest effort to achieve mastery over circumstances. He felt latterly that he had a firm grip on the immediate future. Yet who could tell?

Dusk began to close on the valley while the far, high crests of the mountains still gleamed under a crimson sky. Deep shadows filled every gorge and canyon, crept up and up until only the snowy crests glimmered in the night, ghostly-silver against a sky speckled with stars. The valley itself was shrouded under the dark blanket of the night, through which the river murmured unseen and distant waterfalls roared over rocky precipices. The two Indians attending Lawanne squatted within the red glow of their fire on the bank. Downstream a yellow spot broke out like a candle flame against black velvet.

"There is some one at Bland's now," Hollister said.

"That's their window light, eh?" Lawanne commented. "I may go down and see him in the morning. I am not very keen on two or three weeks alone in these tremendous silences. This valley at night now—it's awesome. And those Siwashes are like dumb men. You wouldn't go bear-hunting, I suppose?"

There was a peculiar gratification to Hollister in being asked. But he had too much work on hand. Neither did he wish to leave Doris. Not because it might be difficult for her to manage alone. It was simply an inner reluctance to be separated from her. She was becoming a vital part of him. To go away from her for days or weeks except under the spur of some compelling necessity was a prospect that did not please him. That which had first drawn them together grew stronger. Love, the mysterious fascination of sex, the perfect accord of the well-mated—whatever it was it grew stronger. The world outside of them held less and less significance. Sometimes they talked of that, wondered about it, wondered if it were natural for a man and a woman to become so completely absorbed in each other, to attain that singular oneness. They wondered if it would last. But whether it should prove lasting or not, they had it now and it was sufficient.

Lawanne went down to Bland's in the morning. He was still there when Hollister climbed the hill to his work.

Before evening he had something else to think about besides Lawanne. A trifle, but one of those trifles that recurs with irritating persistence no matter how often the mind gives it dismissal.

About ten o'clock that morning a logger came up to the works on the hill.

"Can you use another man?" he asked bluntly. "I want to work."

Hollister engaged him. By his dress, by his manner, Hollister knew that he was at home in the woods. He was young, sturdily built, handsome in a swarthy way. There was about him a slightly familiar air. Hollister thought he might have seen him at the steamer landing, or at Carr's. He mentioned that.

"I have been working there," the man replied. "Working on the boom."

He was frank enough about it. He wanted money—a stake. He believed he could make more cutting shingle bolts by the cord. This was true. Hollister's men were making top wages. The cedar stood on good ground. It was big, clean timber, easy to work.

"I'll be on the job tomorrow," he said, after they had talked it over. "Take me this afternoon to get my outfit packed up here."

Hollister was haunted by the man's face at odd times during the day. Not until he was half-way home, until he came out on that ledge from whence he could look— and always did look with a slight sense of irritation— down on Bland's cabin as well as his own, did he recall clearly where and when he had seen Charlie Mills. Mills was the man who sat looking at Myra across the table that winter morning when Hollister was suffering from the brief madness which brought him to Bland's cabin with a desperate project in his disordered mind.

Well, what of it, Hollister asked himself? It was nothing to him. He was a disinterested bystander now. But looking down on Bland's cabin, he reflected that his irritation was rooted in the fact that he did not want to be a bystander. He desired to eliminate Myra Bland and all that pertained to her from even casual contact with him. It seemed absurd that he should feel himself to be in danger. But he had a dim sense of danger. And instead of the aloofness which he desired, he seemed to see vague threads drawing himself and Doris and Myra Bland and this man Mills closer and closer together, to what end or purpose he could not tell.

For a minute Hollister was tempted to turn the man away when he went back up there in the morning. But that, he concluded with a shrug of his shoulders, was carrying a mere fancy too far.

It did not therefore turn his thoughts into a more placid channel to find, when he reached the house, Myra

127

sitting in the kitchen talking to Doris. Yet it was no great surprise. He had expected this, looked forward to it with an uneasy sense of its inevitability.

Nothing could have been more commonplace, more uneventful than that meeting. Doris introduced her husband. They were all at their ease. Myra glanced once at his face and thereafter looked away. But her flow of small talk, the conversational stop-gap of the woman accustomed to social amenities, went on placidly. They were strangers, meeting for the first time in a strange land.

Bland had gone up-river with Lawanne. "Jim lives to hunt," Myra said with a short laugh. It was the first and nearly the last mention of her husband she made that evening. Hollister went out to wash himself in a basin that stood on a bench by the back door. He felt a relief. He had come through the first test casually enough. A slightly sardonic grimace wrinkled his tight-lipped mouth. There was a grim sort of humor in the situation. Those three, whose lives had got involved in such a tangle, forgathered under the same roof in that lonely valley, each more or less a victim of uncomprehended forces both within and exterior to themselves. Yet it was simple enough. Each, in common with all humanity, pursued the elusive shadow of happiness. The diverging paths along which they pursued it had brought them to this common point.

Hollister soaped and scrubbed to clean his hands and face of the sweat and dirt of his day's labor. Above the wash bench Myra's face, delicately pink and white and framed by her hair that was the color of strained honey, looked down at him through an open window. Her blue eyes rested on him, searchingly, he thought, with a curious appraisal, as if he were something to be noted

128

and weighed and measured by the yardstick of her estimation of men. If she only knew, Hollister reflected sardonically, with his face buried in the towel, what a complete and intimate knowledge she had of him!

Looking up suddenly, his eyes met hers fixed unwaveringly upon him and for an instant his heart stood still with the reasonless conviction that she did know, she must know, that she could not escape knowing. There was a quality of awareness in her steady gaze that terrified him for a moment by its implication, which made him feel as if he stood over a powder magazine and that she held the detonator in her hand. But immediately he perceived the absurdity of his momentary panic. Myra turned her head to speak to Doris. She smiled, the old dimpling smile which gave him a strange feeling to see again. Certainly his imagination was playing him tricks. How could she know? And what would she care if she did know—so long as he made no claims, so long as he let the dead past lie in its grave. For Myra was as deeply concerned to have done with their old life as he. He rested upon that assumption and went into the house and sat down to his supper.

Later, towards sundown, Myra went home. Hollister watched her vanish among the thickets, thinking that she too had changed—as greatly as himself. She had been timid once, reluctant to stay alone over night in a house with telephones and servants, on a street brilliantly lighted. Now she could apparently face the loneliness of those solitudes without uneasiness. But war and the aftermath of war had taught Hollister that man adapts himself to necessity when he must, and he suspected that women were not greatly different. He understood that after all he had never really known

129

Myra any more than she had known him. Externally they had achieved knowledge of each other through sight, speech, physical contact, comprehension of each other's habits. But their real selves, the essence of their being, the shadowy inner self where motives and passions took form and gathered force until they were translated for good or evil into forthright action—these they had not known at all.

At any rate he perceived that Myra could calmly enough face the prospect of being alone. Hollister cast his eye up to where the cedars towered, a green mass on the slope above the cliff. He thought of Charlie Mills and wondered if after all she would be alone.

He felt ashamed of that thought as soon as it formed in his mind. And being ashamed, he saw and understood that he still harbored a little bitterness against Myra. He did not wish to bestow bitterness or any other emotion upon her. He wanted her to remain completely outside the scope of his feelings. He would have to try, he perceived, to cultivate a complete indifference to her, to what she did, to where she went, to insulate himself completely against her. Because he was committed to other enterprises, and chiefly because, as he said to himself, he would not exchange a single brown strand of Doris Cleveland's hair for all of Myra's body, even if he had that choice.

The moon stole up from behind the Coast Range after they had gone to bed. Its pale beams laid a silver square upon the dusky floor of their room. Doris reached with one arm and drew his face close up to hers.

"Are you happy?" she demanded with a fierce intensity. "Don't you ever wish you had a wife who could see? Aren't you *ever* sorry?"

"Doris, Doris," he chided gently. "What in the world

put such a notion as that into your head?"

She lay thoughtful for a minute. "Sometimes I wonder," she said at last. "Sometimes I feel that I must reassure myself that you are contented with me. When we come in contact with a woman like Mrs. Bland, for instance—Tell me, Bob, is she pretty?"

"Yes," he said "Very."

"Fair or dark?"

"Fair-skinned. She has blond hair and dark blue eyes, almost purple. She is about your height, about the same figure. Why so curious?"

"I just wondered. I like her very much," Doris said, with some slight emphasis on the last two words. "She is a very interesting talker."

"I noticed that," Hollister observed dryly. "She spoke charmingly of the weather and the local scenery and the mosquitoes."

Doris laughed.

"A woman always falls back on those conversational staples with a strange man. That's just the preliminary skirmishing. But she was here all afternoon, and we didn't spend five hours talking about the weather."

"What did you talk about then?" Hollister asked curiously.

"Men and women and money mostly," Doris replied. "If one may judge a woman by the impressionistic method, I should say that Mrs. Bland would be very attractive to men."

It was on the tip of Hollister's tongue to say, "She is." Instead he murmured, "Is that why you were doubting me? Think I'm apt to fall in love with this charming lady?"

"No," Doris said thoughtfully. "It wasn't anything concrete like that. It's a feeling, a mood, I suppose. And

131

it's silly for me to say things like that. If you grow sorry you married me, if you fall in love with another woman, I'll know it without being told."

She pinched his cheek playfully and lay silent beside him. Hollister watched the slow shift of the moonbeams across the foot of the bed, thinking, his mind darting sketchily from incident to incident of the past, peering curiously into the misty future, until at last he grew aware by her drooped eyelashes and regular breathing that Doris was asleep.

He grew drowsy himself. His eyelids grew heavy. Presently he was asleep also and dreaming of a fantastic struggle in which Myra Bland—transformed into a vulture-like creature with a fierce beaked face and enormous strength—tore him relentlessly from the arms of his wife.

CHAPTER XIII

FROM DAY TO DAY and from week to week, apprehending mistily that he was caught in and carried along by a current—a slow but irresistible movement of events—Hollister pursued the round of his daily life as if nothing but a clear and shining road lay before him; as if he had done for ever with illusions and uncertainties and wild stirrings of the spirit; as if life spread before him like a sea of which he had a chart whereon every reef was marked, every shoal buoyed, and in his hands and brain the instruments and knowledge wherewith to run a true course. He made himself believe that he was reasonably safe from the perils of those uneasy waters. Sometimes he was a little in doubt, not so sure of untroubled passage. But mostly he did not think of these potential dangers.

He was vitally concerned, as most men are, with making a living. The idea of poverty chafed him. He had once been a considerable toad in a sizable puddle. He had inherited a competence and lost it, and power to reclaim it was beyond him. He wasted no regrets upon the loss of that material security, although he sometimes wondered how Myra had contrived to let such a sum slip through her fingers in a little over two years. He assumed that she had done so. Otherwise she would not be sitting on the bank of the Toba, waiting more or less passively for her husband to step into a dead man's shoes.

That was, in effect, Bland's situation. He was an Englishman of good family, accustomed to a definite social standing, accustomed to money derived from a source into which he never troubled to inquire. He had never worked. He never would work, not in the sense of performing any labor as a means of livelihood. He had a small income—fifty or sixty dollars a month. When he was thirty he would come into certain property and an income of so many thousand pounds a year. He and his wife could not subsist in any town on the quarterly dole he received. That was why they had come to live in that cabin on the Toba River. Bland hunted. He fished. To him the Toba valley served well enough as a place to rusticate. Any place where game animals and sporting fish abounded satisfied him temperamentally.

He had done his "bit" in the war. When he came into his money, they would go "home." He was placidly sure of himself, of his place in the general scheme of things. He was suffering from temporary embarrassment, that was all. It was a bit rough on Myra, but it would be all right by and by.

So much filtered into Hollister's ears and understanding before long. Archie Lawanne came back downstream with two grizzly pelts, and Hollister met Bland for the first time. He appraised Bland with some care—this tall, ruddy Englishman who had supplanted him in a woman's affections, and who, unless Hollister's observation had tricked him, was in a fair way to be himself supplanted.

For Hollister was the unwilling spectator of a drama to which he could not shut his eyes. Nor could he sit back in the role of cynical audience, awaiting in cushioned ease the climax of the play and the final exit of the actors.

Mills was the man. Whether he was more than a potential lover, whether Myra in her *ennui,* her hunger for a new sensation—whatever unsatisfied longings led her to exercise upon men the power of her undeniable attraction—had now given her heart into Charlie Mills' keeping, Hollister of course neither knew nor cared.

But he did know that they met now and then, that Mills seemed to have some curious knowledge of when Bland was far afield. Mills could be trusted to appear on the flat in the evening or on a Sunday, if Myra came to see Doris.

He speculated idly upon this sometimes. Myra he knew well enough, or thought he did. He began to regard Mills with a livelier interest, to talk to the man, to draw him out, to discover the essential man under the outward seeming. He was not slow to discover that Mills was something more than so much bone and sinew which could be applied vigorously to an axe or a saw. Hollister's speculations took a new turn when Archie Lawanne and Bland came back from the bear hunt. For Lawanne did not go out. He pitched a tent on the flat below Hollister's and kept one Siwash to cook for him. He made that halt to rest up, to stretch and dry his bear-skins. But long after these trophies were cured, he still remained. He was given to roaming up and down the valley. He extended his acquaintance to the settlement farther down, taking observation of an earnest attempt at cooperative industry. He made himself at home equally with the Blands and the Hollisters.

And when July was on them, with hot, hazy sunshine in which berries ripened and bird and insect life filled the Toba with a twitter and a drone, when the smoke of distant forest fires drifted like pungent fog across the hills, Hollister began to wonder if the net Myra seemed unconsciously to spread for men's feet had snared another victim.

This troubled him a little. He liked Lawanne. He knew nothing about him, who he was, where he came from, what he did. Nevertheless there had arisen between them a curious fellowship. There seemed to reside in the man a natural quality of uprightness, a moral stoutness of soul that lifted him above petty judgments. One did not like or dislike Lawanne for what he did or said so much as for what he suggested as being inherent within himself.

There was a little of that quality, also, about Charlie Mills. He worked in the timber with a fierce energy. His dark face glistened with sweat-beads from morning till night. His black hair stood in wisps and curls, its picturesque disorder heightened by a trick he had of running his fingers through it when he paused for a minute to take breath, to look steadfastly across at the slide-scarred granite face of the north valley wall, with a wistful look in his eyes.

135

"Those hills," he said once abruptly to Hollister, "they were here long before we came. They'll be here long after we're gone. What a helpless, crawling, puny insect man is, anyway. A squirrel on his wheel in a cage."

It was a protesting acceptance of a stark philosophy, Hollister thought, a cry against some weight that bore him down, the momentary revealing of some conflict in which Mills foresaw defeat, or had already suffered defeat. It was a statement wrung out of him, requiring no comment, for he at once resumed the steady pull on the six-foot, cross-cut saw.

"Why don't you take it easier?" Hollister said to him. "You work as if the devil was driving you."

Mills smiled.

"The only devil that drives me," he said, "is the devil inside me.

"Besides," he continued, between strokes of the saw, "I want to make a stake and get to hell out of here."

Hollister did not press him for reasons. Mills did work as if the devil drove him, and in his quiescent moments an air of melancholy clouded his dark face as if physical passivity left him a prey to some inescapable inner gloom.

All about him, then, Hollister perceived strong undercurrents of life flowing sometimes in the open, sometimes underground: Charlie Mills and Myra Bland touched by that universal passion which has brought happiness and pain, dizzy heights of ecstasy and deep abysses of despair to men and women since the beginning of time; Lawanne apparently succumbing to the same malady that touched Mills; Bland moving in the foreground, impassive, stolidly secure in the possession of this desired woman. And all of them

136

bowed before and struggling under economic forces which they did not understand, working and planning, according to their lights, to fulfill the law of their being, seeking through the means at hand to secure the means of livelihood in obedience to the universal will to live, the human desire to lay firm hold of life, liberty, such happiness as could be grasped.

Hollister would sit in the evening on the low stoop before his cabin and Doris would sit beside him with her hand on his knee. A spirit of drowsy content would rest upon them. Hollister's eyes would see the river, gray now with the glacial discharge, slipping quietly along between the fringes of alder and maple, backed by the deeper green of the fir and cedar and groves of enormous spruce. His wife's ears drank in the whispering of the stream, the rumbling of distant waterfalls, and her warm body would press against him with an infinite suggestion of delight. At such times he felt the goodness of being alive, the mild intoxication of the fragrant air which filled the valley, the majestic beauty of those insentient hills upon which the fierce midsummer sun was baring glacial patches that gleamed now like blue diamonds or again with a pale emerald sheen, in a setting of worn granite and white snowdrifts five thousand feet above.

In this wilderness, this vast region of forest and streams and wild mountain ranges, men were infinitesimal specks hurrying here and there about their self-appointed tasks. Those like himself and Doris, who did not mind the privations inseparable from that remoteness, fared well enough. The land held out to them manifold promises. Hollister looked at the red-brown shingle bolts accumulating behind the boom-sticks and felt that inner satisfaction which comes of success achieved by plan and labor. If his mutilated face had been capable of expression, it would have reflected pride, satisfaction. Out of the apparent wreckage of his life he was laying the foundations of something permanent, something abiding, an enduring source of good. He would tangle his fingers in Doris' brown hair and feel glad.

Then perhaps his eyes would shift downstream to where Bland's stark, weather-beaten cabin lifted its outline against the green thickets, and he would think uneasily upon what insecure tenure, upon what deliberate violation of law and of current morality he held his dearest treasure. What would she think, if she knew, this dainty creature cuddling against his knee? He would wake in the night and lie on elbow staring at her face in the moonlight—delicate-skinned as a child's, that lovable, red-lipped mouth, those dear, blind eyes which sometimes gave him the illusion of seeing clearly out of their gray depths.

What would she think? What would she say? What would she do? He did not know. It troubled him to think of this. If he could have swept Myra out of North America with a wave of his hand, he would have made one sweeping gesture. He was jealous of his happiness, his security, and Myra's presence was not only a reminder; it had the effect upon him of a threat he could not ignore.

Yet he was compelled to ignore it. She and Doris had become fast friends. It all puzzled Hollister very much sometimes. Except for the uprooting, the undermining influences of his war experience, he would have been revolted at his own actions. He had committed technical bigamy. His children would be illegitimate before the law.

Hollister's morality was the morality of his early

environment; his class was that magnificently inert middle class which sets its face rigorously against change, which proceeds naively upon the assumption that everything has always been as it is and will continue to be so; that the man and woman who deviates from the accepted conventions in living, loving, marrying, breeding—even in dying—does so because of innate depravity, and that such people must be damned by bell, book and candle in this world, as they shall assuredly be damned in the next.

Hollister could no longer believe that goodness and badness were wholly matters of free will. From the time he put on the king's uniform in a spirit of idealistic service down to the day he met Doris Cleveland on the steamer, his experience had been a succession of devastating incidents. What had happened to him had happened to others. Life laid violent hands on them and tossed them about like frail craft on a windy sea. The individual was caught in the vortex of the social whirlpool, and what he did, what he thought and felt, what he became, was colored and conditioned by a multitude of circumstances that flowed about him as irresistibly as an ocean tide.

Hollister no longer had a philosophy of life in which motives and actions were tagged and labeled according to their kind. He had lost his old confidence in certain arbitrary moral dicta which are the special refuge of those whose intelligence is keen enough to grapple competently with any material problem but who stand aghast, apprehensive and uncomprehending, before a spiritual struggle, before the wavering gusts of human passion.

If he judged himself by his own earlier standard he was damned, and he had dragged Doris Cleveland down with him. So was Myra smeared with the pitch of moral obloquy. They were sinners all. Pain should be their desert; shame and sorrow their portion.

Why? Because driven by the need within them, blinded by the dust of circumstance and groping for security amid the vast confusion which had overtaken them, they reached out and grasped such semblence of happiness as came within reach of their uncertain hands.

The world at large, Hollister was aware, would be decisively intolerant of them all, if the world should by chance be called to pass judgment.

But he himself could no more pass harsh judgment upon his former wife than he could feel within himself a personal conviction of sin. Love, he perceived, was not a fixed emotion. It was like a fire which glows bright when plied with fuel and burns itself out when it is no longer fed. To some it was casual, incidental; to others an imperative law of being. Myra remained essentially the same woman, whether she loved him or some other man. Who was he to judge her? She had loved him and then ceased to love him. Beyond that, her life was her own to do with as she chose.

Nor could Hollister, when he faced the situation squarely, feel that he was less a man, less upright, less able to bear himself decently before his fellows than he had ever been. Sometimes he would grow impatient with thinking and put it all by. He had his moods. But also he had his work, the imperative necessity of constant labor to satisfy the needs both of the present and the future. No man goes into the wilderness with only his hands and a few tools and wins security by any short and easy road. There were a great many things Hollister was determined to have for himself and Doris and their children—for he did not close his eyes to the natural fulfilment of the mating impulse. He did not spare himself. Like Mills, he worked with a prodigious energy. Sometimes he wondered if dreams akin to his own drove Charlie Mills to sweat and strain, to pile up each day double the amount of split cedar, and double for himself the wages earned by the other two men— who were themselves no laggards with axe and saw. Or if Mills fantastically personified the timber as something which stood between him and his aching desire and so attacked it with all his lusty young strength.

Sometimes Hollister sat by, covertly watching Mills and Myra. He could make nothing of Myra. She was courteous, companionable, nothing more. But to Hollister Mills' trouble was plain enough. The man was on his guard, as if he knew betrayal lurked in the glance of his eye, in the quality of his tone. Hollister gauged the depths of Mills' feelings by the smoldering fire in his glance—that glow in Mills' dark eyes when they rested too long on Myra. There would be open upon his face a look of hopelessness, as if he dwelt on something that fascinated and baffled him.

Sometimes, latterly, he saw a hint of that same dubious expression about Archie Lawanne. But there was a diferent temper in Lawanne, a flash of the sardonic at times.

In July, however, Lawanne went away.

"I'm coming back, though," he told Hollister before he left. "I think I shall put up a cabin and winter here."

"I'll be glad to see you," Hollister replied, "but it's a lonely valley in the winter."

Lawanne smiled.

"I can stand isolation for a change," he said. "I want to write a book. And while I am outside I'll send you in

141

a couple that I have already written. You will see me in October. Try to get the shingle-bolt rush over so we can go out after deer together now and then."

So for a time the Toba saw no more of Lawanne. Hollister missed him. So did Doris. But she had Myra Bland to keep her company while Hollister was away at work in the timber. Sometimes Bland himself dropped in. But Hollister could never find himself on any common ground of mutual interest with this sporting Englishman. He was a bluff, hearty, healthy man, apparently without either intellect or affection.

"What do you think of Bland?" he asked Doris once.

"I can't think of him, because I can't see him," she answered. "He is either very clever at concealing any sort of personality, or he is simply a big, strong, stupid man."

Which was precisely what Hollister himself thought.

"Isn't it queer," Doris went on, "how vivid a thing personality is? Now Myra and Mr. Lawanne are definite, colorable entities to me. So is Charlie Mills, quiet as he is. And yet I can't make Bland seem anything more than simply a voice with a slightly English accent."

"Well, there must be something to him, or she wouldn't have married him," Hollister remarked.

"Perhaps. But I shouldn't wonder if she married him for something that existed mostly in her own mind," Doris reflected. "Women often do that—men too, I suppose. I very nearly did myself once. Then I discovered that this ideal man was something I had created in my own imagination."

"How did you find that out before you were committed to the enterprise?" he asked curiously.

"Because my reason and my emotions were in
142

continual conflict over that man," Doris said thoughtfully. "I have always been sure, ever since I began to take men seriously, that I wouldn't get on very long with any man who was simply a strong, healthy animal. And as soon as I saw that this admirable young man of mine hadn't much to offer that wasn't purely physical, why, the glamor all faded."

"Maybe mine will fade too," Hollister suggested.

"Oh, you're fishing for compliments now," she laughed. "You know very well you are. But we're pretty lucky, Robert mine, just the same. We've gained a lot. We haven't lost anything yet. I wouldn't back-track, not an inch. Would you—honest, now?"

Hollister answered that in a manner which seemed to him suitable to the occasion. And while he stood with his arm around her, Doris startled him.

"Myra told me a curious thing the other day," she said. "She has been married twice. She told me that her first husband's name was the same as yours—Bob Hollister—that he was killed in France in 1917. She says that you somehow remind her of him."

"There were a good many men killed in France in '17," he observed. "And Hollister is not such an uncommon name. Does the lady suspect I'm the reincarnation of her dear departed? She seems to have consoled herself for the loss, anyway."

"I doubt if she has," Doris answered. "She doesn't unburden her soul to me, but I have the feeling that she is not exactly a happy woman."

The matter rested there. Doris went away to do something about the house. Hollister stood glowering at the distant outline of Bland's cabin. A slow uneasiness grew on him. What did Myra mean by that confidence? Did she mean anything? He shook himself impatiently.

He had a profound distaste for that revelation. In itself it was nothing, unless some obscure motive lurked behind. That troubled him. Myra meant nothing—or she meant mischief. Why, he could not say. She was quit of him at her own desire. She had made a mouthful of his modest fortune. If she had somehow guessed the real man behind that mask of scars, and from some obscure, perverted motive meant to bring shipwreck to both of them once more, Hollister felt that he would strangle her without a trace of remorse.

CHAPTER XIV

ALL THAT SUMMER the price of cedar went creeping up. For a while this was only in keeping with the slow ascension of commodity costs which continued long after the guns ceased to thunder. But presently cedar on the stump, in the log, in the finished product, began to soar while other goods slowed or halted altogether in their mysterious climb to inaccessible heights—and cedar was not a controlled industry, not a monopoly. Shingles and dressed cedar were scarce, that was all. For the last two years of the war most of the available man power and machinery of British Columbia loggers had been given over to airplane spruce. Carpenters had laid down their tools and gone to the front. House builders had ceased to build houses while the vast cloud of European uncertainty hung over the nation. All across North America the wind and weather had taken toll of roofs, and these must be repaired. The nation did not cease to breed while its men died daily by thousands. And with the signing of the armistice a flood of immigration was let loose. British and French and

Scandinavians and swarms of people from Czecho-Slovakia and all the Balkan States, hurried from devastated lands and impending taxes to a new country glowing with the deceptive greenness of far fields. The population had increased; the housing for it had not. So that rents went up and up until economic factors exerted their inexorable pressure and the tap of the carpenter's hammer and the ring of his saw began to sound in every city, in every suburb, on new farms and lonely prairies.

Cedar shingles began to make fortunes for those who dealt in them on a large scale. By midsummer Carr's mill on the Toba worked night and day.

"Crowd your work, Hollister," Carr advised him. "I've been studying this cedar situation from every angle. There will be an unlimited demand and rising prices for about another year. By that time every logging concern will be getting out cedar. The mills will be cutting it by the million feet. They'll glut the market and the bottom will drop out of this cedar boom. So get that stuff of yours out while the going is good. We can use it all."

But labor was scarce. All the great industries were absorbing men, striving to be first in the field of post-war production. Hollister found it difficult to enlarge his crew. That was a lonely hillside where his timber stood. Loggers preferred the big camps, the less primitive conditions under which they must live and work. Hollister saw that he would be unable to extend his operations until deep snow shut down some of the northern camps that fall. Even so he did well enough, much better than he had expected at the beginning. Bill Hayes, he of the gray mustache and the ear-piercing faller's cry, was a "long-stake" man. That is to say, old Bill knew his weaknesses, the common weaknesses of the logger, the psychological reaction from hard work, from sordid living, from the indefinable cramping of the spirit that grows upon a man through months of monotonous labor. Town—a pyrotechnic display among the bright lights—one dizzy swoop on the wings of fictitious excitement—bought caresses—empty pockets—the woods again! Yet the logger dreams always of saving his money, of becoming a timber king, of setting himself up in some business—knowing all the while that he is like a child with pennies in his hand, unhappy until they are spent. Bill Hayes was past fifty, and he knew all this. He stayed in the woods as long as the weakness of the flesh permitted, naively certain that he had gone on his last "bust", that he would bank his money and experience the glow of possessing capital.

The other man was negligible—a bovine lump of flesh without personality—born to hew wood and draw water for men of enterprise.

And there was always Mills, Mills who wanted to make a stake and "get to hell out of here", and who did not go, although the sum to his credit in Hollister's account book was creeping towards a thousand dollars, so fierce and unceasing an energy did Mills expend upon the fragrant cedar.

Hollister himself accounted for no small profit. Like Mills, he worked under a spur. He wrestled stoutly with opportunity. He saw beyond the cedar on that green slope. With a living assured, he sought fortune, aspired to things as yet beyond his reach—leisure, an ampler way of life, education for his children that were to be.

This measure of prosperity loomed not so distant. When he took stock of his resources in October, he found himself with nearly three thousand dollars in hand and the bulk of his cedar still standing. Half that was directly the gain derived from a rising market. Labor was his only problem. If he could get labor, and shingles held the upper price levels, he would make a killing in the next twelve months. After that, with experience gained and working capital, the forested region of the British Columbia coast lay before him as a field of operations.

Meantime he was duly thankful for daily progress. Materially that destiny which he doubted seemed to smile on him.

Late in October, when the first southward flight of wild duck began to wing over the valley, old Bill Hayes and Sam Ballard downed tools and went to town. The itch of the wandering foot had laid hold of them. The pennies burned their pockets. Ballard frankly wanted a change. Hayes declared he wanted only a week's holiday, to see a show or two and buy some clothes. He would surely be back. "Yes, he'll be back," Mills commented with ironic emphasis. "He'll be broke in a week and the first camp that pays his fare out will get him.

There's no fool like a logger. Strong in the back and weak in the head—the best of us."

But Mills himself stayed on. What kept him, Hollister wondered? Did he have some objective that centered about Myra Bland? Was the man a victim of hopeless passion, lingering near the unobtainable because he could not tear himself away? Was Myra holding him like a pawn in some obscure game that she played to feed her vanity? Or were the two of them caught in one of those inextricable coils which Hollister perceived to arise in the lives of men and women, from which they could not free themselves without great courage and ruthless disregard of consequences?

Sometimes Hollister wondered if he himself were not overfanciful, too sensitive to moods and impressions. Then he would observe some significant interchange of looks between Mills and Myra and be sure of currents of feeling, furtive and powerful, sweeping about those two. It angered him. Hollister was all for swift and forthright action, deeds done in the open. If they loved, why did they not commit themselves boldly to the undertaking, take matters in their own hands and have an end to all secrecy? He felt a menace in this secrecy, as if somehow it threatened him. He perceived that Mills suffered, that something gnawed at the man. When he rested from his work, when he sat quiescent beside the fire where they ate at noon together, that cloak of melancholy brooding wrapped Mills close. He seldom talked. When he did there was in his speech a resentful inflection like that of a man who smarts under some injury, some injustice, some deep hurt which he may not divulge but which nags him to the limits of his endurance.

Hollister was Mills' sole company after the other two men left. They would work within sight of each other all day. They ate together at noon. Now and then he asked Mills down to supper out of pity for the man's complete isolation. Some chord in Hollister vibrated in sympathy with this youngster who kept his teeth so resolutely clenched on whatever hurt him.

And while Hollister watched Mills and wondered how long that effort at repression would last, he became conscious that Myra was watching him, puzzling over him; that something about him attracted and repulsed her in equal proportions. It was a disturbing discovery. Myra could study him with impunity. Doris could not see this scrutiny of her husband by her neighbor. And

Myra did not seem to care what Hollister saw. She would look frankly at him with a question in her eyes. What that question might be, Hollister refused even to consider. She never again made any remark to Doris about her first husband, about the similarity of name. But now and then she would speak of something that happened when she was a girl, some casual reference to the first days of the war, to her life in London, and her eyes would turn to Hollister. But he was always on his guard, always on the alert against these pitfalls of speech. He was never sure whether they were deliberate traps, or merely the half-regretful, backward looking of a woman to whom life lately had not been kind.

Nevertheless it kept his nerves on edge. For he valued his peace and his home that was in the making. There was a restfulness and a satisfaction in Doris Cleveland which he dreaded to imperil because he had the feeling that he would never find its like again. He felt that Myra's mere presence was like a sword swinging over his head. There was no armor he could put on against that weapon if it were decreed it should fall.

Hollister soon perceived that if he were not to lose ground he must have labor. Men would not come seeking work so far out of the beaten track. In addition, there were matters afoot that required attention. So he took Doris with him and went down to Vancouver. Almost the first man he met on Cordova Street, when he went about in search of bolt cutters, was Bill Hayes, sober and unshaven and a little crestfallen.

"Why didn't you come back?" Hollister asked. Hayes grinned sheepishly.

"Kinda hated to," he admitted. "Pulled the same old stuff—dry town, too. Shot the roll. Dang it, I'd ought to had more sense. Well, that's the way she goes. You

149

want men?"

"Sure I want men," Hollister said. "Look here, if you can rustle five or six men, I'll make it easier for you all. I'll take up a cook for the bolt camp. And I won't shut down for anything but snow too deep to work in."

"You're on. I think I can rustle some men. Try it, anyhow."

Hayes got a crew together in twenty-four hours. Doris attended to her business, which required the help of her married cousin and a round of certain shops. Almost the last article they bought was a piano, the one luxury Doris longed for, a treat they had promised themselves as soon as the cedar got them out of the financial doldrums.

"I suppose it's extravagance," Doris said, her fingers caressing the smooth mahogany, feeling the black and ivory of the keyboard, "but it's one of the few things one doesn't need eyes for."

She had proved that to Hollister long ago. When she could see she must have had an extraordinary faculty for memorizing music. Her memory seemed to have indelibly engraved upon it all the music she had ever played.

Hollister smiled indulgently and ordered the instrument cased for shipping. It went up on the same steamer that gave passage to themselves and six woodsmen and their camp cook. There were some bits of new furniture also.

This necessitated the addition of another room. But that was a simple matter for able hands accustomed to rough woodwork. So in a little while their house extended visibly, took on a homier aspect. The sweet-peas and flaming poppies had wilted under the early frosts. Now a rug or two and a few pictures gave to the floors and walls a cheerful note of color that the flowers had given to their dooryard during the season of their bloom.

About the time this was done, and the cedar camp working at an accelerated pace, Archie Lawanne came back to the Toba. He walked into Hollister's quite unexpectedly one afternoon. Myra was there.

It seemed to Hollister that Lawanne's greeting was a little eager, a trifle expectant, that he held Myra's outstretched hand just a little longer, than mere acquaintance justified. Hollister glanced at Mills, sitting by. Mills had come down to help Hollister on the boom, and Doris had called them both in for a cup of tea. Mills was staring at Lawanne with narrowed eyes. His face wore the expression of a man who sees impending calamity, sees it without fear or surprise, faces it only with a little dismay. He set down his cup and lighted a cigarette. His fingers, the brown, muscular, heavy fingers of a stronghanded man, shook slightly.

"You know, it's good to be back in this old valley," Lawanne said. "I have half a notion to become a settler. A fellow could build up quite an estate on one of these big flats. He could grow almost anything here that will grow in this latitude. And when he wanted to experience the doubtful pleasures of civilization, they would always be waiting for him outside."

"If he had the price," Mills put in shortly.

"Precisely," Lawanne returned, "and cared to pay it—for all he got."

"That's what it is to be a man and free," Myra observed. "You can go where you will and when—live as you wish."

"It all depends on what you mean by freedom," Lawanne replied. "Show me a free man. Where is there

151

such? We're all slaves. Only some of us are too stupid to recognize our status."

"Slaves to what?" Myra asked. "You seem to have come back in a decidedly pessimistic frame of mind."

"Slaves to our own necessities; to other people's demands; to burdens we have assumed, or have had thrust upon us, which we haven't the courage to shake off. To our own moods and passions. To something within us that keeps us pursuing this thing we call happiness. To struggle for fulfilment of ideals that can never be attained. Slaves to our environment, to social forces before which the individual is nothing. It's all rot to talk about the free man, the man whose soul is his own. Complete freedom isn't even desirable, because to attain it you would have to withdraw yourself altogether from your fellows and become a law unto yourself in some remote solitude; and no sane person wants to do that, even to secure this mythical freedom which people prattle about and would recoil from if it were offered them. Yes, I'll have another cup, if you please, Mrs. Hollister."

Lawanne munched cake and drank tea and talked as if he had been denied the boon of conversation for a long time. But that could hardly be, for he had been across the continent since he left there. He had been in New York and Washington and swung back to British Columbia by way of San Francisco.

"I read those two books of yours—or rather Bob read them to me," Doris said presently. "You ought to be ashamed of yourself for writing such a preposterous yarn as 'The Worm'."

"Ah, my dear woman," Lawanne's face lit up with a sardonic smile. "I wish my publishers could hear you say that. 'The Worm' is good, sound, trade union goods,

152

turned out in the very best manner of a thriving school of fictionsmiths. It sold thirty thousand copies in the regular edition and tons in the reprint."

"But there never were such invincible men and such a perfect creature of a woman," Doris persisted. "And the things they did—the strings you pulled. Life isn't like that. You know it isn't."

"Granted," Lawanne returned dryly. "But what did you think of 'The Man Who Couldn't Die'?"

"It didn't seem to me," Doris said slowly, "that the man who wrote the last book could possibly have written the first. That *was* life. Your man there was a real man, and you made his hopes and fears, his love and sufferings, very vivid. Your woman was real enough too, but I didn't like her. It didn't seem to me she was worth the pain she caused."

"Neither did she seem so to Phillips, if you remember," Lawanne said. "That was his tragedy—to know his folly and still be urged blindly on because of her, because of his own illusions, which he knew he must cling to or perish. But wait till I finish the book I'm going to write this winter. I'm going to cut loose. I'm going to smite the Philistines—and the chances are," he smiled cynically, "they won't even be aware of the blow. Did you read those books?" He turned abruptly to Myra.

She nodded.

"Yes, but I refuse to commit myself," she said lightly. "There is no such thing as a modest author, and Mrs. Hollister has given you all the praise that's good for you."

Hollister and Mills went back to their work on the boom. When they finished their day's work, Lawanne had gone down to the Blands' with Myra. After supper, as Mills rose to leave for the upper camp, he said to Doris:

"Have you got that book of his—about the fellow that couldn't die? I'd like to read it." Doris gave him the book. He went away with it in his hand.

Hollister looked after him curiously. There was strong meat in Lawanne's book. He wondered if Mills would digest it. And he wondered a little if Mills regarded Lawanne as a rival, if he were trying to test the other man's strength by his work.

Away down the river, now that dark had fallen, the light in Bland's house shone yellow. There was a red, glowing spot on the river bank. That would be Lawanne's camp. Hollister shut the door on the chill October night and turned back to his easy chair by the stove. Doris had finished her work. She sat at the piano, her fingers picking out some slow, languorous movement that he did not know, but which soothed him like a lullaby.

Vigorously he dissented from Lawanne's philosophy of enslavement. He, Hollister, was a free man. Yes, he was free—but only when he could shut the door on the past, only when he could shut away all the world just as he had but now shut out the valley, the cold frosty night, his neighbors and his men, by the simple closing of a door. But he could not shut away the consciousness that they were there, that he must meet Myra and her vague questioning, Mills with his strange repression, his brooding air. He must see them again, be perplexed by them, perhaps find his own life, his own happiness, tangled in the web of their affairs. Hollister could frown over that unwelcome possibility. He could say to himself that it was only an impression; that he was a fool to labor under that sense of insecurity. But he could not help it. Life was like that. No man stood alone. No man could ever completely achieve mastery of his relations to his fellows. Until life became extinct, men and women would be swayed and conditioned by blind human forces, governed by relations casual or intimate, imposed upon them by the very law of their being. Who was he to escape?

No, Hollister reflected, he could not insulate himself and Doris against this environment, against these people. They would have to take things as they came and be thankful they were no worse.

Doris left the piano. She sat on a low stool beside him, leaned her brown head against him.

"It won't be so long before I have to go to town, Bob," she said dreamily. "I hope the winter is open so that the work goes on well. And sometimes I hope that the snow shuts everything down, so that you'll be there with me. I'm not very consistent, am I?"

"You suit me," he murmured. "And I'll be there whether the work goes on or not."

"What an element of the unexpected, the unforeseen, is at work all the time," she said. "A year ago you and I didn't even know of each other's existence. I used to sit and wonder what would become of me. It was horrible sometimes to go about in the dark, existing like a plant in a cellar, longing for all that a woman longs for if she is a woman and knows herself. And you were in pretty much the same boat."

"Worse," Hollister muttered, "because I sulked and brooded and raged against what had overtaken me. Yet if I hadn't reacted so violently, I should never have come here to hide away from what hurt me. So I wouldn't have met you. That would almost make one think there is something in the destiny that you and

155

Lawanne smile at."

"Destiny and chance: two names for the same thing, and that thing wholly unaccountable, beyond the scope of human foresight," Doris replied. "Things happen; that's all we can generally say. We don't know why. Speaking of Lawanne, I wonder if he really does intend to stay here this winter and write a book?"

"He says so."

"He'll be company for us," she reflected. "He's clever and a little bit cynical, but I like him. He'll help to keep us from getting bored with each other."

"Do you think there is any danger of that?" Hollister inquired.

She tweaked his ear playfully.

"People do, you know. But I hardly think we shall. Not for a year or two, anyway. Not till the house gets full of babies and the stale odor of uneventful, routine, domestic life. Then *you* may."

"Huh," he grunted derisively, "catch me. I know what I want and what contents me. We'll beat the game handily; and we'll beat it together.

"Why, good Lord," he cried sharply, "what would be the good of all this effort, only for you? Where would be the fun of working and planning and anticipating things? Nearly every man, I believe," he concluded thoughtfully, "keeps his gait because of some woman. There is always the shadow of a woman over him, the picture of some woman—past, present, or future, to egg him on to this or that."

"To keep him," Doris laughed, "in the condition a poet once described as:

'This fevered flesh that goes on groping, wailing
Toward the gloom.' "

156

They both laughed. They felt no gloom. The very implication of gloom, of fevered flesh, was remote from that which they had won together.

When Hollister went up to the works in the morning, he found Mills humped on a box beside the fireplace in the old cabin, reading "The Man Who Couldn't Die." At noon he was gone somewhere. Over the noon meal in the split cedar messhouse, the other bolt cutters spoke derisively of the man who laid off work for half a day to read a book. That was beyond their comprehension.

But Hollister thought he understood.

Later in the afternoon, as he came down the hill, he looked from the vantage of height and saw Lawanne's winter quarters already taking form on the river bank, midway between his own place and Bland's. It grew to completion rapidly in the next few days, taking on at last a shake roof of hand-dressed cedar to keep out the cold rains that now began to beat down, the forerunner of that interminable downpour which deluges the British Columbia coast from November to April, the torrential weeping of the skies upon a porous soil which nourishes vast forests of enormous trees, jungles of undergrowth tropical in its density, in its variety of shrub and fern.

For a month after that a lull seemed to come upon the slow march of events towards some unknown destiny— of which Hollister nursed a strange prescience that now rose strong in him and again grew so tenuous that he would smile at it for a fancy. Yet in that month there was no slack in the routine of affairs. The machinery of Carr's mill revolved through each twenty-four hours. Up on the hill Hollister's men felled trees with warning shouts and tumultuous crashings. They attacked the prone trunks with axe and saw and iron wedges,

Lilliputians rending the body of a fallen giant. The bolt piles grew; they were hurled swiftly down the chute into the dwindling river, rafted to the mill. All this time the price of shingles in the open market rose and rose, like a tide strongly on the flood, of which no man could prophesy the high-water mark. Money flowed to Hollister's pockets, to the pockets of his men. The value of his standing timber grew by leaps and bounds. And always Sam Carr, who had no economic illusions, urged Hollister on, predicting before long the inevitable reaction.

The days shortened. Through the long evenings Hollister's house became a sort of social center. Lawanne would come in after supper, sometimes inert, dumb, to sit in a corner smoking a pipe—again filled with a curious exhilaration, to talk unceasingly of everything that came into his mind, to thump ragtime on the piano and sing a variety of inconsequential songs in a velvety baritone. Myra came often. So did Bland. So did Charlie Mills. Many evenings they were all there together. As the weeks went winging by, Doris grew less certain on her feet, more prone to spend her time sitting back in a deep arm chair, and Myra began to play for them, to sing for them—to come to the house in the day, and help Doris with her work.

The snow began at last, drifting down out of a windless sky. Upon that, with a sudden fear lest a great depth should fall, lest the river should freeze and make exit difficult, Hollister took his wife to town. This was about the middle of November. Some three weeks later a son was born to them.

CHAPTER XV

WHEN THEY CAME BACK TO THE TOBA, Hollister brought in a woman to relieve Doris of housework and help her take care of the baby, although Doris was jealous of that privilege. She was a typical mother in so far as she held the conviction that no one could attend so well as herself the needs of that small, red-faced, lusty-lunged morsel of humanity.

And as if some definite mark had been turned, the winter season closed upon the valley in a gentle mood. The driving rains of the fall gave way to January snows. But the frost took no more than a tentative nibble now and then. Far up on the mountains the drifts piled deep, and winter mists blew in clammy wraiths across the shoulders of the hills. From those high, cold levels, the warmth of day and the frosts that gnawed in chill darkness started intermittent slides rumbling, growling as they slipped swiftly down steep slopes, to end with a crash at the bottom of the hill or in the depths of a gorge. But the valley itself suffered no extremes of weather. The river did not freeze. It fell to a low level, but not so low that Hollister ever failed to shift his cedar bolts from chute mouth to mill. There was seldom so much snow that his crew could not work. There was growing an appreciable hole in the heart of his timber limit. In another year there would be nothing left of those great cedars that were ancient when the first white man crossed the Rockies, nothing but a few hundred stumps.

With the coming of midwinter a somnolent period seemed also to occur in Hollister's affairs. One day succeeded another in placid routine. The work went on

159

with clock-like precision. It had passed beyond a one-man struggle for economic foothold; it no longer held for him the feeling of a forlorn hope which he led against the forces of the wilderness. It was like a ball which he had started rolling down hill. It kept on, whether he tended it or not. If he chose to take his rifle and go seeking venison, if he elected to sit by his fire reading a book, the cedars fell, their brown trunks were sawn and split, the bolts came sliding down the chute in reckonable, profitable quantities, to the gain of himself and his men.

Mills remained, moody, working with that strange dynamic energy, sparing of words except that now and then he would talk to Hollister in brief jerky sentences, in a manner which implied much and revealed nothing. Mills always seemed on the point of crying out some deep woe that burned within him, of seeking relief in some outpouring of speech—but he never did. At the most he would fling out some cryptic hint, bestow some malediction upon life in general. And he never slackened the dizzy pace of his daily labor, except upon those few occasions when from either Hollister or Lawanne he got a book that held him. Then he would stop work and sit in the bunk house and read till the last page was turned. But mostly he cut and piled cedar as if he tried to drown out in the sweat of his body whatever fever burned within.

Hollister observed that Mills no longer had much traffic with the Blands. For weeks at a time he did not leave the bolt camp except to come down to Hollister's house.

Lawanne seemed to be a favored guest now, at Bland's. Lawanne worked upon his book, but by fits and starts, working when he did work with a feverish concentration. He had a Chinese boy for house-servant. He might be found at noon or at midnight sprawled in a chair beside a potbellied stove, scrawling in an ungainly hand across sheets of yellow paper. He had no set hours for work. When he did work, when he had the vision and the fit was on and words came easily, chance callers met with scant courtesy. But he had great stores of time to spare, for all that. Some of it he spent at Bland's, waging an interminable contest at cribbage with Bland, coming up now and then with the Blands to spend an evening at Hollister's.

"It's about a man who wrecked his life by systematically undermining his own illusions about life," he answered one day Hollister's curious inquiry as to what the new book was about, "and of how finally a very assiduously cultivated illusion made him quite happy at last. Sound interesting?"

"How could he deliberately cultivate an illusion?" Doris asked. "If one's intelligence ever classifies a thing as an illusion, no conscious effort will ever turn it into a reality."

"Oh, I didn't say *he* cultivated the illusion," Lawanne laughed.

"Besides, do you really think that illusions are necessary to happiness?" Doris persisted.

"To some people," Lawanne declared. "But let's not follow up that philosophy. We're getting into deep water. Let's wade ashore. We'll say whatever is is right, and let it go at that. It will be quite all right for you to offer me a cup of tea, if your kitchen mechanic will condescend. That Chink of mine is having a holiday with my shotgun, trying to bag a brace of grouse for dinner. So I throw myself on your mercy."

"This man Bland is the dizzy limit," Lawanne

observed, when the tea and some excellent sandwiches presently appeared. "He bought another rifle the other day—paid forty-five bones for it. That makes four he has now. And they have to manage like the deuce to keep themselves in grub from one remittance day to the next. He's a study. You seldom run across such a combination of physical perfection and childlike irresponsibility. He was complaining about his limited income the other day—'inkum' in his inimitable pronunciation. I suggested that right here in this valley he could earn a considerable number of shekels if he cared to work. He merely smiled amiably and said he didn't think he cared to take on a laborer's job. It left a chap no time for himself, you know. I suppose he'll vegetate here till he comes into that money he's waiting for. He refers to that as if it were something which pertained to him by divine right, something which freed him from any obligation to make any effort to overcome the sordid way in which they live at present."

"He doesn't consider it sordid," Hollister said. "Work is what he considers sordid—and there is something to be said for his viewpoint, at that. He enjoys himself tramping around with a gun, spending an afternoon to catch half a dozen six-inch trout."

"But it is sordid," Lawanne persisted. "Were you ever in their house?"

Hollister shook his head.

"It isn't as comfortable as your men's bunk house. They have boxes for chairs, a rickety table, a stove about ready to fall to pieces. There are cracks in the walls and a roof that a rat could crawl through—or there would be if Mrs. Bland didn't go about stuffing them up with moss and old newspapers. Why can't a gentleman, an athlete and a sportsman make his quarters something

162

a little better than a Siwash would be contented with? Especially if he has prevailed on a woman to share his joys and sorrows. Some of these days Mr. Bland will wake up and find his wife has gone off with some enterprising chap who is less cocksure and more ambitious."

"Would you blame her?" Doris asked casually.

"Bless your soul, no," Lawanne laughed. "If I were a little more romantic, I might run away with her myself. What a tremendous jar that would give Bland's exasperating complacency. I believe he's a hang-over from that prehistoric time when men didn't believe that any woman had a soul—that a woman was something in which a man acquired a definite property right merely by marrying her."

Doris chuckled.

"I can imagine how Mr. Bland would look if he heard you," she said.

"He'd only smile in a superior manner," Lawanne declared. "You couldn't get Bland fussed up by any mere assertion. The only thing that would stir him deeply would be a direct assault on that vague abstraction which he calls his honor—or on his property. Then he would very likely smite the wrongdoer with all the efficiency of outraged virtue."

Hollister continued to muse on this after Lawanne went away. He thought Lawanne's summing up a trifle severe. Nevertheless it was a pretty clear statement of fact. Bland certainly seemed above working either for money or to secure a reasonable degree of comfort for himself and his wife. He sat waiting for a windfall to restore his past splendor of existence, which he sometimes indirectly admitted meant cricket, a country home, horses and dogs, a whirl among the right sort of

163

people in London now and then. That sort of thing and that sort of man was what Myra had fallen in love with. Hollister felt a mild touch of contempt for them both. His wife had also let her thoughts focus on the Blands.

"I wonder," she said, "if they are so very poor? Why don't you offer Bland a job? Maybe he is too proud to ask."

Bland was not too proud to ask for certain things, it seemed. About a week later he came to Hollister and in a most casual manner said, "I say, old man, can you let me have a hundred dollars? My quarterly funds are delayed a bit."

Hollister gave him the money without question. As he watched Bland stride away through the light blanket of snow, and a little later noticed him disappear among the thickets and stumps going towards the Carr camp, where supplies were sold as a matter of accommodation rather than for profit, Hollister reflected that there was a mild sort of irony in the transaction. He wondered if Myra knew of her husband's borrowing. If she had any inkling of the truth, how would she feel? For he knew that Myra was proud, sensitive, independent in spirit far beyond her capacity for actual independence. If she even suspected his identity, the borrowing of that money would surely sting her. But Hollister put that notion aside.

For a long time Myra had ceased to trouble him with the irritating uncertainty of their first meetings. She apparently accepted him and his mutilated face as part of Doris Hollister's background and gave him no more thought or attention. Always in the little gatherings at his house Hollister contrived to keep in the shadow, to be an onlooker rather than a participant—just as Charlie Mills did. Hollister was still sensitive about his face. He

164

was doubly sensitive because he dreaded any comment upon his disfigurement reaching his wife's ears. He had succeeded so well in thus effacing himself that Myra seemed to regard him as if he were no more than a grotesque bit of furniture to which she had become accustomed. All the sense of sinister possibilities in her presence, all that uneasy dread of her nearness, that consciousness of her as an impending threat, had finally come to seem nothing more than mere figments of his imagination. Especially since their son was born. That seemed to establish the final bond between himself and Doris. Myra, the past which so poignantly included Myra, held less and less significance. He could look at Myra and wonder if this was the same woman he had held in his arms, whose kisses had been freely and gladly bestowed upon him; if all the passion and pain of their life together, of their tearing apart, had ever really been. He had got so far beyond that it seemed unreal. And lately there had settled upon him a surety that to Myra it must all be just as unreal—that she could not possibly harbor any suspicion that he was her legal husband, hiding behind a mask of scars—and that even if she did suspect, that suspicion could never be translated into action which could deflect ever so slightly the current of his present existence.

He was working at the chute mouth when Bland came to ask for that loan. He continued to work there. Not long after he noticed Bland leave his own house and go down the flat, he saw Myra coming along the bank. That was nothing. There was a well-beaten path there that she traveled nearly every afternoon. He felt his first tentative misgiving when he saw that Myra did not stop at the house, that she walked past and straight towards where he worked. And this slight misgiving grew to a

165

certainty of impending trouble when she came up, when she faced him. Movement and the crisp air had kindled a glow in her cheeks. But something besides the winter air had kindled an almost unnatural glow in her eyes. They were like dusky pansies. She was, he thought, with curious self-detachment, a strikingly beautiful woman. And he recalled that anger or excitement, any emotion that stirred her, always made her seem more alluring, always made her glow and sparkle as if in such moments she was a perfect human jewel, flashing in the sun of life.

She nodded to Hollister, looked down on the cedar blocks floating in the cold river, stood a moment to watch the swift descent of other bolts hurtling down the chute and joining their fellows with successive splashes.

"You let Jim have some money this morning?" she said then; it was a statement as much as an interrogation.

"Yes," Hollister replied.

"Don't let him have any more," she said bluntly. "You may never get it back. Why should you supply him with money that you've worked for when he won't make any effort to get it for himself? You're altogether too free-handed, Robin."

Hollister stood speechless. She looked at him with a curious half-amused expectancy. She knew him. No one but Myra had ever called him that. It had been her pet name for him in the old days. She knew him. He leaned on his pike pole, waiting for what was to follow. This revelation was only a preliminary. Something like a dumb fury came over Hollister. Why did she reveal this knowledge of him? For what purpose? He felt his secure foundations crumbling.

"So you recognize me?"

"Did you think I wouldn't?" she said slowly. "Did you think your only distinguishing characteristic was the shape of your face? I've been sure of it for months."

"Ah," he said. "What are you going to do about it?"

"Nothing. Nothing. What is there to do?"

"Then why reveal this knowledge?" he demanded harshly. "Why drag out the old skeleton and rattle it for no purpose? Or have you some purpose?"

Myra sat down on a fallen tree. She drew the folds of a heavy brown coat closer about her and looked at him steadily.

"No," she replied. "I can't say that I have any definite purpose except—that I want to talk to you. And it seemed that I could talk to you better if we stopped pretending. We can't alter facts by pretending they don't exist, can we?"

"I don't attempt to alter them," he said. "I accept them and let it go at that. Why don't you?"

"I do," she assured him, "but when I find myself compelled to accept your money to pay for the ordinary necessaries of living, I feel myself being put in an intolerable position. I suppose you won't understand that. I imagine you think of me as a selfish little beast who has no scruples about anything. But I'm not quite like that. It galls me to have Jim borrow from you. He may intend to pay it back. But he won't; it will somehow never be quite convenient. And I've squandered enough of your money. I feel like a thief sometimes when I watch you work. You must hate me. Do you, Robin?"

Hollister stirred the snow absently with the pike-pole point. He tried to analyze his feelings, and he found it difficult.

"I don't think so," he said at last. "I'm rather

167

indifferent. If you meddled with things I'd not only hate you, I think I would want to destroy you. But you needn't worry about the money. If Bland doesn't repay the hundred dollars it won't break me. I won't lend him any more if it disturbs you. But that doesn't matter. The only thing that matters is whether you are going to upset everything in some rash mood that you may sometime have."

"Do you think I might do that?"

"How do I know what you may do?" he returned. "You threw me into the discard when your fancy turned to some one else. You followed your own bent with a certain haste as soon as I was reported dead. I had ceased to be man enough for you, but my money was still good enough for you. When I recall those things, I think I can safely say that I haven't the least idea what you may do next. You aren't faring any too well. That's plain enough. I have seen men raise Cain out of sheer devilishness, out of a desperate notion to smash everything because they were going to smash themselves. Some people seem able to amuse themselves by watching other people squirm. Maybe you are like that. You had complete power over me once. I surrendered to that gladly, then. You appear to have a faculty of making men dance to any tune you care to play. But all the power you have now, so far as I'm concerned, is to make me suffer a little more by giving the whole ugly show away. No, I haven't the least idea what you may do. I don't know you at all."

"My God, no, you don't," she flung out. "You don't. If you ever had, we wouldn't be where we are now."

"Probably it's as well," Hollister returned. "Even if you had been true, you'd have faltered when I came back looking like this."

168

"And that would have been worse than what I did do," she said, "wouldn't it?"

"Are you justifying it as an act of mercy to me?" he asked.

Myra shook her head.

"No. I don't feel any great necessity for justifying my actions. No more than you should feel compelled to justify yours. We have each only done what normal human beings frequently do when they get torn loose from the moorings they know and are moved by forces within them and beyond them, forces which bewilder and dismay them. The war and your idea of duty, of service, pried us apart. Natural causes—natural enough when I look back at them—did the rest. We all want to be happy. We all grab at that when it comes within reach. That's all you and I have done. We will probably continue doing that the same as every one else."

"I have it," Hollister said defiantly. "That is why I don't want any ghosts of the old days haunting me now."

"If you have, you are very fortunate," she murmured. "But don't leave your wife alone in a city throbbing with the fevered excitement and uncertainty of war, where every one's motto is a short life and a merry one! Not if she's young and hot-blooded, if she has grown so accustomed to affection and caresses that the want of them afflicts her with a thirst like that of a man lost in a desert. Because if she has nothing to do but live from day to day on memories and hopes, there will be a time when some man at hand will obscure the figure of the absent one. That is all that happened to me, Robin. I longed for you. Then I began to resent your complete absorption by the war machine. Then you got dim, like the figure of a man walking away down a long road. Do

169

you remember how it was? Leave once in six months or so. A kiss of welcome and a goodbye right on its heels. There were thousands like me in London. The war took our men—but took no account of us. We were untrained. There were no jobs to occupy our hands—none we could put our hearts into—none that could be gotten without influence in the proper quarters. We couldn't pose successfully enough to persuade ourselves that it was a glorious game. They had taken our men, and there was nothing much left. We did not have to earn our keep. If you had only not stuck so closely to the front lines."

"I had to," Hollister said sharply. "I had no choice. The country—"

"The country! That shadowy phantasm—that recruiting sergeant's plea—that political abstraction that is flung in one's face along with other platitudes from every platform," Myra broke out passionately. "What does it really mean? What did it mean to us? Men going out to die. Women at home crying, eating their hearts out with loneliness, going bad now and then in recklessness, in desperation. Army contractors getting rich. Ammunition manufacturers getting rich. Transportation companies paying hundred percent. dividends. One nation grabbing for territory here, another there. Talk of saving the world for democracy and in the same breath throttling liberty of speech and action in every corner of the world. And now that it's all over, everything is the same, only worse. The rich are richer and the poor poorer, and there are some new national boundaries and some blasted military and political reputations. That's all. What was that to you and me? Nothing. Less than nothing. Yet it tore our lives up by the roots. It took away from us something we had that we valued, something that we might have kept. It doesn't matter that you were sincere, that you wanted to serve, that you thought it a worthy service. The big people, the men who run things, they had no such illusions; they had their eye on the main chance all the time. It paid them—if not in money then in prestige and power. How has it paid you? You know, every time you look in a mirror. You know that the men that died were the lucky ones. The country that marched them to the front with speeches and music when the guns were talking throws them on the scrapheap when they come back maimed. I have no faith in a country that takes so much and gives a little so grudgingly. I've learned to think, Robin, and perhaps it has warped me a little. You have suffered. So have I, partly because I was ignorant of the nature I was born with, which you didn't understand and which I'm only myself beginning to understand—but mostly because the seats of the mighty were filled by fools and hypocrites seeking their own advantage. Oh, life is a dreary business sometimes! We want so to be happy. We try so hard. And mostly we fail."

Her eyes filled with tears, round drops that gathered slowly in the corners of her puckered lids and spilled over the soft curves of her cheek. She did not look at Hollister. She stared at the gray river. She made a little gesture, as if she dumbly answered some futile question, and her hands dropped idly into her lap.

"I feel guilty," she continued after a little, "not because I failed to play up to the role of the faithful wife. I couldn't help that. But I shouldn't have kept that money, I suppose. Still, you were dead. Money meant nothing to you. It was in my hands and I needed it, or thought I did. You must have had a hard time, Robin, coming back to civil life a beggar."

"Yes, but not for lack of money," Hollister replied. "I didn't need much and I had enough. It was being scarred so that everybody shunned me. It was the horror of being alone, of finding men and women always uneasy in my presence, always glad to get away from me. They acted as if I were a monstrosity that offended them beyond endurance. I couldn't blame them much. Sometimes it gave me the shivers to look at myself in the glass. I am a horrible sight. People who must be around me seem to get used to me, whether they like it or not. But at first I nearly went mad. I had been uprooted and disfigured. Nobody wanted to know me, to talk to me, to be friendly. However, that's past. I have got a start. Unless this skeleton is dragged out of the closet, I shall get on well enough."

"I shall not drag it out, Robin," she assured him with a faint smile. "Some day I hope I'll be able to give you back that money."

"What became of it?" He voiced a question which had been recurring in his mind for a year. "You must have had over forty thousand dollars when I was reported dead in '17."

Myra shrugged her shoulders.

"We were married six months after that. Jim has some rather well-to-do people over there. They were all very nice to me. I imagine they thought he was marrying money. Perhaps he thought so himself. He had nothing except a quarterly pittance. He has no sense of values, and I was not much better. There is always this estate which he will come into, to discount the present. He had seen service the first year of the war. He was wounded and invalided home. Then he served as a military instructor. Finally, when the Americans came in, he was allowed to resign. So we came across to the States. We went here and there, spending as we went. We cut a pretty wide swath too, most of the time. There were several disastrous speculations. Presently the money was all gone. Then we came up here, where we can live on next to nothing. We shall have to stay here another eighteen months. Looking back, the way we spent money seems sheer lunacy. The fool and his money—you know. And it wasn't our money. That hurts me now. I've begun to realize what money means to me, to you, to everyone. That's why when Jim calmly told me that he had borrowed a hundred dollars from you I felt that was a little more than I could stand. That's piling it on. I wondered why you gave it to him—if you let him have it in a spirit of contemptuous charity. I might have known it wasn't that. But don't lend him any more. He really doesn't need it. Borrowing with Jim is just like asking for a smoke. He's queer. If he made a bet with you and lost he'd pay up promptly, if he had to pawn his clothes and mine too. Borrowed money, however, seems to come in a different category. When this estate comes into his hands perhaps I shall be able to return some of this money that we wasted. I think that—and the fact that I'm just a little afraid to break away and face the world alone—is chiefly what keeps me faithful to him now."

"Is it as bad as that?" Hollister asked.

"Don't misunderstand me, Robin," she protested. "I'm not an abused wife or anything like that. He's perfectly satisfied, as complacent as an English gentleman can be in the enjoyment of possession. But he doesn't love me any more than I love him. He blandly assumes that love is only a polite term for something else. And I can't believe that—yet. Maybe I'm what

Archie Lawanne calls a romantic sentimentalist, but there is something in me that craves from a man more than elementary passion. I'm a woman; therefore my nature demands of a man that he be first of all a man. But that alone isn't enough. I'm not just a something to be petted when the fit is on and then told in effect to run along and play. There must be men who have minds as well as bodies. There must be here and there a man who understands that a woman has all sorts of thoughts and feelings as well as sex. Meanwhile—I mark time. That's all."

"You appear," Hollister said a little grimly, "to have acquired certain definite ideas. It's a pity they didn't develop sooner."

"Ideas only develop out of experience," she said quietly. "And our passions are born with us."

She rose, shaking free the snow that clung to her coat.

"I feel better for getting all that steam off my chest," she said. "It's better, since we must live here, that you and I should not keep up this game of pretence between ourselves. Isn't it, Robin?"

"Perhaps. I don't know." The old doubts troubled Hollister. He was jealous of what he had attained, fearful of reviving the past, a little uncertain of this new turn.

"At any rate, you don't hold a grudge against me, do you?" Myra asked. "You can afford to be indifferent now. You've found a mate, you're playing a man's part here. You're beating the game and getting some real satisfaction out of living. You can afford to be above a grudge against me."

"I don't hold any grudge," Hollister answered truthfully.

"I'm going down to the house, now," Myra said. "I

wanted to talk to you openly, and I'm glad I did. I think and think sometimes until I feel like a rat in a trap. And you are the only one here I can really talk to. You've been through the mill and you won't misunderstand."

"Ah," he said. "Is Charlie Mills devoid of understanding, or Lawanne?"

She looked at him fixedly for a second.

"You are very acute," she observed. "Some time I may tell you about Charlie Mills. Certainly I'd never reveal my soul to Archie Lawanne. He'd dissect it and gloat over it and analyze it in his next book. And neither of them will ever be quite able to abandon the idea that a creature like me is something to be pursued and captured."

She turned away. Hollister saw her go into the house. He could picture the two of them there together. Doris and Myra bending over young Robert, who was now beginning to lie with wide-open blue eyes, in which the light of innocent wonder, of curiosity, began to show, to wave his arms and grope with tiny, uncertain hands. Those two women together hovering over his child— one who was still legally his wife, the other his wife in reality.

How the world would prick up its donkey ears—even the little cosmos of the Toba valley—if it knew. But of course no one would ever know. Hollister was far beyond any contrition for his acts. The end justified the means—doubly justified it in his case, for he had had no choice. Harsh material factors had rendered the decision for him. Hollister was willing now to abide by that decision. To him it seemed good, the only good thing he had laid hold of since the war had turned his world upside down and inside out.

He went about his work mechanically, deep in

thought. His mind persisted in measuring, weighing, turning over all that Myra had said, while his arms pushed and heaved and twisted the pike pole, thrusting the blocks of cedar into an orderly arrangement within the boom-sticks.

CHAPTER XVI

HOLLISTER HAD GONE DOWN TO LAWANNE'S with a haunch of venison. This neighborly custom of sharing meat, when it is to be had for the killing, prevails in the northern woods. Officially there were game seasons to be observed. But the close season for deer sat lightly on men in a region three days' journey from a butcher shop. They shot deer when they needed meat. The law of necessity overrode the legal pronouncement in this matter of food, as it often did in other ways.

While Hollister, having duly pleased Lawanne's China-boy by this quarter of venison, sat talking to Lawanne, Charlie Mills came in to return a book.

"Did you get anything out of that?" Lawanne asked.

"I got a bad taste in my mouth," Mills replied. "It reads like things that happen. It's too blamed true to be pleasant. A man shouldn't be like that, he shouldn't think too much—especially about other people. He ought to be like a bull—go around snorting and pawing up the earth till he gets his belly full, and then lie down and chew his cud."

Lawanne smiled.

"You've hit on something, Mills," he said. "The man who thinks the least and acts the most is the happy man, the contented man, because he's nearly always pleased with himself. If he fails at anything he can usually

176

excuse himself on the grounds of somebody else's damnfoolishness. If he succeeds he complacently assumes that he did it out of his own greatness. Action—that's the thing. The contemplative, analytical mind is the mind that suffers. Man was a happy animal until he began to indulge in abstract thinking. And now that the burden of thought is laid on him, he frequently uses it to his own disadvantage."

"I'll say he does," Mills agreed. "But what can he do? I've watched things happen. I've read what some pretty good thinkers say. It don't seem to me a man's got much choice. He thinks or he don't think, according to the way he's made. When you figure how a man comes to be what he is, why he's nothing but the product of forces that have been working on all the generations of his kind. It don't leave a man much choice about how he thinks or feels. If he could just grin and say 'It doesn't matter', he'd be all right. But he can't, unless he's made that way. And since he isn't responsible for the way he's made, what the hell can he do?"

"You're on the high road to wisdom when you can look an abstraction like that in the face," Lawanne laughed. "What you say is true. But there's one item you overlook. A man is born with, say, certain predispositions. Once he recognizes and classifies them, he can begin to exercise his will, his individual determination. If our existence was ordered in advance by destiny, dictated by some all-conscious, omnipotent intelligence, we might as well sit down and fold our hands. But we still have a chance. Free will is an exploded theory, in so far as it purposes to explain human action in a general sense. Men are biologically different. In some weakness is inherent, in others determination. The weak man succumbs when he is

177

beset. The strong man struggles desperately. The man who consciously grasps and understands his own weaknesses can combat an evil which will destroy a man of lesser perception, lesser will; because the intelligent man will avoid what he can't master. He won't butt his head against a stone wall either intellectually, emotionally, or physically. If the thing is beyond him and he knows it is beyond him, he will not waste himself in vain effort. He will adapt himself to what he can't change. The man who can't do that must suffer. He may even perish.

And to cling to life is the prime law. That's why it is a fundamental instinct that makes a man want to run when he can no longer fight."

Hollister said nothing. He was always a good listener. He preferred to hear what other men said, to weigh their words, rather than pour out his own ideas. Lawanne sometimes liked to talk at great length, to assume the oracular vein, to analyze actions and situations, to put his finger on a particular motive and trace its origin, its most remote causation. Mills seldom talked. It was strange to hear him speak as he did now, to Lawanne.

Mills walked back through the flat with Hollister. They trudged silently through the soft, new snow, the fresh fall which had enabled Hollister to track and kill the big deer early that morning. The sun was setting. Its last beam struck flashing on the white hills. The back of the winter was broken, the March storms nearly at an end. In a little while now, Hollister thought, the buds would be bursting, there would be a new feel in the air, new fragrant smells arising in the forest, spring freshets in the rivers, the wild duck flying north. Time was on the wing, in ceaseless flight.

Mills broke into his reflections.

"Come up in the morning, will you, and check in what cedar I have piled? I'm going to pull out."

"All right." Hollister looked his surprise at the abrupt decision. "I'm sorry you're going."

Mills walked a few paces.

"Maybe it won't do me any good," he said. "I wonder if Lawanne is right? It just struck me that he is. Anyway, I'm going to try his recipe. Maybe I can kid myself into thinking everything's jake, that the world's a fine sort of place and everything is always lovely. If I could just myself think that—maybe a change of scenery will do the trick. Lawanne's clever, isn't he? Nothing would fool him very long."

"I don't know," Hollister said. "Lawanne's a man with a pretty keen mind and a lively imagination. He's more interested in why people do things than in what they do. But I dare say he might fool himself as well as the rest of us. For we all do, now and then."

"I guess it's the way a man's made," Mills reflected. "But it's rather a new idea that a man can sort of make himself over if he puts his mind to it. Still, it sounds reasonable. I'm going to give it a try. I've got to."

But he did not say why he must. Nor did Hollister ask him. He thought he knew—and he wondered at the strange tenacity of this emotion which Mills could not shake off. A deep-rooted passion for some particular woman, an emotion which could not be crushed, was no mystery to Hollister. He only wondered that it should be so vital a force in the life of a man.

Mills came down from the hill camp to settle his account with Hollister in the morning. He carried his blankets and his clothes in a bulky pack on his sturdy shoulders. When he had his money, he rose to go, to catch the coastwise steamer which touched the Inlet's head that afternoon. Hollister helped him sling the pack, opened the door for him—and they met Myra Bland setting foot on the porch step.

They looked at each other, those two. Hollister knew that for a second neither was conscious of him. Their eyes met in a lingering fixity, each with a question that did not find utterance.

"I'm going out," Mills said at last. A curious huskiness seemed to thicken his tongue. "This time for good, I hope. So-long."

"Goodbye, Charlie," Myra said.

She put out her hand. But either Mills did not see it or he shrank from contact, for he passed her and strode away, bent a little forward under his pack. Myra turned to watch him. When she faced about again there was a mistiness in her eyes, a curious, pathetic expression of pity on her face. She went on into the house with scarcely a glance at Hollister.

In another week spring had ousted winter from his seasonal supremacy. The snow on the lower levels vanished under a burst of warm rain. The rain ceased and the clouds parted to let through a sun fast growing to full strength. Buds swelled and burst on willow and alder. The soil, warmed by the sun, sent up the first shoots of fern and grasses, a myriad fragile green tufts that would presently burst into flowers. The Toba rose day by day, pouring down a swollen flood of snowwater to the sea.

And life went on as it always did. Hollister's crew, working on a bonus for work performed, kept the bolts of cedar gliding down the chute. The mill on the river below swallowed up the blocks and spewed them out in bound bundles of roof covering. Lawanne kept close to his cabin, deep in the throes of creation, manifesting strange vagaries of moroseness or exhilaration which in his normal state he cynically ascribed to the artistic temperament. Bland haunted the creeks where the trout lurked, tramped the woods gun in hand, a dog at his heels, oblivious to everything but his own primitive, purposeless pleasures.

"I shouldn't care to settle here for good," he once said to Hollister. "But really, you know, it's not half bad. If money wasn't so dashed scarce. It's positively cruel for an estate to be so tied up that a man can't get enough to live decently on."

Bland irritated Hollister sometimes, but often amused him by his calm assurance that everything was always well in the world of J. Carrington Bland. Hollister could imagine him in Norfolk and gaiters striding down an English lane, concerned only with his stable, his kennels, the land whose rentals made up his income. There were no problems on Bland's horizon. He would sit on Hollister's porch with a pipe sagging one corner of his mouth and gaze placidly at the river, the hills, the far stretch of the forest—and Hollister knew that to Bland it was so much water, so much up-piled rock and earth, so much growing wood. He would say to Myra: "My dear, it's time we were going home", or "I think I shall have a go at that big pool in Graveyard Creek tomorrow", or "I say, Hollister, if this warm weather keeps on, the bears will be coming out soon, eh?", and between whiles he would sit silently puffing at his pipe, a big, heavy, handsome man, wearing soiled overalls and a shabby coat with a curious dignity. He spoke of "family" and "breeding" as if these were sacred possessions which conferred upon those who had them complete immunity from the sort of effort that common men must make.

"He really believes that," Myra said to Hollister once. "No Bland ever had to work. They have always had property—they have always been superior people. Jim's an anachronism, really. He belongs in the Middle Ages when the barons did the fighting and the commoners did the work. Generations of riding in the bandwagon has made it almost impossible for a man like that to plan intelligently and work hard merely for the satisfaction of his needs."

"I wonder what he'd do if there was no inheritance to fall back on?" Hollister asked.

"I don't know—and I really don't care much," Myra said indifferently. "I shouldn't be concerned, probably, if that were the case."

Hollister frowned.

"Why do you go on living with him, if that's the way you feel?"

"You seem to forget," she replied, "that there are very material reasons! And you must remember that I don't dislike Jim. I have got so that I regard him as a big, good-natured child of whom one expects very little."

"How in heaven's name did a man like that catch your fancy in the first place?" Hollister asked. He had never ceased to wonder about that. Myra looked at him with a queer lowering of her eyes.

"What's the use of telling you?" she exclaimed petulantly. "You ought to understand without telling. What was it drove you into Doris Cleveland's arms a month after you met her? You couldn't know her—nor she you. You were lonely and moody, and something about her appealed to you. You took a chance—and drew a prize in the lottery. Well, I took a chance also— and drew a blank. I'm a woman and he's a man, a very good sort of a man for any woman who wants nothing more of a man than that he shall be a handsome, agreeable, well-mannered animal. That's about what Jim is. I may also be good-looking, agreeable, well-mannered—a fairly desirable woman to all outward appearances—but I'm something besides, which Jim doesn't suspect and couldn't understand if he did. But I didn't learn that soon enough."

"When did you learn it?" Hollister asked. He felt that he should not broach these intimately personal matters with Myra, but there was a fascination in listening to her reveal complexes of character which he had never suspected, which he should have known.

"I've been learning for some time; but I think Charlie Mills gave me the most striking lesson," Myra answered thoughtfully. "You can imagine I was blue and dissatisfied when we came here, to bury ourselves alive because we could live cheaply, and he could hunt and fish to his heart's content while he waited to step into a dead man's shoes. A wife's place, you see, is in the home, and home is wherever and whatever her lord and master chooses to make it. I was quite conscious by that time that I didn't love Jim Bland. But he was a gentleman. He didn't offend me. I was simply indifferent—satiated, if you like. I used to sit wondering how I could have ever imagined myself going on year after year, contented and happy, with a man like Jim. Yet I had been quite sure of that—just as once I had been quite sure you were the only man who could ever be much of a figure on my horizon. Do you think I'm facile and shallow? I'm not really. I'm not just naturally a sensation-seeker. I hate promiscuity. *He* convinced me of that."

She made a swift gesture towards Mills' vanishing figure.

183

"I ran across him first in London. He was convalescing from a leg wound. That was shortly after I was married, and I was helping entertain these stray dogs from the front. It was quite the fashion. People took them out motoring and so on. I remembered Mills out of all the others because he was different from the average Tommy, quiet without being self-conscious. I remembered thinking often what a pity nice boys like that must be killed and crippled by the thousand. When we came here, Charlie was working down at the settlement. Somehow I was awfully glad to see him— any friendly face would have been welcome those first months before I grew used to these terrible silences, this complete isolation which I had never before known.

"Well, the upshot was that he fell in love with me, and for awhile—for a little while—I thought I was experiencing a real affection at last, myself; a new love rising fine and true out of the ashes of old ones.

"And it frightened me. It made me stop and think. When he would stare at me with those sad eyes I wanted to comfort him, I wanted to go away with him to some distant place where no one knew me and begin life all over again. And I knew it wouldn't do. It would only be the same thing over again, because I'm made the way I am. I was beginning to see that it would take a good deal of a man to hold my fitful fancy very long. Charlie's a nice boy. He's clean and sensitive, and I'm sure he'd be kind and good to any woman. Still, I knew it wouldn't do. Curious thing—all the while that my mind was telling me how my whole existence had unfitted me to be a wife to such a man—for Charlie Mills is as full of romantic illusions as a seventeen-year-old girl—at the same time some queer streak in me made me long to wipe the slate clean and start all over

184

again. But I could never convince myself that it was anything more than sex in me responding to the passion that so deeply moved him. That suspicion became certainty at last. That is why I say Charlie Mills taught me something about myself."

"I think it was a dear lesson for him," Hollister said, remembering the man's moods and melancholy, the bitterness of frustration which must have torn Mills. "You hurt him."

"I know it, and I'm sorry, but I couldn't help it," she said patiently. "There was a time just about a year ago when I very nearly went away with him. I think he felt that I was yielding. But I was trying to be honest with myself and with him. With all my vagaries, my uncertain emotions, I didn't want just the excitement of an affair, an amorous adventure. Neither did he. He wanted me body and soul, and I recoiled from that finally, because—I was afraid, afraid of what our life would become when he learned that truth which I had already grasped, that life can't be lived on the peaks of great emotion and that there was nothing much else for him and me to go on." She stopped and looked at Hollister.

"I wonder if you think I'm a little mad?" she asked.

"No. I was just wondering what it is about you that makes men want you," he returned.

"You should know," she answered bluntly.

"I never knew. I was like Mills: a victim of my emotions. But one outgrows any feeling if it is clubbed hard enough. I daresay all these things are natural enough, even if they bring misery in their wake."

"I daresay," she said. "There is nothing unnatural in a man loving me, any more than it was unnatural for you to love Doris, or for Doris to have a son. Still you are

185

inclined to blame me for what I've done. You seem to forget that the object of each individual's existence, man or woman, is not to bestow happiness on some one else, but to seek it for themselves."'

"That sounds like Lawanne," Hollister observed.

"It's true, no matter who it sounds like," she retorted.

"If you really believe that, you are certainly a fool to go on living with a man like Jim Bland," Hollister declared. It did not occur to him that he was displaying irritation.

"I've told you why and I do not see any reason for changing my idea," she said coolly. "When it no longer suits me to be a chattel, I shall cease to be one. Meantime—*pax—pax—*

"Where is Doris and the adorable infant?" Myra changed the subject abruptly. "I don't hear or see one or the other."

"They were all out in the kitchen a minute ago, bathing the kid," he told her, and Myra went on in.

Hollister's work lay almost altogether in the flat now. The cut cedar accumulating under the busy hands of six men came pouring down the chute in a daily stream. To salvage the sticks that spilled, to arrange the booms for rafting down stream, kept Hollister on the move. At noon that day Myra and Doris brought the baby and lunch in a basket and spread it on the ground on the sunny side of an alder near the chute mouth, just beyond the zone of danger from flying bolts. The day was warm enough for comfortable lounging. The boy, now grown to be a round-faced, clear-skinned mite with blue eyes like his father, lay on an outspread quilt, waving his chubby arms, staring at the mystery of the shadows cast upon him by leaf and branch above.

Hollister finished his meal in silence, that reflective

silence which always overtook him when he found himself one corner of this strange triangle. He could talk to Myra alone. He was never at a loss for words with his wife. Together, they struck him dumb.

And this day Doris seemed likewise dumb. There was a growing strangeness about her which had been puzzling Hollister for days. At night she would snuggle down beside him, quietly contented, or she would have some story to tell, or some unexpectedness of thought which still surprised him by its clear-cut and vigorous imagery. But by day she grew distrait, as if she retreated into communion with herself, and her look was that of one striving to see something afar, a straining for vision.

Hollister had marked this. It had troubled him. But he said nothing. There were times when Doris liked to take refuge in her own thought-world. He was aware of that, and understood it and let her be, in such moods.

Now she sat with both hands clasped over one knee. Her face turned toward Myra for a time. Then her eyes sought her husband's face with a look which gave Hollister the uneasy, sickening conviction that she saw him quite clearly, that she was looking and appraising. Then she looked away toward the river, and as her gaze seemed to focus upon something there, an expression of strain, of effort, gathered on her face. It lasted until Hollister, watching her closely, felt his mouth grow dry. It hurt him as if some pain, some terrible effort of hers was being communicated to him. Yet he did not understand, and he could not reach her intimately with Myra sitting by.

Doris spoke at last.

"What is that, Bob?" she asked. She pointed with her finger.

"A big cedar stump," he replied. It stood about thirty

feet away.

"Is it dark on one side and light on the other?"

"It's blackened by fire and the raw wood shows on one side where a piece is split off."

He felt his voice cracked and harsh.

"Ah," she breathed. Her eyes turned to the baby sprawling on his quilt.

Myra rose to her feet. She picked up the baby, moved swiftly and noiselessly three steps aside, stood holding the boy in her arms.

"You have picked up baby. You have on a dress with light and dark stripes. I can see—I can see."

Her voice rose exultantly on the last word.

Hollister looked at Myra; she held the boy pressed close to her breast. Her lips were parted, her pansy-purple eyes were wide and full of alarm as she looked at Hollister.

He felt his scarred face grow white. And when Doris turned toward him to bend forward and look at him with that strange, peering gaze, he covered his face with his hands.

CHAPTER XVII

"EVERYTHING IS INDISTINCT, just blurred outlines. I can't see colors only as light and dark," Doris went on, looking at Hollister with that straining effort to see. "I can only see you now as a vague form without any detail."

Hollister pulled himself together. After all, it was no catastrophe, no thunderbolt of fate striking him a fatal blow. If, with growing clarity of vision, catastrophe ensued, then was time enough to shrink and cower. That resiliency which had kept him from going before under terrific stress stood him in good stead now.

"It seems almost too good to be true," he forced himself to say, and the irony of his words twisted his lips into what with him passed for a smile.

"It's been coming on for weeks," Doris continued. "And I haven't been able to persuade myself it was real. I have always been able to distinguish dark from daylight. But I never knew whether that was pure instinct or because some faint bit of sight was left me. I have looked and looked at things lately, wondering if imagination could play such tricks. I couldn't believe I was seeing even a little, because I've always been able to see things in my mind, sometimes clearly, sometimes in a fog—as I see now—so I couldn't tell whether the things I have seen lately were realities or mental images. I have wanted so to see, and it didn't seem possible."

Asking about the stump had been a test, she told Hollister. She did not know till then whether she saw or only thought she saw. And she continued to make these tests happily, exulting like a child when it first walks alone. She made them leave her and' she followed them among a clump of alders, avoiding the trunks when she came within a few feet, instead of by touch. She had Hollister lead her a short distance away from Myra and the baby. She groped her way back, peering at the ground, until at close range she saw the broad blue and white stripes of Myra's dress.

"I wonder if I shall continue to see more and more?" she sighed at last, "or if I shall go on peering and groping in this uncertain, fantastic way. I wish I knew."

"I know one thing," Myra put in quickly. "And that is you won't do your eyes any good by trying so hard to see. You mustn't get excited about this and overdo it. If it's a natural recovery, you won't help it any by trying so hard to see."

"Do I seem excited?" Doris smiled. "Perhaps I am. If you had been shut up for three years in a room without windows, I fancy you'd be excited at even the barest chance of finding yourself free to walk in the sun. My God, no one put here with sight knows the despair that the blind sometimes feel. And the promise of seeing— you can't possibly imagine what a glorious thing it is. Every one has always been good to me. I've been lucky in so many ways. But there have been times—you know, don't you, Bob?—when it has been simply hell, when I struggled in a black abyss, afraid to die and yet full of bitter protest against the futility of living."

The tears stood in her eyes and she reached for Hollister's hand, and squeezed it tightly between her own.

"What a lot of good times we shall have when I get so that I can see just a little better," she said affectionately. "Your blind woman may not prove such a bad bargain, after all, Bob."

"Have I ever thought that?" he demanded.

"Oh, no," she said smiling, "but *I* know. Give me the baby, Myra."

She cuddled young Robert in her arms.

"Little, fat, soft thing," she murmured. "By and by his mother will be able to see the color of his dear eyes. Bless its little heart—him and his daddy are the bestest things in this old world—this old world that was black so long."

Myra turned her back on them, walked away and stood on the river bank. Hollister stared at his wife. He struggled with an old sensation, one that he had thought long put by—a sense of the intolerable burden of existence in which nothing was sure but sorrow. And he was aware that he must dissemble all such feelings. He must not let Doris know how he dreaded that hour in which she should first see clearly his mutilated face.

"You ought to see an oculist," he said at last.

"An oculist? Eye specialists—I saw a dozen of them," she replied. "They were never able to do anything—except to tell me I would never see again. A fig for the doctors. They were wrong when they said my sight was wholly destroyed. They'd probably be wrong again in the diagnosis and treatment. Nature seems to be doing the job. Let her have her way."

They discussed that after Myra was gone, sitting on a log together in the warm sun, with the baby kicking his heels on the spread quilt. They continued the discussion after they went back to the house. Hollister dreaded uncertainty. He wanted to know how great a measure of her sight would return, and in what time. He did not belittle the oculists because they had once mistaken. Neither did Doris, when she recovered from the excitement engendered by the definite assurance that her eyes were ever so slightly resuming their normal function. She did believe that her sight was being restored naturally, as torn flesh heals or a broken bone knits, and she was doubtful if any eye specialist could help that process. But she agreed in the end that it would be as well to know if anything could be done and what would aid instead of retard her recovery.

"But not for awhile," she said. "It's just a glimmer. Wait a few days. If this fog keeps clearing away, then we'll go."

They were sitting on their porch steps. Doris put her arms around him.

"When I can see, I'll be a real partner," she said happily. "There are so many things I can do that can't be done without eyes. And half the fun of living is in sharing the discoveries one makes about things with some one else. Sight will give me back all the books I want to read, all the beautiful things I want to see. I'll be able to climb hills and paddle a canoe, to go with you wherever you want to take me. Won't it be splendid? I've only been half a woman. I have wondered sometimes how long it would be before you grew weary of my moods and my helplessness."

And Hollister could only pat her cheek and tell her that he loved her, that her eyes made no difference. He could not voice the fear he had that her recovered sight would make the greatest difference, that the reality of him, the distorted visage which peered at him from a mirror would make her loathe him. He was not a fool. He knew that people, the women especially, shrank from the crippled, the disfigured, the malformed, the horrible. That had been his experience. It had very nearly driven him mad. He had no illusions about the men who worked for him, about his neighbors. They

192

found him endurable, and that was about all. If Doris Cleveland had seen him clearly that day on the steamer, if she had been able to critically survey the unlovely thing that war had made of him, she might have pitied him. But would she have found pleasure in the sound of his voice, the touch of his hand? Hollister's intelligence answered "No." For externally his appearance would have been a shock, would have inhibited the pleasant intimacy at which they so soon arrived.

Doris made light of his disfigurement. She could comprehend clearly many things unseen—but not that. Hollister knew she must have created some definite image of him in her mind; something, he suspected, which must correspond closely to her ideal of a man, something that was dear to her. If that ideal did not— and his intelligence insisted that he could not—survive the reality, then his house was built on sand and must topple.

And he must dig and pry at the foundations. He must do all that could be done for her eyes. That was her right—to see, to be free of her prison of darkness, to be restored to the sight of beauty, to unclouded vision of the world and all it contained, no matter what the consequence to him. He would play the game, although he felt that he would lose.

A cloud seemed to settle on him when he considered that he might lose everything that made life worth while. And it would be an irrevocable loss. He would never again have courage to weave the threads of his existence into another such goodly pattern. Even if he had the courage, he would never have the chance. No such fortuitous circumstances would ever again throw him into the arms of a woman—not such a woman as Doris Cleveland.

Hollister looked at her beside him, and his heart ached to think that presently she might not sit so with her hand on his knee, looking up at him with lips parted in a happy smile, gray eyes eager with anticipation under the long, curving, brown lashes. She was so very dear to him. Not alone because of the instinctive yearning of flesh to flesh, not altogether because of the grace of her vigorous young body, the comeliness of her face, the shining coils of brown hair that gave him a strange pleasure just to stroke. Not alone because of the quick, keen mind that so often surprised him by its sureness. There was some charm more subtle than these, something to which he responded without knowing clearly what it was, something that made the mere knowledge of her presence in his house a comfort, no matter whether he was beside her or miles away.

Lawanne once said to him that a man must worship a God, love a woman, or find a real friendship, to make life endurable. God was too dim, too nebulous, for Hollister's need. Friendship was almost unattainable. How could a man with a face so mutilated that it was grotesque, repellent, cultivate the delicate flower of friendship? Doris loved him because she could not see him. When she could see, she would cease to love. And there would be nothing left for him—nothing. He would live on, obedient to the law of his being, a sentient organism, eating and sleeping, thinking starkly, without joy in the reluctant company of his fellows, his footsteps echoing hollowly down the long corridor of the years, emptied of hope and all those pleasant illusions by which man's spirit is sustained. But would he? Would it be worth while?

"I must go back to work," he said at last. Doris rose with him, holding him a moment. "Presently I shall be

194

able to come and watch you work! I might help. I know how to walk boom-sticks, to handle timber with a pike pole. I'm as strong as an ox. See!"

She put her arms around him and heaved, lifting the hundred and eighty pounds of his weight clear of the ground. Then she laughed, a low, pleased chuckle, her face flushed with the effort, and turned into the house.

Hollister heard her at the piano as he walked away, thundering out the rollicking air of the "Soldier's Chorus", its naive exultance of victory, it seemed to Hollister, expressing well her mood—a victory that might mean for him an abyss of sorrow and loneliness out of which he might never lift himself.

CHAPTER XVIII

FOR A WEEK HOLLISTER NURSED THIS FEAR which so depressed him, watching the slow return of his wife's vision, listening to her talk of all they could do together when her sight was fully restored. From doubt of ocular treatment she changed to an impatient desire of whatever benefit might lie in professional care. A fever of impatience to see began to burn in her.

So Hollister took her out to Vancouver, thence to Seattle, on to San Francisco, passing from each city to a practitioner of higher standing in the next, until two men with great reputations, and consulting fees in proportion, after a week of observation announced their verdict: she would regain normal vision, provided so and so—and in the event of such and such. There was some mystery about which they were guarded. They spoke authoritatively about infusions into the vitreous humor and subsequent absorption. They agreed in language too technical for a layman to understand that the cause of Doris' blindness was gradually disappearing. Only when they put aside the formal language of diagnosis and advised treatment did Hollister really fathom what they were talking about. What they said then was simple. She must cease to strain for sight of objects. She must live for a time in neutral lights. The clearing up of her eyes could perhaps be helped by certain ray treatments, certain forms of electrical massage, which could be given in Vancouver as well as anywhere.

Whereupon the great men accepted their fees and departed.

So too did Hollister and his wife depart for the North again, where they took a furnished apartment overlooking the Gulf of Georgia, close to a beach where Robert junior could be wheeled in a pram by his nurse. And Hollister settled himself to wait.

But it was weary work to nurse that sense of impending calamity, to find his brain ceaselessly active upon the forecast of a future in which he should walk alone, and while he was thus harassed still to keep up a false cheerfulness before Doris. She was abnormally sensitive to impressions. A tone spoke volumes to her. He did not wish to disturb her by his own anxiety at this critical period.

All the while, little by little, her sight was coming back. She could distinguish now any violent contrast of colors. The blurred detail of form grew less pronounced. In the chaos of sensory impressions she began to distinguish order; and when she began to peer unexpectedly at the people she met, at the chubby boy in his cot, at her husband's face, Hollister could stand it no longer. He was afraid, afraid of what he might see in those gray eyes if she looked at him too long, too closely.

He was doubly sensitive now about his face because of those weeks among strangers, of going about in crowded places where people stared at him with every degree of morbid curiosity, exhibiting every shade of feeling from a detached pity to open dislike of the spectacle he presented. That alone weighed heavily on him. Inaction rasped at his nerves. The Toba and his house, the grim peaks standing aloof behind the timbered slopes, beckoned him back to their impassive, impersonal silences, those friendly silences in which a man could sit and think—and hope. A man doomed to death must prefer a swift end to a lingering one. Hollister gradually came to the idea that he could not possibly sit by and watch the light of comprehension steal slowly into his wife's eyes. Better that she should fully regain her sight, and then see with what manner of man she had lived and to whom she had borne a son. Then if she could look at him without recoiling, if the essential man meant more to her than the ghastly wreckage of his face, all would be well. And if not— well then, one devastating buffet from the mailed fist of destiny was better than the slow agony of daily watching the crisis approach.

So Hollister put forth the plausible fact that he must see about his affairs and took the next steamer for the Toba.

Lawanne, expecting letters, was at the float to meet the steamer. Hollister went upstream with him. They talked very little until they reached Lawanne's cabin. There was a four-mile current to buck, and they saved their breath for the paddles. Myra Bland waved as they passed, and Hollister scarcely looked up. He was in the grip of a strange apathy. He was tired, physically weary.

197

His body was dull and heavy, sluggish. So was his mind. He was aware of this, aware that a nervous reaction of some sort was upon him. He wished that he could always be like that—dull, phlegmatic, uncaring. To cease thinking, to have done with feeling, to be a clod, dead to desires, to high hopes and heartnumbing fears.

"Come in and have a cup of tea and tell me the latest Vancouver scandal," Lawanne urged, when they beached the canoe.

Hollister assented. He was as well there as anywhere. If there were an antidote in human intercourse for what afflicted him, that antidote lay in Archie Lawanne. There was no false sentiment in Lawanne. He did not judge altogether by externals. His was an understanding, curiously penetrating intelligence. Hollister could always be himself with Lawanne. He sat down on the grass before the cabin and smoked while Lawanne looked over his letters. The Chinese boy brought tea and sandwiches and cake on a tray.

"Mrs. Hollister is recovering her sight?" Lawanne asked at length.

Hollister nodded.

"Complete normal sight?"

Hollister nodded again.

"You don't seem overly cheerful about it," Lawanne said slowly.

"You aren't stupid," Hollister replied. "Put yourself in my place."

It was Lawanne's turn to indicate comprehension and assent by a nod. He looked at Hollister appraisingly, thoughtfully.

"She gains the privilege of seeing again. You lose— what? Are you sure you stand to lose anything—or is it

198

simply a fear of what you may lose?"

"What can I expect?" Hollister muttered. "My face is bound to be a shock. I don't know how she'll take it. And if when she sees me she can't stand me—isn't that enough?"

"I shouldn't worry, if I were you," Lawanne encouraged. "Your wife is a little different from the ordinary run of women, I think. And, take it from me, no woman loves her husband for his Grecian profile alone. Nine times out of ten a man's looks have nothing to do with what a woman thinks of him, that is if she really knows him; whereas with a man it is usually the other way about, until he learns by experience that beauty isn't the whole works—which a clever woman knows instinctively."

"Women shy away from the grotesque, the unpleasant," Hollister declared. "You know they do. I had proof of that pretty well over two years. So do men, for that matter. But the women are the worst. I've seen them look at me as if I were a loathsome thing."

"Oh, rats," Lawanne returned irritably. "You're hyper-sensitive about that face of yours. The women— well, take Mrs. Bland as an example. I don't see that the condition of your face makes any great difference to her. It doesn't appear to arouse any profound distaste on her part."

Hollister could not counter that. But it was an argument which carried no weight with him. For if Myra could look at him without a qualm, Hollister knew it must be because her mind never quite relinquished the impression of him as he used to be in the old days. And Doris had nothing like that to mitigate the sweeping impression of first sight, which Hollister feared with a fear he could not shake off by any effort of his will.

199

He went on up to his own house. The maple tree thrust one heavy-leaved branch over the porch. The doors were shut. All about the place hung that heavy mantle of stillness which wraps a foresaken home, a stillness in which not even a squirrel chattered or a blue-jay lifted his voice, and in which nothing moved. He stood amid that silence, hearing only a faint whisper from the river, a far-off monotone from the falls beyond the chute. He felt a heaviness in his breast, a sickening sense of being forsaken.

He went in, walked through the kitchen, looked into the bedroom, came back to the front room, opening doors and windows to let in the sun and air and drive out the faint, musty odor that gathers in a closed house. A thin film of dust had settled on the piano, on chairs, on the table. He stood in the middle of the room, abandoned to a horrible depression. It was so still, so lonely, in there. His mind, quick to form images, likened it to a crypt, a tomb in which all his hopes laid buried. That was the effect it had on him, this deserted house. His intelligence protested against submitting to this acceptance of disaster prior to the event, but his feelings overrode his intelligence. If Doris had been lying white and still before him in her coffin, he could not have felt more completely that sense of the futility of life, of love, of hope, of everything. As he stood there, one hand in his pocket, the other tracing with a forefinger an aimless pattern in the dust on the piano, he perceived with remarkable clarity that the unhappiness he had suffered, the loneliness he had endured before he met Doris Cleveland was nothing to what now threatened, to what now seemed to dog his footsteps with sinister portent.

In the bedroom occupied by their housekeeper stood

the only mirror in the house. Hollister went in there and stood before it, staring at the presentment of himself in the glass. He turned away with a shiver. He would not blame her if with clear vision she recoiled from that. He could expect nothing else. Or would she endure that frightful mien until she could first pity, then embrace? Hollister threw out his hands in a swift gesture of uncertainty. He could only wait and see, and meanwhile twist and turn upon the grid. He could not be calm and detached and impersonal. For him there was too much at stake.

He left all the doors and windows wide and climbed the hill. If he were to withstand the onslaught of these uncertainties, these forebodings which pressed upon him with such damnable weight, he must bestir himself. He must not sit down and brood. He knew that. It was not with any particular enthusiasm that he came upon his crew at work, that his eye marked the widening stump-dotted area where a year before the cedars stood branch to branch, nor when he looked over the long ricks of bolts waiting that swift plunge down the chute.

Bill Hayes gave a terse account of his stewardship during Hollister's absence. So many cords of bolts cut and boomed and delivered to the mill. Hollister's profits were accelerating, the fruit of an insatiable market, of inflated prices. As he trudged down the hill, he reflected upon that. He was glad in a way. If Doris could not or would not live with him, he could make life easy for her and the boy. Money would do that for them. With a strange perverseness, his mind dwelt upon the most complete breaking up of his domestic life. It persisted in shadowing forth scenes in which he and Doris took part, in which it was made plain how and why they could no longer live together. In Hollister's mind these scenes always ended by his crying despairingly "If you can't, why, you can't, I suppose. I don't blame you." And he would give her the bigger half of his funds and go his way. He would not blame her for feeling like that. Nevertheless, Hollister had moments when he felt that he would hate her if she did—a paradox he could not understand.

He slept—or at least tried to sleep—that night alone in his house. He cooked his breakfast and worked on the boom until midday, then climbed the hill to the camp and ate lunch with his men. He worked up there till evening and came down in the dusk. He dreaded that lonely house, those deserted rooms. But he forced himself to abide there. He had a dim idea of so disciplining his feelings, of attaining a numbed acquiescence in what he could not help.

Some one had been in the house. The breakfast dishes were washed, the dust cleared away, the floor swept, his bed made. He wondered, but gave credit to Lawanne. It was like Archie to send his Chinese boy to perform those tasks. But it was Myra, he discovered by and by. He came off the hill in midafternoon two days later and found her clearing up the kitchen.

"You don't mind, do you?" she asked. "I have nothing much to do at home, and it seems a shame for everything here to be neglected. When is Doris coming back?"

"I don't know exactly. Perhaps two or three weeks, perhaps as many months."

"But her eyes will be all right again?"

"So they say."

Hollister went out and sat on the front doorstep. His mind sought to span the distance to Vancouver. He wondered what Doris was doing. He could see her sitting in a shaded room. He could see young Robert waving fat arms out of the cushioned depths of his carriage. He could see the sun glittering on the sea that spread away westward, from beneath the windows of the house where they lived. And Doris would sit there anticipating the sight of all those things which had been hidden in a three-year night—the sea rippling in the sun, the distant purple hills, the nearer green of the forest and of grass and flowers, all the light and color that made the world beautiful. She would be looking forward to seeing him. And that was the stroke which Hollister dreaded, which made him indifferent to other things.

He forgot Myra's presence. Six months earlier he would have resented her being there, he would have been uneasy. Now it made no difference. He had ceased to think of Myra as a possible menace. Lately he had not thought of her or her affairs at all.

She came now and sat down upon the porch step within arm's length of him, looking at him in thoughtful silence.

"Is it such a tragedy, after all?" she said at last.

"Is what?"

He took refuge in refusal to understand, although he understood instantly what Myra meant. But he shrank from her intuitive penetration of his troubled spirit. Like any other wounded animal, he wanted to be left alone.

"You know what I mean," she said. "You are afraid of Doris seeing you. That's plain enough. Is it so terrible a thing, after all? If she can't stand the sight of your face, you're better off without her."

"It's easy to be philosophic about some one else's troubles," Hollister muttered. "You can be off with one love and be reasonably sure of another before long. I can't. I'm not made that way, I don't think. And if I

203

were, I'm too badly handicapped."

"You haven't a very charitable opinion of me, have you, Robin?" she said reflectively. "You rather despise me for doing precisely what you yourself have done, making a bid for happiness as chance offered. Only I haven't found it, and you have. So you are morally superior, and your tragedy must naturally be profound because your happiness seems threatened."

"Oh, damn the moral considerations," he said wearily. "It isn't that. I don't blame you for anything you ever did. Why should I? I'm a bigamist. I'm the father of an illegitimate son. According to the current acceptance of morality, I've contaminated and disgraced an innocent woman. Yet I've never been and am not now conscious of any regrets. I don't feel ashamed. I don't feel that I have sinned. I merely grasped the only chance, the only possible chance that was in reach. That's all you did. As far as you and I are concerned, there isn't any question of blame."

"Are you sure," she asked point-blank, "that your face will make any difference to Doris?"

"How can it help?" he replied gloomily. "If you had your eyes shut and were holding in your hands what you thought was a pretty bird and suddenly opened your eyes and saw it was a toad, wouldn't you recoil?"

"Your simile is no good. If Doris really loved you, it was not because she pictured you as a pretty bird. If she could love you without seeing you, if you appealed to her, why should your marred face make her turn away from you?"

But Hollister could not explain his feeling, his deep dread of that which seemed no remote possibility but something inevitable and very near at hand. He did not want pity. He did not want to be merely endured. He sat

204

silent, thinking of those things, inwardly protesting against this miraculous recovery of sight which meant so great a boon to his wife and contained such fearful possibilities of misery for himself.

Myra rose. "I'll come again and straighten up in a day or two."

She turned back at the foot of the steps. "Robin," she said, with a wistful, uncertain smile, "if Doris *does* will *you* let me help you pick up the pieces?"

Hollister stared at her a second.

"Good God!" he broke out. "Do you realize what you're saying?"

"Perfectly."

"You're a strange woman."

"Yes, I suppose I am," she returned. "But my strangeness is only an acceptance, as a natural fact, of instincts and cravings and desires that women are taught to repress. If I find that I've gone swinging around an emotional circle and come back to the point, or the man, where I started, why should I shrink from that, or from admitting it—or from acting on it if it seemed good to me?"

She came back to where Hollister sat on the steps. She put her hand on his knee, looked searchingly into his face. Her pansy-blue eyes met his steadily. The expression in them stirred Hollister.

"Mind you, Robin, I don't think your Doris is superficial enough to be repelled by a facial disfigurement. She seems instinctively to know and feel and understand so many things that I've only learned by bitter experience. She would never have made the mistakes I've made. I don't think your face will make you any the less her man. But if it does—I was your first woman. I did love you, Robin. I could again. I could creep back into your arms if they were empty, and be glad. Would it seem strange?"

And still Hollister stared dumbly. He heard her with a little rancor, a strange sense of the futility of what she said. Why hadn't she acquired this knowledge of herself long ago? It was too late now. The old fires were dead. But if the new one he had kindled to warm himself were to be extinguished, could he go back and bask in the warmth that smoldered in this woman's eyes? He wondered. And he felt a faint irritation, as if some one had accused him of being faithless.

"Do you think it's strange that I should feel and speak like this?" Myra persisted. "Do people never profit by their mistakes? Am I so unlovable a creature? Couldn't you either forget or forgive?"

He shook his head.

"It isn't that." His voice sounded husky, uncertain. "We can't undo what's done, that's all. I cross no more bridges before I come to them."

"Don't mistake me, Robin," she said with a self-conscious little laugh. "I'm no lovesick flapper. Neither am I simply a voluptuous creature seeking a new sensation. I don't feel as if I couldn't live without you. But I do feel as if I could come back to you again and it would be a little like coming home after a long, disappointing journey. When I see you suffering, I want to comfort you. If she makes you suffer, I shall be unhappy unless I can make you feel that life still holds something good. If I could do that, I should perhaps find life good myself. And it doesn't seem much good to me, any more. I'm still selfish. I want to be happy. And I can't find happiness anywhere. I look back to our old life and I envy myself. If the war marred your face and made you suffer, remember what it has done to me.

Those months and months that dragged into years in London. Oh, I know I was weak. But I was used to love. I craved it. I used to lie awake thinking about you, in a fever of protest because you could not be there with me, in a perfect passion of resentment at the circumstances that kept you away; until it seemed to me that I had never had you, that there was no such man, that all our life together was only a dream. Think what the war did to us. How it has left us—you scarred and hopeless; I, scarred by my passions and emotions. That is all the war did for any one scarred them, those it didn't kill. Oh, Robin, Robin, life seems a ghastly mockery, sometimes. It promises so much and gives so little."

She bent her head. Her shoulders shook with sobs she tried to strangle. Hollister put his hand on the thick coils of honey-colored hair. He was sorry for her—and for himself. And he was disturbed to find that the touch of her hair, the warm pressure of her hands on his knee, made his blood run faster.

The curious outbreak spent itself. She drew herself away from him, and rising to her feet without a word she walked rapidly away along the path by the river.

Hollister looked after her. He was troubled afresh, and he thought to himself that he must avoid scenes like that. He was not, it appeared, wholly immune from the old virus.

And he was clearly conscious of the cold voice of reason warning him against Myra. Sitting there in the shadow of his silent house, he puzzled over these new complexities of feeling. He was a little bewildered. To him Doris meant everything that Myra had once been. He wanted only to retain what he had. He did not want to salvage anything from the wreckage of the past. He was too deeply concerned with the dreadful test that fully restored eyesight would impose on Doris. He knew that Doris Cleveland's feeling for him had been profound and vital. She had given too many proofs for him to doubt that. But would it survive? He did not know. He hoped a little and feared much.

Above this fear he found himself now bewildered by this fresh swirl of emotion. He knew that if Myra had flung herself into his arms he would have found some strange comfort in that embrace, that he could not possibly have repulsed her. It was a prop to his soul—or was it, he asked himself, merely his vanity?—that Myra could look behind the grimness of his features and dwell fondly on the essential man, on the reality behind that dreadful mask.

Still, Hollister knew that to be only a mood, that unexpected tenderness for a woman whom he had hated for betraying him. It was Doris he wanted. The thought of her passing out of his life rested upon him like an intolerable burden. To be in doubt of her afflicted him with anguish. That the fires of her affection might dwindle and die before daily sight of him loomed before Hollister as the consummation of disaster—and he seemed to feel that hovering near, closely impending.

That they had lived together sixteen months did not count. That she had borne him a child—neither did that count. That she had pillowed her brown head nightly in the crook of his arm—that he had bestowed a thousand kisses on her lips, her hair, her neck—that she had lain beside him hour after hour through the long nights, drowsily content—none of these intimacies counted beside vision. He was a stranger in the dark. She did not know him. She heard his voice, knew his tenderness, felt the touch of him—the unseen lover. But there remained for her the revelation of sight. He was still the mysterious, the unknown, about which her fancies played.

How could he know what image of him, what ideal, resided tenaciously in her mind, and whether it would survive the shock of reality? That was the root of Hollister's fear, a definite well-grounded fear. He found himself hoping that promise of sight would never be fulfilled, that the veil would not be lifted, that they would go on as they were. And he would feel ashamed of such a thought. Sight was precious. Who was he to deny her that mercy—she who loved the sun and the hills and the sea; all the sights of earth and sky which had been shut away so long; she who had crept into his arms many a time, weeping passionate tears because all the things she loved were forever wrapped in darkness?

If upon Hollister had been bestowed the power to grant her sight or to withhold it, he would have shrunk from a decision. Because he loved her he wished her to see, to experience the joy of dawn following that long night in which she groped her way. But he dreaded lest that light gladdening her eyes should mean darkness for him, a darkness in which everything he valued would be lost.

Then some voice within him whispered suggestively that in this darkness Myra would be waiting with outstretched hands—and Hollister frowned and tried not to think of that.

CHAPTER XIX

AT NOON NEXT DAY Hollister left the mess-house table and went out to sit in the sun and smoke a pipe beyond the Rabelaisian gabble of his crew. While he sat looking at the peaks north of the valley, from which the June sun was fast stripping even the higher snows, he saw a man bent under a shoulder pack coming up the slope that dropped away westward toward the Toba's mouth. He came walking by stumps and through thickets until he was near the camp. Then Hollister recognized him as Charlie Mills. He saw Hollister, came over to where he sat, and throwing off his pack made a seat of it, wiping away the sweat that stood in shining drops on his face.

"Well, I'm back, like the cat that couldn't stay away," Mills said.

The same queer undercurrent of melancholy, of sadness, the same hint of pain colored his words—a subtle matter of inflection, of tone. The shadowy expression of some inner conflict hovered in his dark eyes. Again Hollister felt that indefinable urge of sympathy for this man who seemed to suffer with teeth grimly clenched, so that no complaint ever escaped him. A strange man, tenacious of his black moods.

"How's everything?" Mills asked. "You've made quite a hole here since I left. Can I go to work again?"

"Sure," Hollister replied. "This summer will just about clean up the cedar here. You may as well help it along, if you want to work."

"It isn't a case of wanting to. I've got to," Mills said under his breath. Already he was at his old trick of absent staring into space, while his fingers twisted tobacco and paper into a cigarette. "I'd go crazy loafing. I've been trying that. I've been to Alaska and to Oregon, and blew most of the stake I made here in riotous living." He curled his lip disdainfully. "It's no good. Might as well be here as anywhere. So I came back— like the cat."

He fell silent again, looking through the trees out over

the stone rim under which Bland's house stood by the river. He sat there beside Hollister until the bolt gang, moving out of the bunk house to work, saw and hailed him. He answered briefly. Then he rose without another word to Hollister and carried in his pack. Hollister saw him go about selecting tools, shoulder them and walk away to work in the timber.

That night Hollister wakened out of a sound sleep to sniff the air that streamed in through his open windows. It was heavy with the pungent odor of smoke. He rose and looked out. The silence of night lay on the valley, over the dense forest across the river, upon the fir-swathed southern slope. No leaf stirred. Nothing moved. It was still as death. And in this hushed blackness— lightened only by a pale streak in the north and east that was the reflection of snowy mountain crests standing stark against the sky line—this smoky wraith crept along the valley floor. No red glow greeted Hollister's sight. There was nothing but the smell of burning wood, that acrid, warm, heavy odor of smoke, the invisible herald of fire. It might be over the next ridge. It might be in the mouth of the valley. It might be thirty miles distant. He went back to bed, to lie with that taint of smoke in his nostrils, thinking of Doris and the boy, of himself, of Charlie Mills, of Myra, of Archie Lawanne. He saw ghosts in that dusky chamber, ghosts of other days, and trooping on the heels of these came apparitions of a muddled future—until he fell asleep again, to be awakened at last by a hammering on his door.

The light of a flash-lamp revealed a logger from the Carr settlement below. The smoke was rolling in billows when Hollister stepped outside. Down toward the Inlet's head there was a red flare in the sky.

"We got to get everybody out to fight that," the man

said. "She started in the mouth of the river last night. If we don't check it and the wind turns right, it'll clean the whole valley. We sent a man to pull your crew off the hill."

In the growing dawn, Hollister and the logger went down through woods thick with smoke. They routed Lawanne out of his cabin; and he joined them eagerly. He had never seen a forest fire. What bore upon the woodsmen chiefly as a malignant, destructive force affected Lawanne as something that promised adventure, as a spectacle which aroused his wonder, his curious interest in vast, elemental forces unleashed. They stopped at Bland's and pressed him into service.

In an hour they were deployed before the fire, marshalled to the attack under men from Carr's, woodsmen experienced in battle against the red enemy, this spoiler of the forest with his myriad tongues of flame and breath of suffocating smoke.

In midsummer the night airs in those long inlets and deep valleys move always toward the sea. But as day grows and the sun swings up to its zenith, there comes a shift in the aerial currents. The wind follows the course of the sun until it settles in the westward, and sometimes rises to a gale. It was that rising of the west wind that the loggers feared. It would send the fire sweeping up the valley. There would be no stopping it. There would be nothing left in its wake but the blackened earth, smoking roots, and a few charred trunks standing gaunt and unlovely amid the ruin.

So now they strove to create a barrier which the fire should not pass. It was not a task to be perfunctorily carried on, there was no time for malingering. There was a very real incitement to great effort. Their property was at stake; their homes and livelihood; even their lives, if they made an error in the course and speed of the fire's advance and were trapped.

They cut a lane through the woods straight across the valley floor from the river to where the southern slope pitched sharply down. They felled the great trees and dragged them aside with powerful donkey engines to manipulate their gear. They cleared away the brush and the dry windfalls until this lane was bare as a traveled road—so that when the fire ate its way to this barrier there was a clear space in which should fall harmless the sparks and embers flung ahead by the wind.

There, at this labor, the element of the spectacular vanished. They could not attack the enemy with excited cries, with brandished weapons. They could not even see the enemy. They could hear him, they could smell the resinous odor of his breath. That was all. They laid their defenses against him with methodical haste, chopping, heaving, hauling the steel cables here and there from the donkeys, sweating in the blanket of heat that overlaid the woods, choking in the smoke that rolled like fog above them and about them And always in each man's mind ran the uneasy thought of the west wind rising.

But throughout the day the west wind held its breath. The flames crawled, ate their way instead of leaping hungrily. The smoke rose in dun clouds above the burning area and settled in gray vagueness all through the woods, drifting in wisps, in streamers, in fantastic curlings, pungent, acrid, choking the men. The heat of the fire and the heat of the summer sun in a windless sky made the valley floor a sweat-bath in which the loggers worked stripped to undershirts and overalls, blackened with soot and grime.

Night fell. The fire had eaten the heart out of a block

half a mile square. It was growing. A redness brightened the sky. Lurid colors fluttered above the hottest blaze. A flame would run with incredible agility up the trunk of a hundred-foot cedar to fling a yellow banner from the topmost boughs, to color the billowing smoke, the green of nearby trees, to wave and gleam and shed coruscating spark-showers and die down again to a dull glow.

Through the short night the work went on. Here and there a man's weariness grew more than he could bear, and he would lie down to sleep for an hour or two. They ate food when it was brought to them. Always, while they could keep their feet, they worked.

Hollister worked on stoically into the following night, keeping Lawanne near him, because it was all new and exciting to Lawanne, and Hollister felt that he might have to look out for him if the wind took any sudden, dangerous shift.

But the mysterious forces of the air were merciful. During the twenty-four hours there was nothing but little vagrant breezes and the drafts created by the heat of the fire itself. When day came again, without striking a single futile blow at the heart of the fire, they had drawn the enemy's teeth and clipped his claws—in so far as the flats of the Toba were threatened. The fire would burn up to that cleared path and burn itself out— with men stationed along to beat out each tiny flame that might spring up by chance. And when that was done, they rested on their oars, so to speak; they took time to sit down and talk without once relaxing their vigilance.

In a day or two the fire would die out against that barrier, always provided the west wind did not rise and in sportive mockery fling showers of sparks across to start a hundred little fires burning in the woods behind their line of defense. A forest fire was never beaten until it was dead. The men rested, watched, patrolled their line. They looked at the sky and sighed for rain. A little knot of them gathered by a tree. Some one had brought a box of sandwiches, a pail of coffee and tin cups. They gulped the coffee and munched the food and stretched themselves on the soft moss. Through an opening they could see a fiery glow topped by wavering sheets of flame. They could hear the crackle and snap of burning wood.

"A forest fire is quite literally hell, isn't it?" Lawanne asked.

Hollister nodded. His eyes were on Bland. The man sat on the ground. He had a cup of coffee in one hand, a sandwich in the other. He was blackened almost beyond recognition, and he was viewing with patent disgust the state of his clothes and particularly of his hands. He set down his food and rubbed at his fingers with a soiled handkerchief. Then he resumed eating and drinking. It appeared to him a matter of necessity rather than a thing from which he derived any satisfaction. Near him Charlie Mills lay stretched on the moss, his head pillowed on his folded arms, too weary to eat or drink, even at Hollister's insistence.

"Dirty job this, eh?" Bland remarked. "I'll appreciate a bath. Phew. I shall sleep for a week when I get home."

By mid-afternoon of the next day, Sam Carr decided they had the fire well in hand and so split his forces, leaving half on guard and letting the others go home to rest. Hollister's men remained on the spot in case they were needed; he and Lawanne and Bland went home.

But that was not the end of the great blaze. Blocked in the valley, the fire, as if animated by some deadly purpose, crept into the mouth of a brushy canyon and ran uphill with demoniac energy until it was burning fiercely over a benchland to the west of Hollister's timber.

The fight began once more. With varying phases it raged for a week. They would check it along a given line and rest for awhile, thinking it safely under control. Then a light shift of wind would throw it across their line of defense, and in a dozen places the forest would break into flame. The fire worked far up the slope, but its greatest menace lay in its steady creep westward.

Slowly it ate up to the very edge of Hollister's timber, in spite of all their checks, their strategy, the prodigious effort of every man to check its vandal course.

Then the west wind, which had held its breath so long, broke loose with unrestrained exhalation. It fanned the fire to raging fury, sent it leaping in yellow sheets through the woods. The blaze lashed eagerly over the tops of the trees, the dreaded crown fire of the North Woods. Where its voice had been a whisper, it became a roar, an ominous, warning roar to which the loggers gave instant heed and got themselves and their gear off that timbered slope.

They could do no more. They had beaten it in the valley. Backed by the lusty pressure of the west wind, it drove them off the hill and went its wanton way unhindered.

In the flat by Hollister's house the different crews came together. There was not one of them but drooped with exhaustion. They sat about on the parched ground, on moss, against tree trunks, and stared up the hill.

Already the westerly gale had cleared the smoke from the lower valley. It brought a refreshing coolness off the salt water, and it was also baring to their sight the spectacular destruction of the forest.

All that area where Hollister's cedars had stood was a red chaos out of which great flames leaped aloft and waved snaky tongues, blood-red, molten gold, and from which great billows of smoke poured away to wrap in obscurity all the hills beyond. There was nothing they could do now. They watched it apathetically, too weary to care.

Hollister looked on the destruction of his timber most stolidly of all. For days he had put forth his best effort. His body ached. His eyes smarted. His hands were sore. He had done his best without enthusiasm. He was not oppressed so greatly as were some of these men by this vast and useless destruction. What did it matter, after all? A few trees more or less! A square mile or two of timber out of that enormous stand. It was of no more consequence in the sum total than the life of some obscure individual in the teeming millions of the earth.

It was his timber. So was his life a possession peculiar to himself. And neither seemed greatly to matter; neither did matter greatly to any one but himself.

It was all a muddle. He was very tired, too tired to bear thinking, almost too tired to feel. He was conscious of himself as a creature of weariness sitting against a tree, his scarred face blackened like the tired faces of these other men, wondering dully what was the sum of all this sweat and strain, the shattered plans, the unrewarded effort, the pain and stress that men endure. A man made plans, and they failed. He bred hope in his soul and saw it die. He longed for and sought his desires always, to see them vanish like a mirage just as they seemed within his grasp.

Lawanne and Bland had gone home, dragging themselves on tired limbs. Carr's men rested where they chose. They must watch lest the fire back down into the valley again and destroy their timber, as it had destroyed Hollister's. They had blankets and food. Hollister gave his own men the freedom of the house. Their quarters on the hill stood in the doomed timber. The old log house would be ashes now.

He wondered what Doris was doing, if she steadily gained her sight. But concrete, coherent thought seemed difficult. He thought in pictures, which he saw with a strange detachment as if he were a ghost haunting places once familiar.

He found his chin sinking on his breast. He roused himself and walked over to the house. His men were sprawled on the rugs, sleeping in grotesque postures. Hollister picked his way among them. Almost by the door of his bedroom Charlie Mills sprawled on his back, his head resting on a sofa cushion. He opened his eyes as Hollister passed.

"That was a tough game," Hollister said.

"It's all a tough game," Mills answered wearily and closed his eyes again.

Hollister went on into the room. He threw himself across the bed. In ten seconds he was fast asleep.

CHAPTER XX

FOR ANOTHER DAY, a day of brilliant sunshine and roaring west wind, the fire marched up over the southern slope. Its flaming head, with a towering crest of smoke, went over a high ridge, and its lower flank smoldered threateningly a little above the valley. The second night the wind fell to a whisper, shifting freakishly into the northeast, and day dawned with a mass formation of clouds spitting rain, which by noon grew to a downpour.

The fire sizzled and sputtered and died. Twenty hours of rain cleared the sky of clouds, the woods of smoke. The sun lifted his beaming face over the eastern sky line. The birds that had been silent began their twittering again, the squirrels took up their exploration among the tree tops, scolding and chattering as they went. Gentle airs shook the last rain drops from leaf and bough. The old peace settled on the valley. There was little to mark the ten days of effort and noise and destruction except a charred patch on the valley floor and a mile-wide streak that ran like a bar sinister across the green shield of the slope south of the Big Bend. Even that desolate path seemed an insignificant strip in the vast stretch of the forest.

Hollister and his men went, after the rain, up across that ravaged place, and when they came to the hollow where the great cedars and lesser fir had stood solemn and orderly in brown-trunked ranks, the rudest of the loggers grew silent, a little awed by the melancholy of the place, the bleakness, the utter ruin. Where the good green forest had been, there was nothing but ashes and blackened stubs, stretches of bare rock and gravelly soil, an odor of charred wood. There was no green blade, no living thing, in all that wide space, nothing but a few gaunt trunks stark in the open; blasted, sterile trunks standing like stripped masts on a derelict.

There was nothing left of the buildings except a pile of stone which had been the fireplace in the log house, and a little to one side the rusty, red skeleton of the mess-house stove. They looked about curiously for a few minutes and went back to the valley.

At the house Hollister paid them off. They went their way down to the steamer landing, eager for town after a long stretch in the woods. The fire was only an exciting incident to them. There were other camps, other jobs.

It was not even an exciting incident to Hollister. Except for a little sadness at sight of that desolation where there had been so much beauty, he had neither been uplifted nor cast down. He had been unmoved by the spectacular phases of the fire and he was still indifferent, even to the material loss it had inflicted on him. He was not ruined. He had the means to acquire more timber if it should be necessary. But even if he had been ruined, it is doubtful if that fact would have weighed heavily upon him. He was too keenly aware of a matter more vital to him than timber or money—a matter in which neither his money nor his timber counted one way or the other, and in which the human equation was everything.

The steamer that took out his men brought in a letter from his wife, which Lawanne sent up by his Chinese boy. He had written to her the day before the fire broke out. He could not recall precisely what he wrote, but he had tried to make clear to her what troubled him and why. And her reply was brief, uncommonly brief for Doris, who had the faculty of expressing herself fully and freely.

Hollister laid the letter on the table. The last line of that short missive kept repeating itself over and over, as if his brain were a phonograph which he had no power to stop playing:

"I shall be home next week on the Wednesday boat."

He got up and walked across the room, crossed and recrossed it half a dozen times. And with each step those words thrust at him with deadly import. He had deluded himself for a while. He had thought he could beat the game in spite of his handicap. He had presumed for a year to snap his fingers and laugh in the face of

220

Fate, and Fate was to have the last laugh.

He seemed to have a fatalistic sureness about this. He made a deliberate effort to reason about it, and though his reason assumed that when a woman like Doris Cleveland loved a man she did not love him for the unblemished contours of his face, there was still that deep-rooted, unreasoning feeling that however she might love him as the unseen, the ideal lover, she must inevitably shrink from the reality.

He stood still for a few seconds. In the living quarters of his house there was, by deliberate intention, no mirror. Among Hollister's things there was a small hand glass before which he shaved off the hairs that grew out of the few patches of unscarred flesh about his chin, those fragments of his beard which sprouted in grotesquely separated tufts. But in the bedroom they had arranged for the housekeeper there was a large oval glass above a dresser. Into this room Hollister now walked and stood before the mirror staring at his face.

No, he could not blame her, any one, for shrinking from *that*. And when the darting shuttle of his thought reminded him that Myra did not shrink from it, he went out to the front room and with his body sunk deep in a leather chair he fell to pondering on this. But it led him nowhere except perhaps to a shade of disbelief in Myra and her motives, a strange instinctive distrust both of her and himself.

He recognized Myra's power. He had succumbed to it in the old careless days and gloried in his surrender. He perceived that her compelling charm was still able to move him as it did other men. He knew that Myra had been carried this way and that in the great, cruel, indifferent swirl that was life. He could understand a great many things about her and about himself, about men as men and women as women, that he would have denied in the days before the war.

But while he could think about himself and Myra Bland with a calmness that approached indifference, he could not think with that same detachment about Doris. She had come, walking fearlessly in her darkened world, to him in his darkened world of discouragement and bitterness. There was something fine and true in this blind girl, something that Hollister valued over and above the flesh-and-blood loveliness of her, something rare and precious that he longed to keep. He could not define it; he simply knew that it resided in her, that it was a precious quality that set her apart in his eyes from all other women.

But would it stand the test of sight? If he were as other men he would not have been afraid; he would scarcely have asked himself that question. But he knew he would be like a stranger to her, a strange man with a repellingly scarred face. He did not believe she could endure that, she who loved beauty so, who was sensitive to subtleties of tone and atmosphere beyond any woman he had ever known. Hollister tried to put himself in her place. Would he have taken her to his arms as gladly, as joyously, if she had come to him with a face twisted out of all semblance to its natural lines? And Hollister could not say. He did not know.

He threw up his head at last, in a desperate sort of resolution. In a week he would know. Meantime—

He had no work to occupy him now. There were a few bolts behind the boom-sticks which he would raft to the mill at his leisure. He walked up to the chute mouth now and looked about. A few hundred yards up the hill the line of green timber ended against the black ruin of the fire. There the chute ended also. Hollister walked on

222

across the rocky point, passed the waterfall that was shrinking under the summer heat, up to a low cliff where he sat for a long time looking down on the river.

When he came back at last to the house, Myra was there, busy at her self-imposed tasks in those neglected rooms. Hollister sat down on the porch steps. He felt a little uneasy about her being there, uneasy for her. In nearly two weeks of fighting fire he had been thrown in intimate daily contact with Jim Bland, and his appraisal of Bland's character was less and less flattering the more he revised his estimate of the man. He felt that Myra was inviting upon herself something she might possibly not suspect. He decided to tell her it would be wiser to keep away; but when he did so, she merely laughed. There was a defiant recklessness in her tone when she said:

"Do you think I need a chaperone? Must one, even in this desolate place, kow-tow to the conventions devised to prop up the weak and untrustworthy? If Jim can't trust me, I may as well learn it now as any other time. Besides, it doesn't matter to me greatly whether he does or not. If for any reason he should begin to think evil of me—well, the filthy thought in another's mind can't defile me. I can't recall that I was ever greatly afraid of what other people might think of me, so long I was sure of myself."

"Nevertheless," Hollister said, "it is as well for you not to come here alone while I am here alone."

"Don't you like me to come, Robin?" she asked.

"No," he said slowly. "That wasn't why I spoke—but I don't think I do."

"Why?" she persisted.

Hollister stirred uneasily.

"Call a spade a spade, Robin," she advised. "Say

what you think—what you mean."

"That's difficult," he muttered. "How can any one say what he means when he is not quite sure what he does mean? I'm in trouble. You're sorry for me, in a way. And maybe you feel—because of old times, because of the contrast between what your life was then and what it is now you feel as if you would like to comfort me. And I don't want you to feel that way. I look at you—and I think about what you said. I wonder if you meant it? Do you remember what you said?"

"Quite clearly. I meant it, Robin. I still mean it. I'm yours—if you need me. Perhaps you won't. Perhaps you will. Does it trouble you to have me a self-appointed anchor to windward?"

She clasped her hands over her knees, bending forward a little, looking at him with a curious serenity. Her eyes did not waver from his. Hollister made no answer.

"I brought a lot of this on you, Robin," she went on in the musical, rippling voice so like Doris in certain tones and inflections as to make him wonder idly if he had unconsciously fallen in love with Doris Cleveland's voice because it was like Myra's. "If I had stuck it out in London till you came back, maimed or otherwise, things would have been different. But we were started off, flung off, one might say, into different orbits by the forces of the war itself. That's neither here nor there, now. You may think I'm offering myself as a sort of vicarious atonement—if your Doris fails you—but I'm not, really. I'm too selfish. I have never sacrificed myself for any man. I never will. It isn't in me. I'm just as eager to get all I can out of life as I ever was. I liked you long ago. I like you still. That's all there is to it, Robin."

She shifted herself nearer him. She put one hand on his shoulder, the other on his knee, and bent forward, peering into his face. Hollister matched that questioning gaze for a second. It was unreadable. It conveyed no message, hinted nothing, held no covert suggestion. It was earnest and troubled. He had never before seen that sort of look on Myra's face. He could make nothing of it, and so there was nothing in it to disturb him. But the warm pressure of her hands, the nearness of her body, did trouble him. He put her hands gently away.

"You shouldn't come here," he said quietly. "I will call a spade a spade. I love Doris—and I have a queer, hungry sort of feeling about the boy. If it happens that in spite of our life together Doris can't bear me and can't get used to me, if it becomes impossible for us to go on together—well, I can't make clear to you the way I feel about this. But I'm afraid. And if it turns out that I'm afraid with good cause—why, I don't know what I'll do, what way I'll turn. But wait until that happens—Well, it seems that a man and a woman who have loved and lived together can't become completely indifferent— they must either hate and despise each other—or else— You understand? We have made some precious blunders, you and I. We have involved other people in our blundering, and we mustn't forget about these other people. I *can't*. Doris and the kid come first—myself last. I'm selfish too. I can only sit here in suspense and wait for things to happen as they will. You," he hesitated a second, "you can't help me, Myra. You could hurt me a lot if you tried—and yourself too."

"I see," she said. "I understand."

She sat for a time with her hands resting in her lap, looking down at the ground. Then she rose.

"I don't want to hurt you, Robin," she said soberly. "I

225

can't help looking for a way out, that's all. For myself, I must find a way out. The life I lead now is stifling me—and I can't see where it will ever be any different, any better. I've become cursed with the twin devils of analysis and introspection. I don't love Jim; I tolerate him. One can't go through life merely tolerating one's husband, and the sort of friends and the sort of existence that appeals to one's husband, unless one is utterly ox-like—and I'm not. Women have lived with men they cared nothing for since the beginning of time, I suppose, because of various reasons—but I see no reason why I should. I'm a rebel—in full revolt against shams and stupidity and ignorance, because those three have brought me where I am and you where you are. I'm a disarmed and helpless *revolte* by myself. One doesn't want to go from bad to worse. One wants instinctively to progress from good to better. One makes mistakes and seeks to rectify them—if it is possible. One sees suffering arise as the result of one's involuntary acts, and one wishes wistfully to relieve it. That's the simple truth, Robin. Only a simple truth is often a very complex thing. It seems so with us."

"It is," Hollister muttered, "and it might easily become more so."

"Ah, well," she said, "that is scarcely likely. You were always pretty dependable, Robin. And I'm no longer an ignorant little fool to rush thoughtlessly in where either angels or devils might fear to tread. We shall see."

She swung around on her heel. Hollister watched her walk away along the river path. He scarcely knew what he thought, what he felt, except that what he felt and thought disturbed him to the point of sadness, of regret. He sat musing on the curious, contradictory forces at

226

work in his life. It was folly to be wise, to be sensitive, to respond too quickly, to see too clearly; and ignorance, dumbness of soul, was also fatal. Either way there was no escape. A man did his best and it was futile—or seemed so to him, just then.

His gaze followed Myra while his thought ran upon Doris, upon his boy, wondering if the next steamer would bring him sentence of banishment from all that he valued, or if there would be a respite, a stay of execution, a miracle of affection that would survive and override the terrible reality—or what seemed to him the terrible reality—of his disfigured face. He had abundant faith in Doris—of the soft voice and the keen, quick mind, the indomitable spirit and infinite patience—but he had not much faith in himself, in his own power. He was afraid of her restored sight, which would leave nothing to the subtle play of her imagination.

And following Myra with that mechanical noting of her progress, his eyes, which were very keen, caught some movement in a fringe of willows that lined the opposite shore of the river some three hundred yards below. He looked more sharply. He had developed a hunter's faculty for interpreting movement in the forest, and although he had nothing more positive than instinct and a brief flash upon which to base conclusions, he did not think that movement of the leaves was occasioned by any creature native to the woods.

On impulse he rose, went inside, and taking his binoculars from their case, focused the eight-power lenses on the screen of brush, keeping himself well within the doorway where he could see without being seen.

It took a minute or so of covering the willows before he located the cause of that movement of shrubbery. But presently he made out the head and shoulders of a man. And the man was Bland, doing precisely what Hollister was doing, looking through a pair of field glasses. Hollister stood well back in the room. He was certain Bland could not see that he himself was being watched. In any case, Bland was not looking at Hollister's house. It was altogether likely that he had been doing so, that he had seen Myra sitting beside Hollister with her hand on his shoulder, bending forward to peer into Hollister's face. And Hollister could easily imagine what Bland might feel and think. But he was steadily watching Myra. Once he turned the glasses for a few seconds on Hollister's house. Then he swung them back to Myra, followed her persistently as she walked along the bank, on past Lawanne's, on towards their own rude shack. And at last Bland shifted. One step backward, and the woods swallowed him. One moment his shoulders and his head stood plain in every detail, even to the brickish redness of his skin and the curve of his fingers about the glasses; the next he was gone.

Hollister sat thinking. He did not like the implications of that furtive observance. A suspicious, watchful man is a jealous man. And a jealous man who has nothing to do but watch and suspect and nurse that mean passion was a dangerous adjunct to an unhappy woman.

Hollister resolved to warn Myra, to emphasize that warning. No one could tell of what a dull egotist like Bland might be capable. The very fact of that furtive spying argued an ignoble streak in any man. Bland was stiff-necked, vain, the sort to be brutal in retaliation for any fancied invasion of his rights. And his conception of a husband's rights were primitive in the extreme. A wife was property, something that was his. Hollister could imagine him roused to blind, blundering fury by the least suspicious action on Myra's part. Bland was the type that, once aroused, acts like an angry bull—with about as much regard or understanding of consequences. Hollister had been measuring Bland for a year, and the last two or three weeks had given him the greatest opportunity to do so. He had appraised the man as a dullard under his stupid, inflexible crust of egotism, despite his veneer of manners. But even a clod may be dangerous. A bomb is a harmless thing, so much inert metal and chemicals, until it is touched off; yet it needs only a touch to let loose its insensate, rending force.

Hollister rose to start down the path after Myra with the idea that he must somehow convey to her a more explicit warning. As he stepped out on the porch, he looked downstream at Bland's house and saw a man approach the place from one direction as Myra reached it from the other. He caught up his glasses and brought them to bear. The man was Mills, whom he had thought once more far from the Toba with the rest of his scattered crew. Nevertheless this was Mills drawing near Bland's house with quick strides.

Hollister's uneasiness doubled. There was a power for mischief in that situation when he thought of Jim Bland scowling from his hiding place in the willows. He set out along the path.

But by the time he came abreast of Lawanne's cabin he had begun to feel himself acting under a mistaken impulse, an exaggerated conclusion. He began to doubt the validity of that intuition which pointed a warning finger at Bland and Bland's suspicions. In attempting to forestall what might come of Bland's stewing in the juice of a groundless jealousy, he could easily precipitate something that would perhaps be best avoided by ignoring it. He stood, when he thought of it,

229

in rather a delicate position himself.

So he turned into Lawanne's. He found Archie sitting on the shady side of his cabin, and they fell into talk.

CHAPTER XXI

LAWANNE HAD BEEN THUMPING A TYPEWRITER for hours, he told Hollister, until his fingers ached. He was almost through with this task, which for months had been a curious mixture of drudgery and pleasure.

"I'm through all but typing the last two chapters. It's been a fierce grind."

"You'll be on the wing soon, then," Hollister observed.

"That depends," Lawanne said absently.

But he did not explain upon what it depended. He leaned back in his chair, a cigarette in his fingers, and stared for a minute up at the trees.

"I'll get the rest of it pounded out in two or three days," he came back to his book, "then I think I'll go up the Little Toba, just to see what that wild-looking gorge is like twenty or thirty miles back. Better come along with me. Do you good. You're sort of at a standstill."

"I can't," Hollister explained. "Doris is coming back next week."

Lawanne looked at him intently.

"Eyes all right?"

"I don't know. I suppose so," Hollister replied. "She didn't say. She merely wrote that she was coming on the Wednesday steamer."

"Well, that'll be all right too," Lawanne said. "You'll get over being so down in the mouth then."

"Maybe," Hollister muttered.

"Of course. What rot to think anything else." Hollister did not contradict this. It was what he wanted to feel and think, and could not. He understood that Lawanne, whatever his thought, was trying to hearten him. And he appreciated that, although he knew the matter rested in his wife's own hands and nothing any one else could do or say had the slightest bearing on it. His meeting with Doris would be either an ordeal or a triumph.

"I might get Charlie Mills to go with me," Lawanne pursued his own thought.

"Mills didn't go out with the rest of the crew?" Hollister asked. He knew, of course, that Charlie Mills was still in the Toba valley because he had seen him with his own eyes not more than half an hour earlier. His question, however, was not altogether idle. He wondered whether Mills had gone out and come back, or if he had not left at all.

"No. He turned back at the last minute, for some reason. He's camping in one of the old T. & T. shacks below Carr's. I rather like Mills. He's interesting when you can get him to loosen up. Queer, tense sort of beggar at times, though. A good man to go into the hills with—to go anywhere with—although he might not show to great advantage in a drawing-room. By Jove, you know, Hollister, it doesn't seem like nine months since I settled down in this cabin. Now I'm about due to go back to the treadmill."

"Do you have to?" Hollister asked. "If this satisfies you, why not come back again after you've had a fling at the outside?"

"I can't, very well," Lawanne for the first time touched on his personal affairs, that life which he led somewhere beyond the Toba. "I have obligations to

231

fulfill. I've been playing truant, after a fashion. I've stolen a year to do something I wanted to do. Now it's done and I'm not even sure it's well done—but whether it's well done or not, it's finished, and I have to go back and get into the collar and make money to supply other people's needs. Unless," he shrugged his shoulders, "I break loose properly. This country has that sort of effect on a man. It makes him want to break loose from everything that seems to hamper and restrain him. It doesn't take a man long to shed his skin in surroundings like these. Oh, well, whether I come back or not, I'll be all the same a hundred years from now."

A rifle shot cut sharp into the silence that followed Lawanne's last words. That was nothing uncommon in the valley, where the crack of a gun meant only that some one was hunting. But upon this report there followed, clear and shrill, a scream, the high-pitched cry that only a frightened woman can utter. This was broken into and cut short by a second whip-like report. And both shots and scream came from the direction of Bland's house.

Hollister rose. He looked at Lawanne and Lawanne looked at him. Across Hollister's brain flashed a thought that would scarcely have been born if he had not seen Bland spying from the willows, if he had not seen Charlie Mills approaching that house, if he had not been aware of all the wheels within wheels, the complicated coil of longings and desires and smoldering passions in which these people were involved. He looked at Lawanne, and he could not read what passed in his mind. But when he turned and set out on a run for that shake cabin four hundred yards downstream, Lawanne followed at his heels.

They were winded, and their pace had slowed to a

232

hurried walk by the time they reached the cabin. The door stood open. There was no sound. The house was as still as the surrounding woods when Hollister stepped across the threshold.

Bland stood just within the doorway, erect, his feet a little apart, like a man bracing himself against some shock. He seemed frozen in this tense attitude, so that he did not alter the rigid line of his body or shift a single immobile muscle when Hollister and Lawanne stepped in. His eyes turned sidewise in their sockets to rest briefly and blankly upon the intruders. Then his gaze, a fixed gaze that suggested incredulous disbelief, went back to the body of his wife.

Myra lay in a crumpled heap, her face upturned, open-eyed, expressionless, as if death had either caught her in a moment of impassivity or with his clammy hands had forever wiped out all expression from her features. There were no visible marks on her—but a red stain was creeping slowly from under her body, spreading across the rough floor.

Mills sat on the floor, his back against the wall, his hands braced on his knees to keep his body erect. And upon him there was to be seen no visible mark of the murderer's bullet. But his dark-skinned face had turned waxy white. His lips were colorless. Every breath he drew was a laborious effort. A ghastly smile spread slowly over his face as he looked up at Hollister and Lawanne.

"You fool. You damned, murdering fool!" Lawanne turned on Bland. "You did this?"

Bland did not answer. He put his hand to his face and wiped away the sweat that had gathered in a shiny film on his skin, from which all the ruddiness had fled. Myra's pale, dead face seemed to hold him in some

233

horrible fascination. Hollister shook him.

"Why did you do that?" he demanded. Bland heaved a shuddering sigh. He looked up and about him stupidly.

"I don't know," he croaked. "I don't know—I don't know."

A gleam of something like reason came into his eyes.

"I suppose I shall have to give myself up to the authorities," he mumbled. "My God!"

The last two words burst from his lips like a cry, as for the first time he saw the full import of what he had done, realized the horror, the madness, and the consequences of his act. He shrank against the wall with a groan, putting out his hands as if to ward off some invisible enemy. Then, thrusting Hollister aside, he rushed out of the door, his rifle still clasped in both hands. He ran down the bank, out into the shallows of the river, splashing through water to his knees. He gained the opposite side where the heavy woods lifted silent and solemn, full of dusky places. Into that— whether for sanctuary or driven by some unreekoning panic, they did not know—but into that he plunged, the last sight either Hollister or Lawanne ever had of him.

They turned to Mills. Myra was dead. They could do nothing for her. But Mills still lived. The sound of his labored breathing filled the room. He had shifted a little, so that he could reach out and lay one hand on the dead woman's face, where it rested, with a caressing touch. A red pool was gathering where he sat.

"How bad are you hurt, Charlie?" Hollister said. "Let me see."

"No use," Mills said thickly. "I'm done. He got me right through the middle. And I wouldn't live if I could. Not now.

"Don't touch me," he protested, as they bent over him.

234

"You can't do anything. There's a hole in me you could put your hand in. But it don't hurt. I won't last more than a minute or two, anyway."

"How did it happen?" Lawanne asked.

"I was sitting here talking to her," Mills said. "There was nothing wrong—unless it's wrong for a man to love a woman and tell her so. I found her sitting here, crying. She wouldn't tell me why. And I suppose maybe that stirred me up. I hadn't meant to start it again—because we'd had that out long ago. But I tried to persuade her to go away with me—to make a fresh start. I wanted her—but I've been doing that for a long time. She's only stuck to this Bland—because—oh, I don't know why. I don't savvy women. She liked me. But not enough. I was trying to persuade her to break loose. I don't remember—maybe I had hold of her hand. A man doesn't remember when he's begging for a chance. I don't know where he came from. Maybe he heard what I was saying. Maybe it just didn't look good to him. I know his face was like a wild man's when I saw him in the door."

Mills paused to catch his breath. The words tumbled out of him as if he had much to say and knew his time was short.

"Don't think he meant to kill her. He popped me. Then she screamed and jumped in front of me with her arms out—and he gave it to her."

Mills' voice broke. His fingers stroked feebly at the twisted coils of Myra's pale, honey-colored hair. His lips quivered.

"Finished. All over—for both of us. Butchered like beef by a crazy fool. Maybe I'm crazy too," he said in a husky whisper. "It don't seem natural a man should feel like I've felt for months. I didn't want to feel like that.

235

Couldn't help it. I've lived in hell—you won't savvy, but it's true. I'm glad it's over. If there is any other life—maybe that'll be better. I hope there isn't. I feel as if all I want is to sleep forever and ever. No more laying awake nights thinking till my head hurts and my heart is like a lump of lead. By God, I *have* been crazy."

His body began to sag, and Hollister knelt beside him and supported him. He shook his head when Lawanne offered him a drink. His eyes closed. Only the feeble motion of his fingers on the dead woman's face and the slow heave of his breast betokened the life that still clung so tenaciously to him.

He opened his eyes again, to look at Hollister. "I used to think dying—was tough," he whispered. "It isn't. Like going—to sleep—when you're tired—when you're through—for the day."

That was his last word. He went limp suddenly and slid out of Hollister's grasp. And they let him lie, a dead man beside the dead woman on the floor. They stood up themselves and stared at the bodies with that strange incredulity men sometimes feel in the face of sudden death.

Both Lawanne and Hollister were familiar with death, death by the sniper's bullet, by machine gun and shell, by bayonet and poison gas. This was different. It was not war. It was something that touched them more deeply than any of the killing they had seen in war. The low hum of foraging bees about the door, the foxglove swaying in summer airs, the hushed peace of the distant hills and nearer forest—this was no background for violence and death. It shocked them, chilled and depressed them. Hollister felt a new sort of ache creep into his heart. His eyes stung. And Lawanne suddenly turned away with a choking sound muffled in his throat.

They went out into the sunlight. Away down the valley a donkey engine tooted and whirred. High above them an eagle soared, wheeling in great circles about his aerial business. The river whispered in its channel. The blue jays scolded harshly among the thickets, and a meadow lark perched on a black stump near at hand, warbling his throaty song. Life went on as before.

"What'll we do?" Lawanne said presently. "We've got to do something."

"There's not much we can do, now," Hollister replied. "You go down to Carr's and tell them to send a man with a gas-boat out to Powell River with word to the Provincial Police of what has happened. I'll keep watch until you come back."

In an hour Lawanne returned with two men from the settlement. They laid the bodies out decently on a bed and left the two men to keep vigil until sundown, when Hollister and Lawanne would take up that melancholy watch for the night.

"I wonder," Hollister said to Lawanne, as they walked home, "what'll become of Bland? Will he give himself up, or will they have to hunt him?"

"Neither, I think," Lawanne answered slowly, "A man like that is certainly not himself when he breaks out like that. Bland has the cultural inheritance of his kind. You could see that he was stupefied by what he had done. When he rushed away into the woods I think it was just beginning to dawn on him, to fill him with horror. He'll never come back. You'll see. He'll either go mad, or in the reaction of feeling he'll kill himself."

They went into Lawanne's cabin. Lawanne brought out a bottle of brandy. He looked at the shaking of his fingers as he poured for Hollister and smiled wanly.

"I don't go much on Dutch courage, but I sure need it

now," he said. "Isn't it queer the way death affects you under different circumstances? I didn't see such an awful lot of action in France, but once a raiding party of Heinies tumbled into our trench, and there was a deuce of a ruction for a few minutes. Between bayonets and bombs we cleaned the lot, a couple of dozen of them. After it was all over, we stacked them up like cordwood—with about as much compunction. It seemed perfectly natural. There was nothing but the excitement of winning a scrap. The half-dozen of our own fellows that went west in the show—they didn't matter either. It was part of the game. You expected it. It didn't surprise you. It didn't shock you. Yet death is death. Only, there, it seemed a natural consequence. And here it—well, I don't know why, but it gives me a horror."

Lawanne sat down.

"It was so unnecessary; so useless," he went on in that lifeless tone. "The damned, egotistic fool! Two lives sacrificed to a stupid man's wounded vanity. That's all. She was a singularly attractive woman. She would have been able to get a lot out of life. And I don't think she did, or expected to."

"Did you have any idea that Mills had that sort of feeling for her?" Hollister asked.

"Oh, yes," Lawanne said absently. "I saw that. I understood. I was touched a little with the same thing myself. Only, *noblesse oblige.* And also I was never quite sure that what I felt for her was sympathy, or affection, or just sex. I know I can scarcely bear to think that she is dead."

He leaned back in his chair and put his hands over his eyes. Hollister got up and walked to a window. Then on impulse he went to the door. And when he was on the threshold, Lawanne halted him.

238

"Don't go," he said. "Stay here. I can't get my mind off this. I don't want to sit alone and think."

Hollister turned back. Neither did he want to sit alone and think. For as the first dazed numbness wore off, he began to see himself standing alone—more alone than ever—gazing into a bottomless pit, with Fate or Destiny or blind Chance, whatever witless force was at work, approaching inexorably to push him over the brink.

CHAPTER XXII

TO THE WORLD OUTSIDE the immediate environs of the Toba, beyond those who knew the people concerned, that double murder was merely another violent affair which provided material for newpapers, a remote event allied to fires, divorces, embezzlements, politics, and scandals in high finance;—another item to be glanced quickly over and as quickly forgotten.

But one man at least could not quickly forget or pass it over lightly. Once the authorities—coming from a great distance, penetrating the solitude of the valley with a casual, business-like air—arrived, asked questions, issued orders, sent two men abroad in search of the slayer, and removed—the bodies to another jurisdiction, Hollister had nothing more to do with that until he should be called again to give formal testimony.

He was left with nothing to do but brood, to sit asking unanswerable questions of a world and a life that for him was slowly and bewilderingly verging upon the chaotic, in which there was no order, no security, no assurance of anything but devastating changes that had neither rhyme nor reason in their sequence. There might be logical causes, buried obscurely under remote events, for everything that had transpired. He conceded that point. But he could not establish any association; he could not trace out the chain; and he revolted against the common assumption that all things, no matter how mysterious, work out ultimately for some common good.

Where was the good forthcoming out of so much that was evil, he asked? Looking back over the years, he saw much evil for himself, for everything and every one he cared about, and mingled with it there was little good, and that good purely accidental, the result of fortuitous circumstances. He knew that until the war broke out he had lived in a backwater of life, himself and Myra, contented, happy, untried by adversity. Once swung out of that backwater they had been swept away, powerless to know where they went, to guess what was their destination.

Nothing that he could have done would have altered one iota the march of events. Nothing that he could do now would have more than the slightest bearing on what was still to come. He was like a man beaten to a dazed state in which he expects anything, in which his feeble resistance will not ward off a single blow aimed at him by an unseen, inscrutable enemy.

Hollister, sitting on the bank of the river, looked at the mountains rising tier upon tier until the farthest ranges were dazzling white cones against a far sky line. He saw them as a chaos of granite and sandstone flung up by blind forces. Order and logical sequence in the universe were a delusion—except as they were the result of ordered human thought, effected by patient, unremitting human effort, which failed more often than it succeeded.

He looked at one bold peak across the valley,

standing so sheer above the Black Hole that it seemed to overhang from the perpendicular; a mass of bald granite, steep cliff, with glacial ice and perpetual snow lurking in its crevasses. Upon its lower slopes the forest ran up, a green mantle with ragged edges. From the forest upward the wind wafted seeds to every scanty patch of soil. They took root, became saplings, grew to substantial trees. And every winter the snow fell deep on that mountain, piling up in great masses delicately poised, until a mere nothing—a piece of stone loosened by the frost; a gust of wind; perhaps only the overhanging edge of a snow-drift breaking under its own weight—would start a slide that gathered speed and bulk as it came down. And as this insensate mass plunged downward, the small trees and the great, the thickets and the low salal, everything that stood in its path, was overwhelmed and crushed and utterly destroyed. To what end? For what purpose?

It was just the same with man, Hollister thought. If he got in the way of forces greater than himself, he was crushed. Nature was blind, ruthless, disorderly, wantonly destructive. One had to be alert, far-seeing, gifted with definite characteristics, to escape. Even then one did not always, or for long, escape being bruised and mauled by the avalanches of emotion, the irresistible movement of circumstance over which one could exert no control.

How could it be otherwise? Hollister thought of all that had happened to all the people he knew, the men he had seen killed and maimed, driven insane by the shocks of war; of Doris, stricken blind in the full glow of youth; Myra pulled and hauled this way and that because she was as she was and powerless to be otherwise; himself marred and shunned and suffering intolerable agonies of spirit; of Bland, upon whom had fallen the black mantle of unnecessary tragedy; and Mills, who had paid for his passion with his life.

All these things pressed upon Hollister; a burden of discouragement, of sadness. Not one of all these, himself included, but wanted happiness according to his conception of happiness. And who and what was responsible for each one's individual conception of what he wanted? Not one of them had demanded existence. Each had had existence thrust upon him. Nature, and a thousand generations of life and love and pain, such environment in which, willy-nilly, they passed their formative years, had bestowed upon each his individual quota of character, compounded of desires, of intellect, of tendencies. And the sum total of their actions and reactions—what was it? How could they have modified life, bent it purposefully to its greatest fulfilment?

Hollister tried to shake himself free of these morbid abstractions. He was alive. He had a long time yet to live. He was a strong man, in whom the fire of life burned with an unquenchable flame. He had a great many imperative requisitions to make on life's exchequer, and while he was now sadly dubious of their being honored, either in full or in part, he must go on making them.

There was a very black hole yawning before him. The cumulative force of events had made him once more profoundly uncertain. All his props were breaking. Sometimes he wondered if the personal God of the Christian orthodoxy was wreaking upon him some obscure vengeance for unknown sins.

He shook himself out of this depressing bog of reflection and went to see Archic Lawanne. Not simply

242

for the sake of Lawanne's society, although he valued that for itself. He had a purpose.

"That boat's due tomorrow at three o'clock," he said to Lawanne. "Will you take my big canoe and bring Doris up the river?

"I can't," he forestalled the question he saw forming on Lawanne's lips. "I can't meet her before that crowd—the crew and passengers, and loggers from Carr's. I'm afraid to. Not only because of myself, but because of what effect the shock of seeing me may have on her. Remember that I'll be like a stranger to her. She has never seen me. It seems absurd, but it's true. It's better that she sees me the first time by herself, at home, instead of before a hundred curious eyes. Don't you see?"

Lawanne saw; at least, he agreed that it was better so. And after they had talked awhile, Hollister went home.

But he was scarcely in his own dooryard before he became aware that while he might plan and arrange, so also could others; that his wife was capable of action independent of him or his plans.

He glanced down the river and saw a long Siwash dugout sweep around the curve of the Big Bend. It straightened away and bore up the long stretch of swift water that ran by his house. Hollister could distinguish three or four figures in it. He could see the dripping paddles rise and fall in measured beat, the wet blades flashing in the sun.

He gained the porch and turned his glasses on the canoe. He recognized it as Chief Aleck's dugout from a rancherie near the mouth of the river, a cedar craft with carved and brilliantly painted high-curving ends. Four Siwash paddlers manned it. Amidships two women sat. One was the elderly housekeeper who had been with them since their boy's birth. The other was Doris, with the baby in her lap.

A strange panic seized Hollister, the alarm of the unexpected, a reluctance to face the crisis which he had not expected to face for another twenty-four hours. He stepped down off the porch, walked rapidly away toward the chute mouth, crossed that and climbed to a dead fir standing on the point of rocks beyond. From there he watched until the canoe thrust its gaudy prow against the bank before his house, until he saw the women ashore and their baggage stacked on the bank, until the canoe backed into the current and shot away downstream, until Doris with the baby in her arms—after a lingering look about, a slow turning of her head—followed the other woman up the porch steps and disappeared within. Then Hollister moved back over the little ridge into the shadow of a clump of young firs and sat down on a flat rock with his head in his hands, to fight it out with himself.

To stake everything on a single throw of the dice—and the dice loaded against him! If peace had its victories no less than war, it had also crushing defeats. Hollister felt that for him the final, most complete *débacle* was at hand.

He lifted his head at a distant call, a high, clear, sweet "Oh-*hoo-oo-oo*" repeated twice. That was Doris calling him as she always called him, if she wanted him and thought he was within range of her voice. Well, he would go down presently.

He looked up the hill. He could see through a fringe of green timber to a place where the leaves and foliage were all rusty-red from the scorching of the fire. Past that opened the burned ground—charred, black, desolate. Presently life would be like that to him; all the years that stretched ahead of him might be as barren as that black waste.

His mind projected itself into the future from every possible angle. He did not belittle Doris' love, her sympathy, her understanding. He even conceded that no matter how his disfigurement affected her, she would try to put that behind her, she would make an effort to cling to him. And Hollister could see the deadly impact of his grotesque features upon her delicate sensibility, day after day, month after month, until she could no longer endure it, or him. She loved the beautiful too well, perfection of line and form and color. Restored sight must alter her world; her conception of him must become transformed. The magic of the unseen would lose its glamor. All that he meant to her as a man, a lover, a husband, must be stripped bare of the kindly illusion that blindness had wrapped him in. Even if she did not shrink in amazed reluctance at first sight, she must soon cease to have for him any keener emotion than a tolerant pity. And Hollister did not want that. He would not take it as a gift—not from Doris; he could not.

Love, home, all that sweet companionship which he had gained, the curious man-pride he had in that morsel of humanity that was his son—he wondered if he were to see all these slowly or swiftly withdrawn from him?

Well, he would soon know. He stood up and looked far along the valley. Suddenly it seemed a malevolent place, oppressive, threatening, grim in spite of its beauty. It seemed as if something had been lurking there ready to strike. The fire had swept away his timber. In that brilliant sunshine, amid all that beauty, Myra's life had been snuffed out like a blown candle flame—to no purpose. Or was there some purpose in it all? Was some

245

sentient force chastening him, scourging him with rods for the good of his soul? Was it for some such inscrutable purpose that men died by the hundred thousand in Europe? Was that why Doris Cleveland had been deprived of her sight? Why Myra had been torn by contradictory passions during her troubled life and had perished at last, a victim of passions that burst control? All this evil that some hidden good might accrue? Hollister bared his teeth in defiance of such a concluion. But he was in a mood to defy either gods or devils. In that mood he saw the Toba valley, the whole earth, as a sinister place—a place where beauty was a mockery, where impassive silence was merely the threatening hush before some elemental fury. This serene, indifferent beauty was hateful to him in that moment, the Promethean rock to which circumstance had chained him to suffer. It needed only as a capsheaf the gleam of incredulous dismay which should appear in his wife's eyes when she looked first upon the mutilated tissue, the varying scars and cicatrices, the twisted mask that would be revealed to her as the face of her husband.

This test was at hand. He reassured himself, as he had vainly reassured himself before, by every resource his mind and courage could muster, and still he was afraid. He saw nothing ahead but a black void in which there was neither love nor companionship nor friendly hands and faces, nothing but a deep gloom in which he should wander alone—not because he wished to, but because he must.

He turned with a sudden resolution, crossed the low rocky point and went down to the flat. He passed under the trestle which carried the chute. The path to the house turned sharply around a clump of alder. He rounded these leafy trees and came upon Doris standing by a low

246

stump. She stood as she did the first time he saw her on the steamer, in profile, only instead of the steamer rail her elbow rested on the stump, and she stared, with her chin nestled in the palm of one hand, at the gray, glacial stream instead of the uneasy heave of a winter sea. And Hollister thought with a slow constriction gathering in his breast that life was a thing of vain repetitions; he remembered so vividly how he felt that day when he stood watching her by the rail, thinking with a dull resentment that she would presently look at him and turn away. And he was thinking that again.

Walking on soft leaf-mold he approached within twenty feet of her, unheard. Then she lifted her head, looked about her.

"Bob!"

"Yes," he answered. He stopped. She was looking at him. She made an imperative gesture, and when Hollister still stood like a man transfixed, she came quickly to him, her eyes bright and eager, her hands outstretched.

"What's the matter?" she asked. "Aren't you glad to see me?"

"Are you glad to see me?" he countered. "Do you see me?"

She shook her head.

"No, and probably I never shall," she said evenly. "But you're here, and that's just as good. Things are still a blur. My eyes will never be any better, I'm afraid."

Hollister drew her close to him. Her upturned lips sought his. Her body pressed against him with a pleasant warmth, a confident yielding. They stood silent a few seconds, Doris leaning against him contentedly, Hollister struggling with the flood of mingled sensations that swept through him on the heels of this vast relief.

"How your heart thumps," Doris laughed softly. "One would think you were a lover meeting his mistress clandestinely for the first time."

"You surprised me," Hollister took refuge behind a white lie. He would not afflict her with that miasma of doubts and fears which had sickened him. "I didn't expect you till tomorrow afternoon."

"I got tired of staying in town," she said. "There was no use. I wasn't getting any better, and I got so I didn't care. I began to feel that it was better to be here with you blind, than alone in town with that tantalizing half-sight of everything. I suppose the plain truth is that I got fearfully lonesome. Then you wrote me that letter, and in it you talked about such intimately personal things that I couldn't let Mrs. Moore read it to me. And I heard about this big fire you had here. So I decided to come home and let my eyes take care of themselves. I went to see another oculist or two. They can't tell whether my sight will improve or not. It may go again altogether. And nothing much can be done. I have to take it as it comes. So I planned to come home on the steamer tomorrow. You got my letter, didn't you?"

"Yes."

"Well, I happened to get a chance to come as far as the Redondas on a boat belonging to some people I knew on Stuart Island. I got a launch there to bring me up the Inlet, and Chief Aleck brought us up the river in the war canoe. My, it's good to be with you again."

"Amen," Hollister said. There was a fervent quality in his tone.

They found a log and sat down on it and talked. Hollister told her of the fire. And when he saw that she had no knowledge of what tragedy had stalked with bloody footprints across the Big Bend, he put off telling

248

her. Presently she would ask about Myra, and he would have to tell her. But in that hour he did not wish to see her grow sad. He was jealous of anything that would inflict pain on her. He wanted to shield her from all griefs and hurts.

"Come back to the house," Doris said at last. "Baby's fretting a little. The trip in a small boat rather upset him. I don't like to leave him too long."

But Robert junior was peacefully asleep in his crib when they reached the house. After a look at him, they went out and sat on the porch steps. There, when the trend of their conversation made it unavoidable, he told her what had overtaken Charlie Mills and Myra Bland.

Doris listened silently. She sighed.

"What a pity," she murmured. "The uselessness of it, the madness—like a child destroying his toys in a blind rage. Poor Myra. She told me once that life seemed to her like swimming among whirlpools. It must have been true." How true it was Hollister did not dare reveal. That was finished, for Myra and himself. She had perished among the whirlpools. He scarcely knew how he had escaped.

"How lucky we are, you and I, Bob," Doris said after a time. She put her arms around him impulsively. "We might so easily be wandering about alone in a world that is terribly harsh to the unfortunate. Instead—we're here together, and life means something worth while to us. It does to me, I know. Does it to you?"

"As long as I have you, it does," he answered truthfully. "But if you could see me as I really am, perhaps I might not have you very long."

"How absurd," she declared—and then, a little thoughtfully, "if I thought that was really true, I should never wish to see again. Curiously, the last two or three

249

weeks this queer, blurred sort of vision I have seems quite sufficient. I haven't wanted to see half so badly as I've wanted you. I can get impressions enough through the other four senses. I'd hate awfully to have to get along without you. You've become almost a part of me—I wonder if you understand that?"

Hollister did understand. It was mutual—that want, that dependence, that sense of incompleteness which each felt without the other. It was a blessed thing to have, something to be cherished, and he knew how desperately he had reacted to everything that threatened its loss.

Hollister sat there looking up at the far places, the high, white mountain crests, the deep gorges, the paths that the winter slides had cut through the green forest, down which silvery cataracts poured now. It seemed to have undergone some subtle change, to have become less aloof, to have enveloped itself in a new and kindlier atmosphere. Yet he knew it was as it had always been. The difference was in himself. The sympathetic response to that wild beauty was purely subjective. He could look at the far snows, the bluish gleam of the glaciers, the restful green of the valley floor, with a new quality of appreciation. He could even—so resilient and adaptable a thing is the human mind—see himself engaged upon material enterprises, years passing, his boy growing up, life assuming a fullness, a proportion, an orderly progression that two hours earlier would have seemed to him only a futile dream.

He wondered if this would endure. He looked down at his wife leaning upon his knee, her face thoughtful and content. He looked out over the valley once more, at those high, sentinel peaks thrusting up their white cones, one behind the other. He heard the river. He saw the foxglove swaying in the wind, the red flare of the poppies at his door. He smelled the fragrance of wild honeysuckle, the sharp, sweet smells blown out of the forest that drowsed in the summer heat.

It was all good. He rested in that pleasant security like a man who has fought his way through desperate perils to some haven of safety and sits down there to rest in peace. He did not know what the future held for him. He had no apprehension of the future. He was not even curious. He had firm hold of the present, and that was enough. He wondered a little that he should suddenly feel so strong a conviction that life was good. But he had that feeling at last. The road opened before him clear and straight. If there were crooks in it, pitfalls by the way, perils to be faced, pains to be suffered, he was very sure in that hour that somehow he would find courage to meet them open-eyed and unafraid.

We hope that you enjoyed reading this
Sagebrush Large Print Western.
If you would like to read more Sagebrush titles,
ask your librarian or contact the Publishers:

United States and Canada

Thomas T. Beeler, *Publisher*
Post Office Box 659
Hampton Falls, New Hampshire 03844-0659
(800) 818-7574

United Kingdom, Eire, and
the Republic of South Africa

Isis Publishing Ltd
7 Centremead
Osney Mead
Oxford OX2 0ES England
(01865) 250333

Australia and New Zealand

Bolinda Publishing Pty. Ltd.
17 Mohr Street
Tullamarine, 3043, Victoria, Australia
(016103) 9338 0666